THUNDER ISLAND

Focusing on novels with contemporary concerns, Bantam New Fiction introduces some of the most exciting voices at work today. Look for these titles wherever Bantam New Fiction is sold:

WHITE PALACE by Glenn Savan
SOMEWHERE OFF THE COAST OF MAINE by Ann Hood
COYOTE by Lynn Vannucci
VARIATIONS IN THE NIGHT by Emily Listfield
LIFE DURING WARTIME by Lucius Shepard
THE HALLOWEEN BALL by James Howard Kunstler
PARACHUTE by Richard Lees
THUNDER ISLAND by James Howard Kunstler

Also by James Howard Kunstler

THE WAMPANAKI TALES
A CLOWN IN THE MOONLIGHT
THE LIFE OF BYRON JAYNES
AN EMBARRASSMENT OF RICHES
BLOOD SOLSTICE
THE HALLOWEEN BALL

BANTAM NEW FICTION

THUNDER ISLAND

JAMES HOWARD KUNSTLER

BANTAM BOOKS

TORONTO · NEW YORK · LONDON · SYDNEY · AUCKLAND

THUNDER ISLAND
A Bantam Book / June 1988

*Grateful acknowledgment is made for permission to
reprint the following: "BEING FOR THE BENEFIT OF
MR. KITE," words and music by John Lennon and
Paul McCartney. Copyright © 1967 by NOTHERN SONGS
LIMITED. All rights for the U.S., Canada and
Mexico controlled and administered by BLACKWOOD
MUSIC INC., under license from ATV MUSIC (MACLEAN),
all rights reserved. International copyright secured,
used by permission.*

All rights reserved.
Copyright © 1988 by James Howard Kunstler.
Cover art copyright © 1988 by John Jinks.
Book design by Barbara N. Cohen.

*No part of this book may be reproduced or transmitted
in any form or by any means, electronic or mechanical,
including photocopying, recording, or by any information
storage and retrieval system, without permission in
writing from the publisher.*
For information address: Bantam Books.

Library of Congress Cataloging-in-Publication Data

Kunstler, James Howard.
  Thunder Island.

  (Bantam new fiction)
  I. Title.
PS3561.U55T48 1988 813'.54 87-47909
ISBN 0-553-34514-1

Published simultaneously in the United States and Canada

Bantam Books are published by Bantam Books, a division of Bantam Doubleday Dell Publishing Group, Inc. Its trademark, consis-
ting of the words "Bantam Books" and the portrayal of a rooster, is
Registered in U.S. Patent and Trademark Office and in other countries. Marca Registrada. Bantam Books, 666 Fifth Avenue, New
York, New York 10103.

PRINTED IN THE UNITED STATES OF AMERICA

FG   0 9 8 7 6 5 4 3 2 1

This book is for Chris Dunworth

CHAPTER ONE

A half day's drive east of New York City, below the tail of the great fish-shaped heap of land known as Long Island, lies a slender barrier beach. It is twenty-two miles long, yet no more than five hundred yards across at its widest point. The surf is wilder there than at any beach along the Atlantic coast except Cape Hatteras, while its treacherously shifting shoals have wrecked as many ships. The Shinnecock Indians who lived on the nearby mainland three hundred years ago logically named it after another familiar but fearsome element of nature, calling it Thunder Island.

Now, on a Tuesday morning in late June of the year 1967, a young man could be observed laboring in the hot sun with a shovel at a point roughly halfway between the bay and the ocean. The young man was named Andy Newmark. He was a few months shy of his eighteenth birthday, five feet nine inches tall, boyishly slender, and clad only in a pair of cutoff blue-jeans shorts. He was barefoot. Though he'd arrived on Thunder Island just ten days earlier, he had a good start on a suntan, and his longish brown hair was already beginning to turn blonde at the tips.

1

The task he was laboring at was to shovel ankle-deep sand off a long concrete walkway. There were no true roads on Thunder Island, and the only automobiles allowed were the police and fire vehicles and a handful of jeeps licensed as beach taxis that ran up and down between the scattered towns. Getting around otherwise meant bicycling or walking on the narrow concrete footpaths that crisscrossed the towns. Going barefoot was a proud and cherished tradition among the summer folk, young and old. At the ferry landing on a June day, they could be seen kicking off their shoes for the summer like savages who had been kept in a civilized place too long.

The concrete walkway Andy worked on was over a thousand feet long. It was the second time in a week he'd had to shovel it off, and he was beginning to suspect that it would become a regular and hateful feature of his summer job, though his boss, Ted Bass, hadn't made a special point of mentioning it.

Shoveling the walk clear took Andy several hours. The walk was laid through a windswept hundred-fifty-acre parcel of dune grass, wild rose, poison ivy, and scrub holly dotted with only twenty-three summer houses. The rest was undeveloped land. It all belonged to a group of well-to-do Irish Catholic families allied into the Thunder Island Association. This association, called "the Club" by its members, functioned as a real estate company. Its hidden purpose was to keep the land out of the hands of non-Catholics.

This might have seemed a sinister scheme had Catholics been in the majority on Thunder Island. But the town of Ocean Breeze, adjoining the Club's one hundred fifty acres (the biggest of all seven towns along the twenty-two-mile-long beach) was populated overwhelmingly by Jewish families, while Holly Wood, on the far side of Ocean

Breeze, was an even more restrictive colony of old-money Protestants, and had a chain-link fence topped with barbed wire along its village boundary—*like a concentration camp!* the Ocean Breezers said. Six miles further east beyond a long, empty stretch of wild national seashore lay the town of Piney Grove, which was virtually all homosexuals.

Andy Newmark thought it was kind of funny that the club had hired him, a Jewish kid, for the job of steward's assistant. Then again, the club steward, Ted Bass, was also Jewish.

"They like the idea of hiring us as help," Bass had explained to Andy with the foxy good humor that made people think he'd be good on TV. "Kind of like they're evening the score a little around here. Only it makes them nervous if they see you hanging around their daughters," he added, and then Andy couldn't tell whether Bass was kidding or not.

Andy blundered into the Club job because the camp in Maine where he had been a counselor the summer before refused to hire him back due to a disgraceful drunken episode at the final night's awards dinner. So he had gone out to Thunder Island on the Memorial Day weekend, to his Uncle Jack's house in Ocean Breeze, to look for something else. There, on the beach, he ran into Debbie Klinger, a girl from his school back in the city. She was sitting in a crowd of young people, mostly college kids. Presiding over them—on account of seniority, it might be said—was Ted Bass, twenty-four, a graduate student in American studies from Yale who had been a fixture around the beach for years, though he had no family on the island. Bass himself had only just arrived that weekend—driving down from Connecticut on his Bultaco motorcycle—to open up the Club for his second year as its steward. He was having trouble finding an assistant, though.

3

Nobody wanted the job, for some reason. Andy innocently volunteered his services—while some kids in the crowd whispered behind their hands and seemed to snigger. Bass hired him on the spot. It was as simple as that. A week later, Andy came back out with a big suitcase and a duffle bag to stay for the season.

The job paid $58 a week plus room and board. The club maintained its headquarters in a semiwreck of an old Coast Guard station on the bay side of its holdings. Here was the bar and dining room where the members and their guests came to supper on Fridays and Saturdays in the season—always the same supper, too: fish on Fridays and steamship roast on Saturdays. Andy's duties were to assist the cook on weekends, wash the dishes and mop the floors, fetch the provisions from the freight boat down at the ferry landing in Ocean Breeze on Tuesdays and Thursdays, and "generally help out around the place," Bass put it vaguely, failing to mention the walks that needed frequent shoveling.

Bass—virtually everyone called him solely by his last name—lived in a room with an adjoining bath on the first floor behind the club barroom, with its old stuffed and varnished game fish leaking sawdust and 1930s vintage chrome bar-stools. Andy's room was upstairs under a gable in what had long ago been a chief petty officer's quarters. There was a single bed and a table in front of a window that looked out north over the bay and, on clear days, to the pale green sliver of mainland twenty miles distant. The room was bright, clean, and cheerful, and Andy was altogether quite pleased with it. He was not unhappy with the pay, either. It topped his salary as a camp counselor by $9 a week, and he didn't have to share a cabin with five screaming nine-year-old brats.

The rest of the upstairs of the old Coast Guard station was divided into two suites reserved for club guests—

4

mainly prospective lot buyers—and another small room reserved for the cook, who stayed there only on weekends. Finally, there was the old square tower on the third floor, really just a glorified widow's walk, but with a fine view above the club members' scattered houses clear over the dunes to the ocean. And pervading all this loveliness of clear ocean light and invigorating salt air was a ceaseless pounding, the roar of the surf, like perpetual distant thunder on a fine summer day.

Now, the reason it was so important to shovel off the walk this Friday morning was that it was the Club's official opening day for the season. Practically all the Club families were expected to arrive in the next twelve hours. This meant they would be lugging their belongings over from the ferry dock in Ocean Breeze. The customary way to do this on an island where there were no cars was with a child's American Flyer wagon. Each family in Ocean Breeze kept such a wagon, almost always painted in a wildly distinctive manner, with the family's name or the house's name emblazoned on it. There was even a special paddock for the wagons next to the ferry dock where the families kept them locked up between visits.

The little wagons didn't work very well, however, if the concrete walks were covered with sand. In Ocean Breeze proper, where the houses stood cheek by jowl, this was never a problem. But out on the Club property walks, where the sand constantly blew across the vacant land, it was a problem, and Mrs. Dern, the ferocious Club president, made a special point of telling Bass to "get those goddam walks cleared" by opening day.

Bass, of course, had turned around and told Andy to do it. Also this morning, Andy had to take the club hand-truck down to the ferry dock to meet the eleven o'clock freight boat for a big shipment of meat and produce, and the club hand-truck was an eight-foot-long, two-hundred-pound iron and wood monstrosity with ridiculous three-inch caster wheels that was considerably harder to push through a thousand feet of sand than a child's wagon.

Shoveling the long walk was more mind-numbing than strenuous. It wasn't until he was halfway done that Andy glanced at his wristwatch and realized that a hundred miles away in the hot city, at this very hour, his high school graduation was taking place. He felt a deep sense of satisfaction that he had arranged to miss the ceremony, for he had loathed his four years of high school with the profound loathing a released prisoner feels for the penitentiary.

As Andy imagined his classmates crossing the stage to pick up their diplomas, a jet plane roared down the beach out of the east. From his vantage point the plane appeared to scarcely skim the tops of the beachfront dunes, though it actually flew at an altitude of eight hundred feet. It was an F-104 out of Snell Air Force Base on the South Fork. The pilots liked to skim the barrier beaches, supposedly looking for girls.

The jet was gone in another moment, the roar of its engines merging back into the tireless crash of the surf. But seeing it reminded Andy of the various wars going on in the world. Dominating the news that June week in the year 1967 was the war between Israel and its Arab neighbors. The whole fight had taken only six days from start to finish. Around New York City, with its massive Jewish population—more than twice the entire population of Israel—there was an air of jubilation that at times seemed downright smug. The Israeli victory was so delicious that stand-up comics were doing war jokes on TV. The Israeli thrust across the Sinai was labeled "the blintzkrieg," their troops "the Bagel Lancers."

Andy leaned against his shovel, gazing into the empty blue sky above the dunes where the plane had disappeared. Only now did his thoughts turn to that other war, the one in Vietnam. It was a lot harder to understand Vietnam than the Six-Day War, if only because it had been going on for so many years. In the last year or so people were beginning to say that President Lyndon Johnson was a scoundrel like Adolf Hitler. Andy didn't go along with that. He still remembered the LBJ of the Civil Rights days, a southerner who stood up against southern prejudice and injustice.

Seeing the jet plane while imagining his high school graduation also reminded Andy that he did not have any college to go to in the fall. It had begun to dawn on him lately that unless he got into a college, he could get drafted and sent to Vietnam. The reason it dawned on him so slowly was because he didn't know anybody who had been drafted. In his world, the draft was an abstraction, something that happened to farm boys from Missouri. In fact, he didn't know anyone his age who *wasn't* headed for college in the fall. Andy hadn't gotten into a college for a number of reasons, though he'd applied to several and had been rejected. But until lately he hadn't worried much about it. Surely, he thought, some college would take him in the three months remaining before the fall term began. Anyway, he wouldn't have to register for the draft until he turned eighteen in October. This is what he thought as he leaned on his shovel, gazing out over the distant dunes. Then he resumed shoveling the walk, knowing now that the sand would all blow back in a few days.

The trip to the ferry landing was just over a mile. The

Club walk led directly into Ocean Breeze's "Midway," the central avenue down the spine of the island, midway between the bay and the ocean. Every two hundred feet or so this Midway was intersected by a "street"—another concrete footpath—each named after a different plant that flourished on the island: Holly, Juniper, Hawthorne, Bayberry, and so on. (There was an Ivy minus the Poison.) These streets each led up to the beach. Though the lots in Ocean Breeze were small, the houses were rather expensive. Many of them were wild architectural fantasies of glass, cedar shakes, iron pipe railings, decking, and lattice. Every now and then a bicyclist peddled by, rang his bell and said hello to Andy pushing the clunky handtruck. Ocean Breeze seemed a friendly place, the islanders' good spirits emblematic of all the promise that June held for a fine summer ahead.

When he got "downtown"—three blocks of shopfronts and bars along an oblong village square—he practically ran into someone with his hand-truck, a man whose face was at once familiar, but whom he could not place to save his life. The man, a trim, dark-haired guy in his late twenties with a metropolitan pallor, carried a small suitcase, and also appeared to have trouble identifying Andy. The two smiled and pointed at each other awkwardly for a moment.

"Where do I know you from?" the man asked, seeming to enjoy his own bewilderment.

"You're . . . you're . . ."

"Tommy Oldfield?" the man said, as though unsure of his own name.

"You're the bartender from Maxwell's Plum," Andy said, finally placing him. Maxwell's Plum was a trendy new watering hole a couple of blocks from Andy's and his mother's apartment on 70th Street and 2nd Avenue. It was one of the few bars in New York that Andy could get served in without being asked for identification. Andy had been frequenting the place weekend nights his last few months of high school, trying to get the feel of being grown up.

"I knew I knew you from somewhere," Tommy Oldfield said, lighting a Chesterfield.

"It's this setting." Andy gestured at the village. "You could see your own mother in some weird setting and not recognize her."

"This is some weird setting," Oldfield agreed. "Oooo, that sunlight," he winced jokingly.

"So what're you doing here, anyway?" Andy asked.

"Got a job. Shaking drinks over there for the summer," Oldfield said, pointing to a handsome old white clapboard restaurant at one end of the oblong village square. A big sign decorated with a painted red lobster over the front said MCCAULEY'S SEAFOOD AND LEGAL BEVERAGES.

"Hey, no kidding?"

"I start tonight."

"God, that's really great," Andy said, and he meant it because he'd already been asked for I.D. in several of the Ocean Breeze bars and now with Tommy Oldfield working out here he'd have a place to buy beers on his nights off.

Saying good-bye to Tommy Oldfield, and proceeding to the ferry landing, Andy was soon stopped by a policeman in the Ocean Breeze service uniform.

"Hey, pal," the policeman said. "From now on better wear a shirt downtown. This weekend we start enforcing the ordinances."

"Okay," Andy replied, trying to appear innocent and earnest. "Sure."

9

"The Flannery kids think they own this place," Ted Bass had told him while giving Andy the lowdown on the various families who comprised the club membership. "They'll go right behind the bar and snitch beers, give you a hard time, try to blow your mind. But they're good kids. The whole family's a bunch of jokers, from the old man on down. The oldest, Terry, is my age. Only he won't be here this summer. He got married last month out in California. One of them's about your age: Tim. I'm sure he'll try to bust your balls. The kid's never been serious a moment in his life. There's—I dunno—a half dozen more of them. You kind of lose track, know what I mean? Typical Catholics." Bass grinned.

Andy grinned back, although he wasn't exactly sure what Bass meant by that. Growing up on Manhattan's East Side, Andy had never really been personally acquainted with any Catholics, and what he knew about them came mainly from old Hollywood pictures like *Going My Way* and *Boys Town*.

At one-fifteen in the afternoon that same Friday, then, he had just barely returned from the ferry landing with five hundred pounds of meat, produce, canned goods, and liquor, and was busy putting it all away when he heard what at first sounded like a cavalry charge thundering up the Club's front stairway. Shortly the sound of the Beatles singing "Roll Over Beethoven" resounded in the Club's dining room. Coming out from the kitchen to investigate, Andy first encountered a teenager in the bar. He was reaching into the cooler where the beers lay in cool wet rows.

"Hey, what are you doing?" Andy said.

"It's okay," the kid said, holding a couple of dripping Miller bottles by their necks. Scrawny and freckled, he looked about sixteen.

"What do you mean, 'it's okay'? It's not okay. Put 'em back."

The boy stood up to his full height, which was five foot six.

"You think I'm not going to sign for these, right?"

"I think you're a kid, is what I think," Andy said.

At this, the boy cracked up, or appeared to, doubling over with laughter. It stopped abruptly.

"I'm not a kid," he said with sudden gravity. "I'm a hard-working father of four. This is what it does to you—"

"Hey, Shawn, where's those beers," another male voice bellowed from the dining room.

"Coming, Mother," the kid said, his voice ululating comically. Andy followed him into the dining room. There he saw a somewhat smaller and blonder boy dancing with a girl wearing blue jeans with so many velvet patches sewn on that only about half the old faded denim was left showing. Both she and the boy danced quite expertly to the fast tune. She was wearing a T-shirt that advertised Hanson surfboards, and Andy was a little startled to observe her breasts jiggling loosely within it as she jitterbugged. Suddenly the song ended. The two stopped dancing. The girl cut a guarded glance over to Andy, then followed the blonde boy and yet another, smaller, brown-haired boy over to the jukebox, where they all proceeded to argue about which song to play next.

"This must be the new slave," came the voice that had called Shawn from another corner. The owner of this voice was a young man seated with his bare feet up at one of the Club's square formica tables beside a window that overlooked the bay. He looked a lot like Shawn, but was obviously a couple of years older. His features resembled a face off the cover of a biography Andy's mother

11

had been reading, the face of the boozy Celtic playwright, Brendan Behan—puffy, yet dignified by intelligence.

"I beg your pardon?" Andy said, failing to understand him.

"The new slave," the older boy repeated, accepting one of the beer bottles Shawn had popped open with a church key he wore on a leather thong around his neck and fishing an unfiltered cigarette out of his madras shirt's breast pocket. He lit the cigarette with a Zippo lighter and took a sip out of the beer bottle. "Every year they hire some poor schnook to work here. You must be *it*. You have our sympathy."

"Hear! Hear!" Shawn agreed, toasting Andy with his bottle. He too had lit a cigarette. "Our sincere regrets."

Just then the ballad "Surfer Girl" by the Beach Boys came scratchily on the jukebox. The lone girl tried to get one of the younger boys to slow dance with her, but the boy kept squirming out of her grasp.

"A poor schnook?" Andy repeated, bracing a hand on his hip. "Who the hell are you, anyway?"

"I'm Dean Rusk," the oldest one said, totally retaining his poise. "And this is Hubert Humphrey," he added, indicating Shawn.

"Quit being a little asshole and dance!" the girl said.

"You're Flannerys, aren't you?"

Shawn nodded. "We're Flannerys," he confessed gravely, his eyelids closed.

"I've heard about you," Andy said.

"Our legend precedes us," the oldest one said.

"We did it," Shawn said. "Whatever it is that was done, it was us. We didn't mean to, you understand. But what were we to do? There were the little ones to consider. We did the only thing we could do. We did the decent thing."

"He runs on at the mouth, doesn't he?" the oldest one said. "Well, surf's up." He swung his legs down from the table and got on his feet. His belly bulged slightly over the brass belt buckle. Andy self-consciously measured himself against this Flannery. They were exactly the same height.

"Really," the oldest one said, putting his hand on Andy's bare shoulder, "we admire enterprise."

"If there's one thing this generation could do with more of, it's that," Shawn concurred.

The two older Flannerys marched back down the long dining room to the door. The younger two followed closely behind, with the girl taking up the rear. She glanced emphatically at Andy as she hurried past him and even mumbled the word "hi," but didn't stop when he said "hi" in return.

CHAPTER TWO

Minutes after the Flannerys' departure, Ted Bass arrived with the Club's new chef for the summer, a Greco-Parisian named Anatole with an unpronounceable last name a yard long that ended in *opolis*. About sixty, white-haired, no taller than Shawn Flannery, and with a permanently stiff neck cocked to the left side ("war wound"), Anatole greeted Andy almost sheepishly. But within a half hour back in the kitchen, without Bass around, he proved to be a formidable tyrant.

"No, not like that!" He angrily snatched a cook's knife away from Andy, who had been told to peel and chop up twenty heads of garlic. "Like *this*! *Imbecile!*"

The long afternoon and evening proceeded in this vein, with Andy trying to carry out Anatole's increasingly curt and mumbled instructions at a long list of tedious culinary chores—chopping parsley, peeling potatoes and carrots, mixing batter by hand for two dozen tins of corn muffins, cutting the crusts off toasts for the nasty-looking anchovy paste and chopped egg canapés that Anatole concocted as an hors d'oeuvre for the bar crowd, squeezing a whole crate of lemons and then a whole crate of limes by hand for Bass to make daiquiries and scotch sours with behind the bar, and much more.

15

At precisely five o'clock the screen door on the Club entrance began to slap repeatedly as the members trooped in en masse for cocktails. Bass put one of the Club's Vaughn Monroe albums on the record player that was hooked into the public address system and presided behind the bar, shaking cocktails expertly, greeting the many faces familiar from the previous year, joining the fathers in deploring what was happening to today's youth, and dazzling their wives with his incandescent smile and orthodontically perfect teeth.

The scene back in the kitchen, meanwhile, might have been a vignette from an up-to-date version of hell for teenaged Manhattanite infidels. Anatole, Andy observed, was already quite drunk on the cooking wine. Implements no longer stayed in his hands. Plates crashed to the floor off his central preparation table. The sheet cake he had baked for dessert came out so scorched that Andy had to scrape off the blackened top before it could be frosted.

In the spirit of self-sufficiency, the members employed their own teenaged daughters as waitresses for the Friday and Saturday night suppers that constituted the Club's social life. Among them, Andy noticed the same Flannery girl who had been there earlier.

"Never mind what my brothers said," she whispered to him apologetically, as she and the six other girls in white uniforms lined up with their trays to receive dinner plates. "They didn't mean to be snotty."

Andy was about to ask what her brothers' problem was, anyway, when Anatole dropped an entire sheet pan of baked flounder turbans on the linoleum floor. Cursing, muttering imprecations in French, and blaming the mess on Andy, the drunken chef angrily ordered him to rescue the delicate filets with a spatula. Then, by the time all one hundred thirty-four persons had been served their entree,

16

Anatole had collapsed in a chair in the corner beside the walk-in refrigerator, his eyes catatonically open and his mouth agape with fatigue and alcohol. It was left to Andy to portion out one hundred thirty-four servings of yellow cake with white frosting, and by the time he finished that a tower of dirty dinner plates had been piled up by the waitresses on the counter beside the deep stainless steel sinks.

For the next two hours he was deep in suds, hand-washing the dishes. It was something he happened to do well, though he was keenly aware of what a ridiculous thing it was to excel at in the world. Before he was done washing the dinner plates, the dessert plates were piled up. Meanwhile, Anatole slipped out of the kitchen and disappeared upstairs to his quarters. Andy was relieved to be rid of him.

When he had put the last plate back on the shelves, he tackled the pots and pans, which took another two hours. By the time they were put away, coffee cups, saucers, and ashtrays began to collect beside his sinks. Luckily, Bass was washing most of the cocktail glasses up at the bar. Finally, after wiping down the stove and the prep table, Andy took out the garbage and mopped down the kitchen floor. It was eleven o'clock when he was done.

Befouled with grease and food smarm, but still wide awake and eager to have a look around downtown Ocean Breeze, Andy hurried through the still-busy bar to the stairway and then to the employees' bathroom above. In the hall upstairs, he passed Anatole's room. The door was open and he could see the chef asleep, still dressed in his soiled cooking togs, his face to the wall, snoring musically. The overhead light shed a grim glare over him, like in a drawing of a sleeping peasant by Van Gogh. Andy switched it off and shut the door, as much for his benefit as Anatole's.

The hot shower was sublime. He felt like the victim of some atrocious skin disease whose revolting sores were being washed away by a miracle cure. Then he padded back down the hall to his room, put on a pair of jeans and a green alligator shirt, and grabbed his khaki windbreaker. He didn't bother with any shoes. The island's barefoot tradition extended even to the nightspots downtown. (It was one of the more ironic peculiarities of village law that people downtown caught without shirts on were issued summonses, while everybody except the police went barefoot.)

At last, feeling clean, alert, and happy, and with $10 in his wallet, Andy headed back downstairs. He was un-nerved to find the older Flannery boy—Tim, he supposed—sitting by himself at the end of the bar drinking a beer, while a still-raucous crowd of middle-aged moms and dads enjoyed their after-dinner drinks noisily in the background. Some of them sang along with a Frank Sinatra record that was playing over the P.A.

"Can I buy you a beer, Slave?" Flannery asked Andy.

"I've got a name, you know, just like you," Andy told him cooly.

"What a coincidence! You mean we're both named Tim Flannery? Imagine what the mathematical probability of that must be."

"I've been working my ass off for—let's see—about twelve hours now. Don't you have anything better to do than bust my balls?"

"Hey, I'm just kidding around. You're pretty sensitive."

"No I'm not."

"Okay, let's argue about that, then. Can I buy you a beer anyway? This is what's known as a goodwill gesture."

Andy regarded Flannery with a curious glance, seeing in his intelligent eyes a glimmer of something more sub-stantial than all his superficial bantering betokened.

18

"To tell you the truth, I'm underage," Andy said. "It's probably not cool for me to be seen drinking here around the Club. It'd only get Bass in hot water."

"Un-huh," Flannery said neither agreeing nor arguing.

"I was just on my way downtown," Andy explained. "A guy I know from the city is bartending at McCauley's. I figure he won't hassle me there."

"Want some company? I've had enough of these old farts."

Andy hesitated another moment. "All right," he said. "By the way, my name's Andy Newmark."

"Tim Flannery, raconteur, man-about-the-beach, knight of Columbus, heartbreaker extraordinaire, leader of men." He stuck out his hand to shake with a big smile.

Andy shook his hand. "Lead on, then, Flannery," he said.

Outside, before they even escaped the glare of the Club's lights, Tim Flannery lit a cigarette and passed it to Andy.

"No thanks, I've got my own," he said. "How can you smoke those nonfilters?"

"It's not what you think," Tim said, and by then Andy could detect the sweet, burning hay smell of marijuana.

"Oh," he said, trying not to appear foolish, and taking the joint.

"Hey, look," Tim said, trying to talk and hold in the smoke at the same time. Up in one of the windows of the dining room, old Charlie Dern, husband of Edna, the Club president, could be seen putting a lampshade on his head. In his other hand he held a pony glass of green creme de menthe. "I don't know how they can drink that shit," Tim said. "Jews never drink that kind of garbage, do they?"

"Some probably do."

"Let's get away from here," Tim said. "I can't stand it another moment."

So they headed off past the darkened vacant lots of the Club property toward Ocean Breeze. The concrete was cold on Andy's bare feet. The sky glittered with stars, so unlike the city where they could hardly be noticed beyond the combined glow of a billion electric light bulbs. A breeze so mild it could barely be felt rattled the bamboolike stems of the bushy-headed dune reeds.

"Tell me the story of your life," Tim said as they walked.

"It'd bore you to death."

"You from the city?"

"Yes. You?"

"Shaker Heights, Ohio. Isn't that romantic?"

"It's exotic. I don't know about romantic."

"Exotic! You crack me up."

"Is it a small town?"

"Hell, no, it's a suburb of Cleveland."

"Oh. It had sort of a small-town ring to it."

"Actually it's no different than goddam New Jersey, which is where we moved from six years ago. Anyway, I don't care one way or the other because I'll be going down to Tennessee this fall."

"Tennessee! Now that's exotic. You go to school there?"

"Yeah. That is, I'm supposed to start this fall. U. T. Knoxville. Rah-rah."

"How'd you ever pick that school?"

"A bunch of the guys out here go there. I'm just going to try it for one semester, then maybe go somewhere else. How about you?"

"I don't know yet."

"You don't know yet? It's getting awfully late to be undecided, don't you think?"

"I'll get in somewhere," Andy said, dismissing the unpleasant subject. "Where's your brother Shawn, by the way?"

"He's got his own friends. I don't hang around with a bunch of sixteen-year-olds."

By this time they had crossed over into Ocean Breeze. Many of the houses that had stood dark and silent since Andy arrived on the island were now lighted and rang with life. Tim stooped down and carefully snuffed out what remained of the joint on the walk, then stuck the roach in his shirt pocket. Andy felt the familiar warm sensation in his stomach that signaled he was getting high. An elderly couple passed them on the Midway. The man held a tiny poodle in his arms. The dog was peach-colored with a sculpted pompadour of fur on its head, and it growled at them. The woman wore a hairdo that was astoundingly similar to the dog's. Andy and Tim both cracked up at the sight of them.

"Down this way," Tim said, tugging Andy's jacket sleeve, and they both hooked a left down Juniper. Andy was laughing so hard he had to stop and wait, doubled over. "Hey, it wasn't *that* funny," Tim said, but the idea only made Andy crack up again. It was awhile longer before he could continue walking toward the lights of downtown Ocean Breeze.

It seemed to take an hour for them to get there but it was only a few minutes. The village square had taken on a carnival atmosphere this first big weekend night of the summer. Dozens of teenagers too young to get into the bars hung out along the knee-high concrete wall that surrounded the grassy village square.

"Let's sit down and watch the show for a while," Tim suggested, and he indicated a part of the wall sufficiently far away from the cluster of younger teens so that no one

21

would think they were part of that crowd. A song called "Light My Fire" by a new band called the Doors poured out of the Sandpiper, a bar in a spot that, for some mysterious reason, was always unlucky. Whatever bar opened there each June always failed to attract a crowd and went under by August. It was one of the places that Andy had been asked for I.D.

The village was jammed and it was indeed a fascinating spectacle. The passersby were largely young people in their twenties and thirties. Many of them wore hippie garb—bell-bottom jeans, beads—whether they were office workers from Manhattan or college students. Usually, the students had longer hair. But many of the grown-ups worked in artistic fields like television, or the record industry, or the theater, where it was getting to be okay to let your hair grow or sport a beard. It was also becoming fashionable for women to go around without a certain article of underclothing and Andy soon realized that one of the reasons Tim picked this particular seat was that a silhouette of the passing women's bodies could be starkly seen through their shirts as they walked past the Sandpiper's chest-high pink neon sign in the window.

A tall, athletic-looking guy with a halo of kinky blond hair passed by saying, "Hey, Flannery," with a kind of perfunctory snort that denoted acquaintance without true friendliness.

"That's Duff Perleman," Tim explained after the guy had passed. "Goes to Syracuse. Old man made a fortune on this stuff that cleans your toilet bowl. Had a heart attack two years ago and croaked. Pretty young: around forty-two. Kind of tragic. Anyway, his son hates my guts. Biggest phony on the whole beach."

"Why'd he say hello to you then?"

"We work together."

"What's your job?"

"O.B. lifeguard."

"You? A lifeguard?" Andy said and felt the laughter well up inside him again.

"Incredible—but true. I'm a guard."

"How'd you get that job?"

"My brother Terry was a guard. I guess I inherited his spot."

"But you don't live in the town."

"It doesn't matter. The head guard is a guy named Dale Hummer. Family practically founded the Club single-handedly after World War Two, but they still own about half of Ocean Breeze. So, a lot of the guards are from the Club. It's all who you know, like everything else in life."

"Do they need any more guys to work there?"

"You mean you're not enchanted with your position at the Club?"

"I'd rather be a lifeguard."

"I'm sorry to disappoint you, but it's totally out of the question."

"I was a waterfront counselor at a camp in Maine last summer. I've got Red Cross certification and everything."

"Doesn't matter. Practically every one of us has got brothers waiting in line to get on the crew. Shawn's already a guard. First year. He has to stay down at the bay swimming area and watch over the little babies. We all had to start there. Now my other brother Brian's waiting behind Shawn. And this is just one family. See what I mean?"

"I see what you mean," Andy echoed him glumly. "So you work up on the ocean, then, huh?"

"Yeah. I'm a hero. I admit it. I try to wear the mantle of greatness lightly—"

"Hi, Tim."

A girl with short black hair and dark intense eyes had stopped right in front of them. She wore a faded denim skirt, a white peasant blouse, and a severe-looking necklace of polished brass and copper. She was smoking a cigarette in a very anxious, self-conscious manner, gripping the elbow of the hand that held the cigarette with her free hand. She looked as though she was trying to be charming, though it was obvious she was hopping mad.

"Hello, my little love," Tim said.

"Did you have a nice winter?" She asked with a sardonic edge, as if she hoped he'd been miserable and tormented.

"It was nothing short of the sheerest delight. Yourself?"

"I had a nervous breakdown."

"How avant-garde," Tim said.

"I spent three weeks in Payne-Whitney."

"Really? What's that?"

"It's a loony bin on York Avenue and Sixty-eighth Street."

"Hey, that's near where I live," Andy interjected.

The girl glanced at him as though he were an earthworm.

"I hope it didn't interfere with your schoolwork," Tim said.

"Ha-ha," she said, feigning a laugh. Andy noticed that her fingernails were all bitten down. He also observed her nipples through the sheer cotton peasant blouse. They were dark and surprisingly wide. Seeing them made his breathing quicken. "Anyway, I'm fine now," the girl said, taking a theatrical drag on her cigarette.

"I'm so glad to hear that," Tim said, standing up. "Don't think it hasn't been a treat to see you again. Shall we be on our way, my good man?" he asked Andy.

The girl flashed a nervous smile at Andy, as though merely by standing up he had proved to be something more than an earthworm.

"Call me," she said nervously to Tim.

"You bet," he assured her. "Well, ta-ta."

A moment later they were walking quickly away from the square and the girl.

"Who was that?" Andy asked as they hurried along.

"Her name is Meg Marvin," Tim said. "She's an artist. She don't look back."

"I know the type."

"Junior at the Little Red Schoolhouse," Tim said, alluding to a certain private Manhattan prep school with a distinctly left-wing political orientation where a number of nouveau-riche liberal Thunder Islanders sent their offspring out of guilt for having made so much money. "Unless she got left back, which sounds like a definite possibility. She was my girlfriend last summer for about five days."

"You broke her heart, I'd say."

"I had to. She gave me the crabs."

Andy glanced back sharply to where they had been, but the girl had vanished into the parade of strollers.

"Well now, I have built me up a mighty big thirst with all this confabulation," Tim declared. "What do you say we go have that beer now?"

"Okay."

Their first stop was at the far end of town, an establishment called Clausen's Hotel & Restaurant. The restaurant part was an old-fashioned taproom with a bowling machine, a dart board, and a dozen square tables with red gingham vinyl tablecloths. The joint was very quiet considering the crowds on the street. Not more than a dozen people sat at the bar. They were strictly proletarian types—a couple of garbagemen, Al Coombs, the plumber, some of the dock crew.

"This is not where it's happening this year," Tim said at a glance. "Last year, everybody hung out here. C'mon, let's go."

25

They retraced their steps back to the Sea Witch, a discotheque that some Manhattan sharpie had sunk $100,000 into remodeling. A live rock 'n' roll band could be heard thumping and twanging inside, and they sounded pretty good from out on the sidewalk. But there was a line about fifty people long waiting to get in and Tim and Andy agreed that they were too thirsty to wait in it like a couple of tourists. There was Dixie's, a restaurant and piano bar popular with the middle-aged set and therefore an extremely undesirable place to go at this hour. There was the Bayside, favored by the thirtyish crowd. The Sandpiper was out of the question, as though it were a house that some plague had visited and claimed lives. Finally, there was only McCauley's, so they went down there.

McCauley's was packed with young people, including many who seemed to know Tim Flannery. Andy bought a couple of large beers from Tommy Oldfield. Drafts came in two sizes: 15 cents for the small six-ounce glass, and 25 cents for a twelve-ounce tumbler. Bob Dylan's single "Just Like a Woman" was playing on the jukebox.

McCauley's consisted of two rooms: the front barroom and the larger dining room out back, which at this hour had been cleared of people eating supper and was now full of a mostly collegiate crowd. Tim, who had been chatting with a wasted-looking hippie, signaled Andy with his head to follow him into the back room. There they were fortunate to find a small round table at the very rear, with a good view of the whole room.

"Do you think Dylan's got brain damage?" Andy asked, referring to the fact that almost nothing had been heard from the rock star in the year since his motorcycle wreck the summer of '66.

"No," Tim replied. "I'd think he had brain damage if he tried to top his last album."

26

"Then you don't care if he ever makes another record?"

"I'm afraid he might have shot his wad." Tim drained his beer glass. "In a few years he could be making hula movies like Elvis."

"What a dismal thought."

"Hey, you never know. Want another?"

"Sure."

Flannery came back a few minutes later with four large beers, two for each of them.

"Ever been to McSorley's in the East Village?" Tim asked.

"No."

"Whenever you order a beer, they always bring you two. It's a sort of custom."

"What if you only want one?"

"It doesn't matter. They always bring you two. It's a groovy place. We ought to go there sometime."

"Fine," Andy said, though the prospect of returning to New York City in the heat of high summer sent a pang of nausea through him.

"Do you know a lot of these people?" Andy asked.

"Practically all of them. Since we were babies."

"Who's that tiny chick with the long black hair standing under the lobster trap?"

"Karen Koenigsburg. Father was a famous artist: Lee Koenigsburg—"

"Hey, I've heard of him."

"—did all these giant squiggle paintings. Died right out here in the surf two years ago. Drowned."

"She's beautiful."

"She's about as hard to get as a haircut."

"God . . ." Andy said, observing the exquisite small-ness of her sharp features and her fine olive skin. "She couldn't be eighteen."

"She's not."

"Oh."

"Sixteen."

"Who's that blonde dish in the baggy chinos dancing with that square-jawed guy?"

"That's Kelly Donovan. Her brothers are both guards, Van and Hughie. Their folks have a house out at the Club. The guy she's dancing with is Robbie Kugel."

"A lifeguard, no doubt."

"But of course. He's pretty much a phony too, but a *sincere* phony, know what I mean? It's like he can't help it. I think it's because of his looks. Guys that handsome are really cursed. Everybody expects them to grow up and be a movie star. I feel sorry for the guy, I really do. He's a good surfer, though. Oh, wait a minute, there's an interesting little number. See the reddish brown-haired cutie in the lacy shirt and striped pants over by the jukebox?"

"Yeah."

"Guess her age."

"I dunno. Sixteen?"

"Thirteen."

"Come on."

"I'm not kidding. She's thirteen. Last year, she was coming to the bars when she was twelve. She wasn't even a goddam teenager yet."

"She's pretty well-developed for a thirteen-year-old. But it's kind of decadent, don't you think?"

"Hey, it's even sicker than that. Her parents are divorced, right?"

"Uh-huh."

"And her mother takes off and leaves her alone at the house for weeks at a time. See that guy she's with?"

"Yeah."

"He's twenty-five. He was one of the senior guards

when my big brother, Terry, first got promoted up to the beach. He works on goddam Wall Street now."

"That's really sick."

"This island is a sick goddam place. You'll see."

"God, only thirteen," Andy said to himself. "Hey, that girl who was in the club this afternoon, your sister—"

"Uh, friend of the family."

"Come on, I know she's your sister. I met her again in the kitchen."

"All right. She's my sister."

"What's her name and how old is she?"

"Her name's Frances and she's fourteen and she'll probably try to get you to debauch her. Try to resist the temptation. There's plenty of other girls out here. Okay?"

"Okay," Andy said, adding, as though it required clarification, "I'm not interested in fourteen-year-olds."

Tim nodded.

"See that guy in the striped pullover standing by himself next to that old buoy?" he said. "That's Mike Lovett, best surfer on the island, maybe even on the whole East Coast. Stayed out here at the beach straight through last winter. Doesn't have any job. Very mysterious guy. Lives in a shack made of driftwood on the far side of Holly Wood out where the national seashore starts. He's like God out here."

"Are you one of his followers?"

"Hell no," Tim said, draining the second of his two beers. "I'm an atheist."

CHAPTER THREE

Saturday was, if anything, even more of a horror show for Andy than Friday had been. For one thing, he woke up with a whomping headache and a feeling like his body had been dragged through a keyhole—the effects of eleven large draft beers consumed between the hours of midnight to three A.M., and, of course, little sleep. Four aspirin and a quart of orange juice got rid of the headache, but his nerves remained raw all through the morning. And, unlike Friday, there was a special luncheon that he had to help Anatole prepare—for a meeting of the Club's board of directors—and clean up after, and then supper to start without so much as a chance to step outside the back door for a breath of fresh air.

All afternoon—as he wallowed in grease and slashed his finger slicing cold cuts and stifled in the heat of the kitchen, which was a good deal hotter than the ninety-two-degree high the radio reported from the mainland at three o'clock—Andy thought nostalgically of those fine days beside Long Lake in Maine at Camp Algonquin the summer before, of how good it had felt to stand on the pier in the sun lording it over the splashing kiddies, of how reassuring it was to wear a whistle on a lanyard around his neck and be looked up to—compared to this lowly, loathsome, hateful, disgusting job as second banana to a washed-up souse of a chef. What a mistake he had made! How he rued that stupid vodka spree during the awards dinner (he had stashed a bottle in the room where the kids kept their tennis racquets)!

Chef Anatole spiraled into unconsciousness about the same time as he had on Friday, but not before he had carved the steamship roasts and dispatched the dinner plates to the dining room. Andy was again left to portion out one hundred thirty-four desserts before he faced the awesome tower of dirty dishes and the piles of scorched roasting pans. Tim Flannery's sister had come in to wait on tables, of course, and observing her closely Andy saw how she might feasibly be only fourteen years old. But he couldn't quite imagine the clear-eyed, freckle-faced girl as a seductress, no matter what her brother said.

By eleven-thirty Andy began the final mop-up, while the bar still resounded with the hubbub of the after-dinner crowd, and Martin Donovan—father of Van, Hugh, and Kelly—sat down at the Club piano to bang out some of his favorite Broadway show tunes. Andy was bone weary without being at all sleepy, and he had made up his mind to go downtown by himself when he heard a voice at the back screen door.

"Hay, Slave."

"Flannery?" He was so thrilled at the prospect of some companionship that it took him another moment to say, "Jesus, when are you gonna quit calling me that?"

"When are you gonna quit calling me Jesus?" Tim said out in the darkness. All that could be seen of him through the screen was the glowing orange tip of his cigarette.

"I'm serious," Andy said, angrily thrusting his mop in the bucket of gray-brown water.

"Well, look at yourself. What a pitiful sight you are."

Andy indeed looked down at himself, at his bare feet all white and wrinkled from standing in sink slop and mop water, at his T-shirt stained with roast beef juice and salad dressing, and the expression on his face must have been one of near-suicidal despair, because Tim hastened to add: "In the years to come you'll probably look back on all this and think what a groovy time you had here. And how character-building it was. Really."

"I hate this goddam job so much I can't believe it," Andy said, fighting to choke back tears of frustration. "When I think about how easy I had it last summer I could . . . kill myself."

"It's all in your attitude. This is actually an extremely stimulating job, and a springboard for great things. I've known all your predecessors going back more than a decade, and today many of them are executives in some of America's leading corporations. Besides, you have tomorrow off."

"Fuck you. I want a drink."

"I've got something even better."

"Pot?"

"Sssshh. For chrissake!"

"Sorry."

"Hurry up and wash the crud off yourself. I'll be out at the bar, in my usual spot, listening to the legendary Martin Donovan tickle the ivories."

Fifteen minutes later, Andy came down showered and changed and met Tim at the bar. Tim hooked a couple of beers from the cooler and they departed just as Martin Donovan began to sing the tune "You'll Never Walk Alone," by Rodgers and Hammerstein. Once outside, Andy stopped and chug-a-lugged half his bottle as though to make emphatic his displeasure with everything that was his present lot in life.

"I really needed that," he gasped, and then he shivered in the clammy offshore breeze. "God, what a day! What a night!"

"Try this," Tim said, proffering what looked like a scrap of paper about an inch square.

Andy took it and peered at the scrap in the weak light that shone from the Club porch. There was a tiny picture of the cartoon character Krazy Kat printed on it. "What is it?"

"Mind detergent."

"What?"

"Blotter acid," Tim said.

Andy looked back at Tim, bewildered.

"The acid's in the little picture. Just put it in your mouth and suck on it."

Andy put it in his mouth, chewed on it, made a face, and washed it down with a slug of beer.

"You swallow it?" Tim asked.

"Yeah."

"I guess it'll work just as well."

"Sure it will."

"Ever do acid before?"

"No," Andy said. "But I did mushrooms about a month ago."

"This stuff makes mushrooms feel like a cup of coffee."

"Uh-oh."

"Nothing to worry about. Relax."

"I hope you took some too."

"Of course. Just before you came down."

"Obviously you've dropped acid before."

"Oh yeah, lots."

"It's cold out. Can we walk?"

"I dunno. *Can* we walk?" Tim asked. He started lurching forward, like Frankenstein's monster. "Look! I'm walking, mother! Here, take my crutches!" he said. "And I owe it all to the power of prayer. Thank you, Jesus."

"You're an asshole."

"I give you good wholesome drugs and you call me names. I really must object."

"All right, you're a sterling fellow and I apologize. Got a cigarette? I left mine at the Club."

Tim gave Andy an unfiltered Camel and flicked his Zippo lighter for him.

"Yccch," Andy said, exhaling. "These things are horrible. How can you smoke them?"

Tim shrugged. In a little while, they neared the houses of Ocean Breeze.

"You feel anything yet?" Andy asked.

"Naw. It takes forty-five minutes to get off."

"Oh."

"By the way, there's big doings in town tonight. Your people are throwing a benefit dance for Israel. There's gonna be a live band and everything."

"My people," Andy quietly chuckled to himself.

The benefit dance really was quite an extravaganza. It was being held at the Ocean Breeze Community Center, a clapboard auditorium that was generally used to show movies. Tonight, however, after the seven o'clock show of *Thoroughly Modern Millie*, all the wooden folding chairs were cleared out of the way and the screen was rolled up, leaving a small proscenium stage open for a band calling itself the Molten Heads to use. The Molten Heads' lead guitarist and singer was Jeff Blum, a nineteen-year-old University of Wisconsin student and older brother of Seth

Blum, seventeen, who was running the light show for the affair. Both were O.B. lifeguards.

They were in the middle of their second set, doing a somewhat discordant version of the song "Groovy Kind of Love," when Tim and Andy arrived. An hour of speeches by O.B. Mayor Arthur Schwartzkoph, up-and-coming movie director Barry Bluestone, actor Harv Stern, author Herman Weiser (*Hitler's Offspring*) and other summering dignitaries had preceded the band. There was a $3 "donation" charge at the door, but the person sitting behind the table when Tim and Andy arrived happened to be the Blum brothers' sister, Beth, eighteen, an overweight Swarthmore freshman with hair like rusty steel wool, who carried a torch for Tim Flannery, and she let them in for free.

The room looked big with the chairs cleared aside and weird colored lights swerving all around the noisy crowd. Every once in awhile Andy whiffed the sweet-acrid smell of marijuana. "You Jews really know how to throw a party," Tim remarked as they entered.

"I'm beginning to think you're a very prejudiced person, Flannery," Andy said, speaking directly into Tim's ear because the guitars were so loud. "You Catholics seem to do a pretty good job of having a good time too."

"If that's what you call a good time: sitting around a piano crooning show tunes and drinking creme de menthe until you puke."

"It's quaint," Andy said.

"Quaint," Tim snorted. "See that babe over there?" Tim dipped his head to indicate a woman in her forties wearing a low-cut, scoop-necked, tie-dyed T-shirt that allowed her to display her deeply tanned cleavage to excellent effect. Her ash-blonde hair was woven into a single long braid that swung this way and that as she did

36

the watusi with a man half her age. "Now there's a hot tamale, wouldn't you agree?"

"Definitely an attractive female," Andy said. "For an older woman."

"It's Duff Perleman's mother."

"That lifeguard you don't get along with?"

"Yeah."

"Jeez. He's got some mother."

"Yeah. And since the hubbie croaked she's about as hard to get as the twenty-four-hour virus."

"Get out of here."

"She's a regular nymphomaniac. The genuine article."

Andy watched the woman shimmy her hips with her hands on her young partner's shoulders.

"God," he said, trying to imagine for a moment what it might be like in her boudoir, and wondering whether this made her a despicable person or an asset to the community. Then, as if coming out of a brief trance, he said, "You're just telling me this because her son hates your guts."

"No, it's well known. She's banged some of the other guards."

"You're making this up."

"Nope. Jeff Blum, the guy who's up there singing, was humping her all last summer, and he's two years younger than Duff. And she showed Robbie Kugel the ropes when he was just fifteen."

"That's sick."

"Hey, it's a sick place. The whole island's sick. I thought we already established that."

"One thing about you Catholics, boy. At least you're not getting divorced every five minutes or screwing your kids' friends."

"Yeah, we're really healthy and upright," Tim said with a mordant laugh. "C'mon, let's get a drink."

There was a makeshift bar set up along the far side of the room with a beer keg stuck in a washtub full of ice. They were selling drafts for 50 cents a cup. Tim plunked down a dollar and got two, handing one to Andy.

"You start feeling that acid yet?" Andy asked.

"Not really," Tim said. "My palms are a little sweaty is all."

They watched the crowd for a while. Andy caught sight of Karen Koenigsburg, the tiny, exquisite girl Tim had told him about the night before at McCauley's. That she was no more than five feet tall and yet had all the curves of a fully formed woman was ineffably charming and beautiful to him. She was dancing with a thickset, clumsy man who appeared to be in his thirties.

"Who's the guy she's with?"

"Max something-or-other. An artist."

"Oh, I get it," Andy said. "Father replacement."

"That's probably not far off the mark," Tim said. "The guy makes huge sculptures of food out of fiberglass. Big six-foot-long hot dogs and gigantic hamburgers and banana splits and crap like that. It's stupid, if you ask me, but I guess it sells."

Andy was about to agree when something extremely peculiar happened. It started when Seth Blum, at the control panel of his light show, threw the switch that turned on the strobe lights. The strobe lights made everybody look as though their movements were jerky and mechanical, like characters in an old silent film comedy. That in itself was not the weird part, because Andy had seen strobe lights quite a few times before during the past year. The weird part was that Andy felt his beer cup slip out of his hand. He glanced down and saw the cup fall to the floor. It seemed as though it had fallen from a five-story window, it took so long to reach the floor. Then, when it hit the floor, it shattered into a million dazzling fragments, like diamonds, glinting prismatic colors in the flickering strobe lights. But this wasn't all. As Andy stared down at the floor in amazement, he suddenly saw all the dazzling fragments come together again and turn back into his beer cup, which then proceeded to fly back into his hand. The whole thing couldn't have taken more than a couple of seconds.

"Holy shit," he said.

"What?" Tim said.

"Did you see that?"

"Who?"

"No, that thing with my cup."

"What . . . ?"

"I dropped it and it shattered into a million pieces and flew back together again."

"It's still in your hand."

"I know."

"You hallucinated it."

"Oh God."

"Besides, it's plastic. It couldn't shatter even if you dropped it from the Empire State Building. You must be getting off. I'm starting to feel a little trippy myself, frankly."

Andy lifted his plastic cup and cautiously took a sip of beer. The cup was there, all right. The beer tasted strongly metallic. Next, he tried to listen to the band but the words they were singing (to the rockabilly song "Kansas City") seemed to come out of their mouths not so much as sound but as filmy blobs of color, like the kind of goop they used to sell for kids to blow giant plastic bubbles with. As for sound, his ears were beginning to fill up with a noise that felt like the roar of a mighty engine—like the jet airplane that had streaked down the beach the day before. For the first time, he noticed the heat inside the community center. It was suffocating.

Anxious about what might happen next, and what to do about it, he shifted his weight nervously from one foot to the other—and then the next thing did happen. He felt as though he had stepped through the floorboards, or rather that they had been replaced with some kind of yielding stuff like marshmallow fluff.

"Omigod," he said.

"What?" Tim asked.

"I've gotta get out of here."

"Let's stick around awhile—"

"No, you don't understand. I can't stay here."

"Sure you can."

"I can't."

An electrical current seemed to roll up his spine and ignite a blue light in his head. Suddenly everything looked blue. He became aware of his heart racing. His shirt was damp and he couldn't breathe.

"Really," he gasped, suddenly seizing Tim by the arm with both of his hands. "I can't stay here."

"You're just getting off," Tim tried to reassure him. "That's all."

"I don't want to get off. I want it to stop," Andy said, with increasing panic. He was squirming in place like a little kid, and despite the myriad bewildering new sensations, part of him remained an observer, and he was embarrassed by his own behavior. "Really," he told Tim, still clinching his arm. "I gotta get out of here."

"Okay," Tim said.

"You gotta come with me. I'm scared. I don't want to be alone."

"Okay," Tim said. He turned toward the entrance where

they had come in. "Could you not dig your fingernails into my arm, though?"

"I'm sorry."

One of the O.B. police officers was standing near the door, craning his neck to see the goings-on within, and he stopped Tim and Andy on their way out.

"No open containers outside, you two," he told them gruffly.

"Sure, Jojo," said Tim, who evidently knew him.

"S'matter with your buddy?" the cop asked, dipping his capped head toward Andy, who looked seasick.

"The depravity in there has turned his stomach," Tim said, and the cop only craned his neck harder, trying to see what Tim was talking about. Meanwhile, Tim knocked back the rest of his beer and Andy's beer too, and helped him outside.

"How's that fresh air feel?" he asked as they stood beside the privet hedge that surrounded the community center.

"It feels super cold like airplane glue."

At midnight Saturday on this first weekend of the summer, downtown was packed shoulder to shoulder with revelers, and all of them looked like characters out of a Fellini movie that Andy had seen just before leaving the city. Their features all seemed hideously exaggerated. A man with a dark beard and a gold chain around his neck appeared Satanic. A fat woman with lipstick on looked like one of Fellini's smirking whores. A parade of human grotesques passed by the hedge, all seeming to bore their eyes accusingly into Andy, as though they were some gigantic jury passing judgment on him.

"Feeling better?" Tim asked delicately.

"No."

"Want to go into McCauley's? It'd be a little quieter."

"No. I gotta get out of here. You gotta take me away from here."

Tim sighed in resignation.

"I should have given you only half."

"Please. I can't stay here another minute."

"Want to go up to the beach? It'll be deserted up there. Just nature."

"Okay, fine. Let's go up to the beach."

"Only you gotta stop hanging onto me like this. People are gonna think we're a couple of queers from Piney Grove."

"I'm sorry. I'm so scared. I can't help it," Andy said as all the lights of downtown appeared to pulsate with the beating of his heart.

CHAPTER FOUR

Every step up to the beach Andy felt the ground giving way beneath his feet and the notion seized him that he might somehow slip through the concrete walk into some terrifying abyss at the planet's core. He recalled, from a book of unexplained happenings called *Stranger Than Science,* an incident involving a Pennsylvania farmer who vanished from the face of the earth in full view of his family. One scientist was quoted in the book as saying that "just possibly" the farmer's bodily molecules "slipped through" the molecules of the cornfield he was standing on.

By the same token, Andy was equally afraid of looking up at the sky, for he felt that nothing, besides invisible gravity, really tethered him to the ground, and that he might just float off into the interstellar ethers. Then, when they reached the end of Juniper Street and climbed the wooden stairway over the dunes, Andy felt suddenly overwhelmed by the dark vastness of the ocean and reached for Tim's arm again.

"I'm sorry," Andy said. "I'm not a queer or anything. I'm just a very frightened normal person. I keep on thinking I'm gonna float away."

"We're perfectly safe. The tide's going out."

"How can you tell it's going out?"

"Hey, you work as a lifeguard, you get to know the tides."

"Oh," Andy said. "Anyway, that's not what I mean. I mean float off the earth."

Tim laughed. "Believe me, you're not gonna float off the earth."

"Omigod! What the hell is that?"

"Just a beach taxi."

"I thought it was . . . I dunno what. A dinosaur."

"Want to sit down awhile?"

"Not really," Andy said. The sand felt icy cold on his bare feet. "To tell you the truth, I'm a little sorry we came out here. I'm very uncomfortable here."

"You want to go back to the Club?"

"No!"

"Well, there's the lifeguard shack." Tim pointed to a boxy, ramshackle structure perched on stilts on the crest of a nearby dune. "We can go up there for a while."

"What's in there?"

"Not much. A bunch of wet jockstraps, some towels."

"It's just that I'm having kind of a rough time with the sky and the ocean and all," Andy tried to explain. "I keep feeling like I'm going to disappear off the face of the earth."

"Okay, then. We'll go up to the guard shack. You'll be okay there."

Tim worked the combination lock on the shack's door by the light of his Zippo lighter. Inside was a room about twelve feet long by eight feet wide. Hooks along the walls were festooned with sweatshirts bearing college insignia, towels, and official O.B. lifeguard red bathing suits. There were a couple of beat-up folding chairs like the ones down in the community center. Tim soon found a flashlight and a portable radio. He turned on the radio and got WABC in the city. Something that sounded like a brand-new song by the Beatles was playing. The song was about getting by, and getting high, with a little help from your friends.

"That's the spirit," Tim said to the radio. Meanwhile, Andy slunk off into a corner and wrapped a huge towel around himself like a blanket. The towel was damp. Everything in the shack was damp and smelled like unwashed laundry. Tim propped the flashlight against the wall so it provided a soft indirect light and sat on one of the two chairs.

"Feeling better now?"

"Yeah, actually."

"Still seeing things?"

"Yeah. Colors. The whole world seems to all turn one color, like a wash. Back in town it was this cold creepy blue."

"What's it now?"

"Sort of warmer yellowish. I guess it's 'cause of the flashlight. I dunno."

"I feel responsible," Tim said, leaning forward on the chair.

"For what?"

"For you having a shitty time."

"You're not responsible. I absolve you. It's totally my fault."

"Well, it's going to last awhile," Tim said, quickly adding, "but it'll probably get better."

"I hope so. I feel pretty terrible now."

"How, exactly?"

"Just scared. Totally, thoroughly, completely scared."

"What of?"

"I don't know. That's the weird part. Everything. Stupid things. The sky. The earth. I'm scared of the goddam universe."

"Tell me your life story," Tim said.

"My life story!" Andy echoed him in amazement. "Ha!"

"It'll take your mind off the universe."

"I wouldn't know where to begin."

"Okay, I'll ask questions. You just answer them. It'll be fun, like an interview for *Playboy*."

"Okay, I'll pretend I'm Bob Dylan."

"No, just be yourself."

"Okay, I'll be myself."

Tim lit two cigarettes and passed one to Andy, who shivered under the towel.

"What's your family like?" Tim asked.

"Oh, Jesus, you sure picked a great topic to kick off with."

"I keep telling you, I'm not Jesus. Now, come on. What's your family like?"

"My family . . ." Andy took a deep drag of his cigarette and looked up at the ceiling, where several surfboards lay across the ceiling joists. "Let's see. There's my mom, and my dad, and there's me."

"No brothers or sisters?"

"Nope. Not a one."

"That must be weird."

"There's one good reason: My parents are divorced."

"Oh. Since you were little?"

"Not that little. Eight."

"That's not so little."

"Who knows. Anyway, no siblings."

"And you live in the city?"

"Yeah. Seventieth Street."

46

"With your mom?"

"Yeah," Andy sighed. "What a drag."

"Where's your old man live?"

"Out in Los Angeles. He's married to this other lady, Charlotte, my stepmother. She's about twenty-five. Imagine having a stepmother a few years older than you are?"

"Weird."

"I only met her a couple of times, actually. Dear old Dad and I don't get along too well. I think it's because he hates my mom's guts. I mean, these two people really despise each other. It's a wonder that they ever got married in the first place. I can't imagine that they ever were, to tell you the truth, even though I remember us all living together. They haven't spoken to each other, except through lawyers, ever since they split up. That's one of the reasons I don't have anywhere to go for college."

"How's that?"

"They were so busy arguing through their lawyers about which one of them was going to get stuck paying for my college that I got sick of it all and screwed up my applications on purpose. I wrote witty answers to all the questions and I pasted a picture of Cassius Clay up in the box where you're supposed to paste a photo of yourself. It was stupid, but I was pretty depressed about it all."

"Seems to me the father's the one who's supposed to pay for a kid's college in our society," Tim observed. "If he's got the dough. What does your old man do for an occupation?"

"It's embarrassing. He produces daytime TV shows."

"What kind of shows?"

"The really stupid ones."

"Which ones?"

Andy exhaled a long plume of cigarette smoke. "*Double-or-Nothing, The Hot Seat, Question Box.* The stupidest shows on the air."

"They're pretty stupid, all right," Tim agreed, with another hearty laugh. Andy appreciated the fact that Tim didn't try to pretend that the shows were splendid highbrow entertainment just to make him feel better. "He must have a pretty good income from that, though, your old man."

"Oh, sure. Lives in a big house with a pool and everything. He's got a sailboat."

"So why won't he pay for your college?"

"It's not that he says straight out that he won't pay. I haven't even gotten in anywhere. It's that every time I talk to the bastard, which is about every other month, the first thing he says to me is, 'Have you spoken to your mother about how you're going to finance your college education?' That's all he ever says. It seems pretty obvious that he doesn't intend to foot the bill."

"Well, how's your mom supposed to pay for it?"

"That's another thing. She's got an occupation that's pretty well-paying too. She owns this art gallery."

"So they're both well-off?"

"Yeah, basically."

"And neither of them'll pay for your college?"

"I guess both of them are more interested in fighting over it between themselves than doing anything about it."

"That's a shitty deal," Tim said. "Hey, don't you love this song?"

The tune was "Carrie-Anne" by the Hollies. It had a catchy hook and nice harmonies.

"Yeah, it's a good song," Andy said.

"So, anyway, why don't you go to some real cheap college you can work your way through? City College. That's free, isn't it, if you're a city resident?"

"I'm through living in New York City," Andy declared, stubbing his cigarette out angrily on the floor. "I hate the city so much I can hardly begin to express it."

"How could you hate New York?"

"You ever actually live there?"

"No, but—"

"You ought to try living in the goddam place. Or going to school there. That was another thing. School. My goddam parents were so wrapped up arguing about money that I was stuck going to these disgusting city schools. After grammar school all my friends went to private schools, where at least you can learn something. You should have seen the junior high school I went to. It was like goddam Guatemala. I think they taught English as a second language there. You couldn't walk around the halls with more than a nickel in your pocket because you'd get robbed."

"Where'd you go to high school?"

"This place called the High School of Music and Art."

"Hey, I know someone from out here on the beach who goes there," Tim said.

"Debbie Klinger, right?"

"Yeah, Debbie Klinger. She raves about it."

"Well, maybe she had a grand time, but I hated it. First of all, the goddam school is located right smack-dab in the middle of Harlem. I had to take this goddam number three bus every day for three goddam years and ride for an hour up Fifth Avenue to One hundred tenth Street and then up Morningside Avenue to One hundred thirty-fifth Street, and it was the most depressing ride you could imagine. Slums, junkies, burned-out tenements. And then an hour back in the afternoon. I got robbed five times. Then, because it's this so-called 'special' school that you have to take an exam to get into, they've got kids from all over the five boroughs coming to school there. I admit, a lot of them had much longer rides than I did, and were a lot more worse off familywise. But hardly any of them lived on the east side of Manhattan, and to tell you the truth it was goddam lonely. You didn't have any friends. They all lived two hours away. You never saw anybody outside of school. They didn't have any extracurricular activities. They didn't have any teams. Hell, they didn't have sports, period. You don't know how badly I wanted to see a normal high school football game. Just smell some autumn leaves burning and listen to a band play. I never did get to see one."

"They're not so wonderful," Tim said. "Believe me."

"I bet you went to a normal high school, though."

"Normal," Tim snorted sardonically. "Rah-rah."

"It might seem stupid, but I really envy that."

"You want to know how normal school was for me?" Tim said. "I got left back in the tenth grade."

"Left back?"

"That's right. I bet you didn't think they really did that anymore in this modern age of miracles. Well, they did it to me."

"God. What a bummer. How come?"

"Simple. I flunked all my subjects except two."

"Oh, Jesus. How'd you do that? Obviously you're not stupid."

"Funny, they said exactly the same thing," Tim said, taking out another cigarette and lighting it pensively.

"What *didn't* you flunk?" Andy asked.

"Social studies and English."

"Oh. I wasn't too swift in math or science either. Except biology. I'm interested in animals. And plants."

"Hey, I *almost* flunked English too. I got a seventy. Social studies I got an eighty-five in. I'm very interested in current events. That's all it takes. An interest."

"I gave up in math when this old bag tried to explain to me that any number multiplied to the zero power equals one," Andy said. "I still don't get it. She gave me a sixty-five. It dragged down my whole grade-point average. I'm not sure I could get into a decent college now with my average, even if I did fill out the goddam application correctly. God, did I hate math."

"I got a forty in geometry," Tim said. "Talk about fucking up your average. I don't see the point of giving someone a mark twenty-five points below the failing grade. Why not just stop at sixty-five?"

"I don't know. School is so ridiculous. Maybe it's a good thing I don't have any college to go to."

"Not with the war on it's not. You're going to have to get in somewhere before the summer is over. Besides, college is fun. You only go to a couple of classes a day. It's a joke compared to high school."

"How the hell did you manage to get into the University of Tennessee, if your grades were so lousy?"

"I got them up a bit after that sophomore year that I got left back. My folks were pretty alarmed, naturally. They arranged for some tutoring so I could pass algebra, and then you didn't have to take any more math. It was all electives after that. I finally graduated with about an eighty-two average, not counting that year they made me do over. Besides, the Donovans both go to Tennessee. Van's gonna be a senior this year and Hughie's a sophomore. It's partly knowing people, like everything else in life."

"How much does it cost?"

"About fifteen hundred dollars for out-of-staters. That's for everything: tuition, room, and board."

"You think I should apply there?"

"Sure. Why not? What was your average, by the way?"

"About eighty. High seventies, actually. They'd think I was a mongoloid idiot."

"You could say you know me and Hughie and Van.

There's this part of the application—it takes up about one quarter of it—where you're supposed to list family members or friends who went there. It's probably more important than your goddam grades or your test scores."

"I got some decent test scores, at least," Andy said. "I qualified for this thing they have in New York called a regent's scholarship. It's good for about four hundred dollars a year. The only catch is that you've got to use it in New York state."

"So apply to some state schools."

"I already got rejected out at Stony Brook."

"Get in wherever you can," Tim said. "You don't have to stay there for four years. Just show them that you're not a total cretin for your freshman year, and then you can transfer somewhere else."

"Fine, except how am I gonna pay for it?"

"Sell sandwiches in the dorms."

Andy was thunderstruck by the idea.

"Sell sandwiches in the dorms!" he said.

"Sure. Or something. It's not that hard to make fifteen hundred dollars in a whole year's time. If you made fifty cents profit off a single sandwich, all you'd have to do is sell three thousand sandwiches."

"How many sandwiches is that per day?"

"You're asking me?" Tim said and then began to laugh.

Andy also cracked up. He began rolling on the floor, still wrapped up in his towel.

"C'mon," Tim said, "let's figure it out. There's probably some formula, right?"

"You . . . you *are* lousy in . . . in math," Andy said, laughing so hard he could hardly speak.

"It sounds like one of those questions on the goddam SAT exam. If Leroy has twelve cents and Fred has twenty-seven cents, blah, blah, blah."

"You . . . you divide . . . the number of days by the . . . by the number of . . . sandwiches," Andy managed to say before he exploded in laughter again.

"Hey, I think you've got it there. Let's see, now. That's—what'd we say?—three thousand sandwiches into three hundred sixty-five days. Uh-oh, you can't divide a smaller number by a larger number. Can you?"

This time Andy was laughing too hard to answer. All he could do was nod his head.

"I forgot how to do that," Tim said matter-of-factly. He got up and fetched a clipboard that was hanging from a nail on the wall. Attached to it was a pencil on a string. "Here, you figure it out."

With some difficulty Andy sat up and propped the clipboard on his knees.

"We already fucked up," he said and cracked up again. It made his stomach hurt.

"How's that?"

"It's the other way around. Sandwiches divided by days."

Still chuckling, Andy worked on the figures.

"Let me see that," Tim said, reaching for the clipboard. "Hmmm. Eight-point-two sandwiches per day. That's a breeze."

"You're absolutely right. It's a great idea. I don't know why I never thought of it myself."

"You could probably start with an investment of under fifty dollars. Just buy some peanut butter and jelly and some tuna fish and mayo and bread and a knife and some tinfoil."

"I could get some of that stuff at home."

"Well, there you go. Eight-point-two little sandwiches a day."

"It's truly amazing."

"Isn't math great?"

"You can really see how the human race has solved a lot of problems with it. It's too bad the only people who teach it are a bunch of disgusting old bats with bad breath."

"With good teachers, we might have been headed for careers in the space program."

"What a waste."

"How do you feel now?" Tim asked.

"Better. Not so bent out of shape."

"Still seeing colors?"

"Oh, God, yes. Everything has these little prismlike auras around them."

"You want to go back downtown?"

Andy hesitated before answering. "I'm sorry, but I don't think I could handle it."

Tim shrugged his shoulders and glanced at his watch. "It's two-thirty, anyhow. Nothing left down there but the dregs of the night."

"It's weird, though. I don't feel the least bit sleepy."

"Acid's like that. Keeps you wired. You want to go back to the Club?"

"Not until this wears off a little."

"It's liable to be a while yet."

"Just do me a favor and don't leave me alone. You can crawl off into a corner and go to sleep if I'm boring you, but please stick around."

"Well, I couldn't sleep either. I'll stick around."

Tim turned down the radio when a disc jockey wouldn't stop yammering about acne medicine and for a while they sat listening to the even pounding of the surf against the beach.

"Isn't it amazing that the ocean keeps going all night long?" Andy said.

"They used to turn it off after dark in the old days," Tim said. "In the forties this scientist figured out how to keep it going around the clock using math."

"Probably the same guy who came up with the A-bomb."

Tim rummaged around on the floor and came up with the latest issue of *Time* magazine, its pages already swollen from the dank sea air.

"Hey, dig this. A cover story about the hippies." He held it up for Andy to see the psychedelic illustration.

"Groovy."

Tim quickly leafed through the pages to find the article and began reading, at first quietly to himself, then out loud.

" 'Whatever their meaning and wherever they may be headed, the hippies have emerged on the U.S. scene in about eighteen months as a wholly new subculture, a bizarre permutation of the middle-class American ethos from which it evolved.' "

"That's us all right," Andy agreed.

" 'San Francisco's Haight-Ashbury district is the vibrant center of the hippie movement. Fog sweeps past the gingerbread houses of "The Hashbury," shrouding the shapes of hirsute, shoeless hippies huddled in doorways, smoking pot, "rapping" (achieving rapport with random talk)—' "

"Hey, that's what we've been doing: rapping."

"Isn't it nice to know that there's a word for it?"

"Oh, yes, a great comfort."

" 'In a sense, hippiedom is a transplanted *Lost Horizon,* a Shangri-La au go-go blending Asian resignation and American optimism in a world where no one grows old.' "

"Good name for a band: Shangri-La au go-go."

"Or a bar. Get this: 'In a recent study, three University of Southern California graduate students interviewed eighteen randomly selected LSD-users for a period of four months and found that the primary quality in common was a history of unhappy family life.' "

"Now that's bullshit," Andy said. "You come from a perfectly happy family and you take acid all the time. My family is all split up and I never took the stuff until tonight."

"Listen, there's more: 'All the acidheads were loners and losers, with few friends and few accomplishments before they dropped out.' "

"Uh-oh, we're in trouble."

"You think we're more loners than losers or the other way around?"

"You're obviously not a loner," Andy said. "It seems like you know practically everyone out here."

"Yeah, but most of them hate my guts."

"Only that lifeguard whose mother screws everybody."

"You don't know. There's a few other guys around here who aren't too fond of me."

"Anyway, you're no loser."

"Thanks for the testimonial."

"Me," Andy said, "I'm definitely a loner. Maybe if I went to a normal high school I wouldn't have been, but it sure ended up that way."

"Get a load of this: 'Central to the drug scene is marijuana, the green-flowered cannabis herb that has been turning men on since time immemorial. Virtually every hippie uses it—sometimes up to three times a day.' "

Tim chucked the magazine to the floor with a derisive snort. Another Beatles song came over the radio airwaves so he turned the volume back up. Like the earlier number, it too was a new tune that neither had heard before.

"What's he singing? 'Lucy in the Sky with Diamonds'?"

"What's that supposed to mean?"

"Who knows?"

They listened to the song until it was over.

"I guess it's about taking an acid trip," Tim concluded.

"That's all we're going to hear about this summer. Hippies and acid," Andy said. "I feel okay enough to go back to the Club now."

"You sure?"

"Yeah. What time is it?"

"Twenty after three."

Andy finally got up from his place on the floor and hung the towel up on a wooden peg. Tim turned off the radio and put the flashlight back in the footlocker where a lot of the equipment was stored to keep it out of the corrosive salt air. Leaving the shack, Andy was stunned to see a full moon hanging about twenty degrees above the horizon of the ocean. This time it didn't frighten him.

"Wow," he said. "What a moon!"

Tim turned from securing the combination lock on the door and the two of them stood on the little eight-foot-wide porch that fronted the guard shack.

"Quite a sight," Tim agreed. "Hey, look down there!"

"Where?"

"That speck in the water, out past the break."

"It's a person!"

"Yeah."

They watched as the speck rode the swells in the reflection of the moonlight.

"It's Mike Lovett."

"The surfer?"

"Yeah," Tim said with boundless admiration.

"That's a weird thing to do: go surfing at night all by yourself. I'd be scared shitless."

"Lovett's not afraid of anything."

"I'd be afraid of a shark. A shark's something."

"Lovett's got true ocean karma," Tim said.

"Now you sound like some stupid hippie."

"Ssshhh. Just watch."

The surfer continued to sit out on the swells, waiting. Eventually a swell larger than those preceding it came into view out of the vast silvery green distance.

"That's the one he's been waiting for."

The surfer saw the swell now and began paddling his board to build up enough speed to catch the wave. As it rolled toward shore, the swell rose into a concavity, glassy green at the crest where the moonlight blazed through it. He stopped paddling and stood up in what seemed like a single fluid motion. Riding the forward end of the board for several seconds, he whirled his body in a three-hundred-sixty-degree turn, letting out a whoop of delight that was audible all the way up to the guard shack. A moment later, the wave broke with a crisp tearing noise, like somebody ripping a gigantic sheet, followed by the hiss of foam. The surfer soon reappeared, retrieved his board in the slop, and headed back out past the break.

"That was incredible," Andy said.

"He's a very spiritual guy," Tim said quietly.

"Maybe." Andy couldn't help but join in admiration for what he had just witnessed. "But if it was me, I'd probably worry about the sharks."

CHAPTER FIVE

When Andy returned to the Club—which looked like a scene straight out of an Edward Hopper painting in the early morning light—he was still too much under the influence of LSD to be able to sleep. Instead he sat at his table with a pen and his letter tablet and painstakingly figured out the details of the sandwich-selling scheme that was going to put him through college.

He soon realized, of course, that such an enterprise would have to be based on less than three hundred sixty-five days of potential sales. To begin, then, he lopped off the twelve weeks of summer vacation. This left two hundred eighty-one days. Next he subtracted forty remaining weekends. This left two hundred one days. After that he knocked off two more vacations of two weeks each—Christmas and Easter—leaving one hundred seventy-three days. He rounded this figure out to one hundred seventy to account for Election Day, Veterans Day, and Washington's Birthday, and also because it was easier to work with an even number. The final revised estimate was seventeen-point-six-five sandwiches per day at 50 cents profit per sandwich in order to make enough money to pay for a year's college. Even in the clear light of day the scheme still seemed perfectly workable. And so at quarter to ten, greatly pleased with himself and optimistic about his future for the first time in months, Andy rolled onto his bed and sank into a restless, febrile slumber.

The ninety-degree heat woke him up in mid-afternoon, and though he was not completely rested from the LSD experience of the night before, he couldn't get back to sleep in the small, stifling room. He was also ravenously hungry. So, he put on a pair of cutoff jeans, went downstairs to rummage in the pantry where he and Bass kept some of the staples they were entitled to, and rustled up a steel mixing bowl full of Rice Krispies and milk. Finally he departed the empty Club for the beach.

Only a handful of people—middle-aged married couples with their crossword puzzles and thermoses of martinis—lay scattered on blankets on the stretch of beach that belonged to the Club, so Andy began walking down to the O.B. stretch a half mile distant. The surf was unusually small by Thunder Island standards, little three-foot tubes that broke close to the beach. A few surfers sat listlessly on their boards, bobbing on the swells beyond the break as though out of a sense of duty, like sentinals, without any apparent serious intent to catch waves and ride them. One of the surfers, Andy noticed, was another of Tim Flannery's younger brothers—Brian, he supposed—the blond-headed one younger than Shawn who had been dancing with Frances that first day at the Club.

Between the Club and Ocean Breeze an enormous sea turtle the size of a coffee table lay dead on its back in the sand, having washed up with the tide early in the morning. The turtle had been attracting a small, constantly changing crowd of beach strollers all day long, and many of them speculated about what might have killed the animal—pollution? a swallowed fish hook? old age?—

since it bore no obvious wounds. Its great size amazed Andy, and yet it seemed like only a small token of the more monstrous secrets that the ocean concealed. The crowd contained many children who took great pleasure in poking the dead creature with driftwood sticks. After a day in the hot sun, the turtle stank ferociously. Everything about its present disposition seemed to Andy to compromise the turtle's essential and monumental dignity and he wished he was able to bury it or return it to the sea, but either course of action would have been too much trouble, and probably unpopular, so he merely continued on down the beach.

At the Ocean Breeze stretch there were many more people scattered on the sand, including in particular, Andy was quick to apprehend, a great many nubile teenage girls gathered in gossiping clusters. Radios blared and the coconut scent of suntan lotion mingled with the tangy salt air. A swimming area was demarcated by two green flags stuck in the sand about two hundred yards apart. Centered between them was the ten-foot-high wooden lifeguard chair. It was presently occupied by Van Donovan, twenty-one, who at six foot three, dark-haired, and with a suntan that turned his skin very reddish, had the stately look of an Indian warrior and the self-possessed personality to go with it. The only element distinctly un-Indian about him was his bomber pilot's sunglasses.

"Is Tim Flannery around today?" Andy inquired of Donovan, who sat in the lofty chair as though it were a throne.

"Up at the shack," the lifeguard told him pleasantly.

At the shack, someone was sitting on a milk crate reading, holding a newspaper up in front of his face.

" 'Scuse me. Is Flannery up there?"

Tim lowered the newspaper and with a big grin said, "Hey, Slave!"

"Aw, hell, are we back to that again?"

"Sorry. I take it back. Can I take it back?"

"Yeah, I guess," Andy said and started up the steps.

"Uh, you can't come up here. It's not cool right now," Tim said, indicating ruefully with a tilt of his head the presence of some authority inside the shack. "Hummer's around," he explained. "Head honcho. Only guards are supposed to be up here."

"Oh. I just wanted to let you know I was okay and all. Made it through the morning with my brain intact."

"Sure. I knew you would."

"And thanks for sticking around last night when it got weird."

"Aw, it was nothing," Tim said. "Hey, you hear the news?"

"What news?"

Tim held the paper up to show Andy down below.

"I can't make out the words from here."

" 'Sentencing of Two Young Pop Musicians Arouses Storm in Britain,' " Tim read out loud. Then he summarized the story: "Mick Jagger and Keith Richard got the book thrown at them. Jagger got three months for having four hits of speed in his pocket. Keith got a year. Get this: 'Mr. Richard was convicted of letting his house be used for the smoking of Indian hemp.' That's priceless, isn't it? Indian hemp. Ha!"

"But, God, that's terrible about the Stones."

"I'm not God, and don't worry about the Stones," Tim said. "They're both out on bail. The whole thing's on appeal. That's what this story is about. There's this furor over it in England. Street protests and everything. Those guys won't spend five minutes behind bars when it's all over. By the way, here's another one that may interest you: 'Draft Extended Under Old Rules Four More Years.' "

"Great," Andy said glumly, but he quickly brightened again. "Hey, I worked out that whole deal with the sandwiches. I've got all the figures. We forgot to consider vacations and weekends. But you know something? It's still a great idea."

"Of course it is. Gonna give me a cut of the profits?"

"How about a plaque of appreciation?"

"Terrific. I can start a trophy room—"

Just then, a scowling, thick-torsoed man strode out onto the narrow porch from inside the guard shack. Dale Hummer, thirty, a schoolteacher in the off-season—math, as chance would have it—wore his hair in a brush-cut of the sort that they give to recruits in the armed services—carved practically down to the scalp on the sides with just a flat tuft at the front. He would have appeared comical in an era when things that smacked of militarism were less malevolent.

"You're on duty, Flannery," he told Tim in a manner that could not be construed as friendly.

"Yessir, Dale, sir," Tim replied, saluting and taking no pains to hide his lack of respect for the chief guard as he climbed down the steps to the sand. "I gotta go be a hero now," he told Andy. "Catch you later."

Andy watched Tim exchange places with Van Donovan up in the high chair. When Donovan came down from his stint, he grabbed one of the surfboards stuck in the sand behind the chair and headed out toward the water with the huge, sleek fiberglass board tucked under his arm. Up above, Tim blew his whistle twice and stood up, gesturing with broad sweeps of his arms to a pair of swimmers who had strayed beyond the green flag to the left. Andy, meanwhile, searched the beach from his spot beside the chair to see if he could locate anyone he knew, specifically Debbie Klinger, his classmate from high school. She was nowhere to be seen, but some one hundred feet away he did spot Ted Bass reclining beside a blonde girl in a red bikini with white polka-dots, and he slogged through the hot sand over to them.

"Well, hello Andrew," Bass said with his customary humorous formality.

The blonde girl looked over her shoulder at Andy and he was astonished to see how beautiful her face was. From behind, the curve of her figure had been exaggerated by the way she reclined on her towel, propped up on one elbow, and he had assumed she was an older college girl. Now he could see by the youthfulness of her face that she was a teenager, probably younger than he was. Where he was standing, practically looming over her, he could also see straight down the front of her bikini top and he could not help but notice one pink nipple pressed against the inside of her right cup. The sight made his head suddenly feel like a soda bottle that someone had shaken up and then opened.

"Andrew, this is Kathy Craig," Bass said with the aplomb of a host on one of the TV game shows Andy's father produced. "She's a mother's helper over here in O.B. Andrew is my assistant over at the Club, and one of the best ones they've ever had in that position. Why, just this morning Mrs. Dern—the old bitch who's president," Bass explained to Kathy "—was telling me what a great job Andrew's doing keeping the walks clear and washing the dishes. . . ."

Bass went on, but Andy was so embarrassed to be depicted as something tantamount to a janitor that he stopped listening. He wished that he could just scuttle beneath the sand and vanish like one of those little crabs in the cool damp layer of sand a yard below the hot surface. And yet, while Bass kept extolling Andy's dishwashing talents, Kathy Craig continued to gaze up at him over her shoulder with a look of friendly openness that left him dizzy.

"Hey, you feeling all right?" Bass finally paused to ask.

"Sure, I'm okay," Andy replied after the one-second lag it took for him to realize that Bass was asking him a question.

"Maybe you ought to sit down," Bass suggested.

Andy caught a final glimpse of Kathy Craig's nipple before walking around to the front of her and sitting down Indian-style in the sand beside her towel, with Bass to his left.

For the next several minutes Bass finished telling Kathy the story he had been in the middle of when Andy came over—all about his exciting motorcycle adventure riding down from Yale—while Kathy listened raptly. But when he was finished, he abruptly excused himself and headed back down the beach toward the Club, leaving Andy alone with the beautiful girl.

"How do you know Bass?" he eventually asked when the breach in the conversation became unendurable.

"He's an old friend of the lady I work for, Jane Anne Lillienthal," Kathy said, then leaned forward. "I think they were real close friends awhile back, if you know what I mean."

"How old is this lady?"

"About thirty."

"Hmmm," Andy said reflectively, picturing a much younger Bass having a torrid affair with this mother who was now practically middle-aged. At the same time, he couldn't help picturing Bass having a torrid affair with the angelic Kathy Craig, and the image sent a shiver of jealousy up his spine. "How many kids do you have to help this mother with?" Andy asked to keep the conversation going. He couldn't believe how beautiful Kathy Craig was.

"Just one. Thank God. Jason, the world's biggest brat. He's five."

"Last summer I was a counselor at this camp in Maine. I had a whole bunk full of nine-year-olds to take care of. That was truly hell," Andy said. "Except all-in-all I think the camp job was better than this thing at the Club," he quickly added. "I just sort of fell into it."

Kathy asked him why he didn't go back to Maine, and Andy told her the story of his vodka spree on awards night, which began to seem funnier in retrospect, and by the time he finished he had relaxed enough to recline in the sand at her level.

"We ought to meet downtown some night this week for a beer or something," Andy suggested.

"I'm underage," she said. "I can't go into a bar."

"Sure you can. I'm underage and I go in all the time. How old are you?"

"Fifteen," she said.

Hearing this rocked him like a punch in the head. She was so beautiful—and only fifteen? It blew his mind.

"You can get in. No problem. They serve twelve-year-olds down in McCauley's."

"Well, maybe some night," she said, smiling, after a moment's thought. Andy had no doubt from the way she smiled that this girl would become a movie star in a matter of a few years. "I'm afraid I've got to go now," she said, standing up and rubbing the sand off the perfect oval of her belly. "Jason," she explained, and she wrinkled her nose.

They said good-bye. Andy stood up and watched her disappear up the steps that led over the dunes to Holly Street. Feeling as though he had achieved something momentous by meeting this beautiful girl, already nervous about the prospect of wooing her in a dark booth at

McCauley's, and emotionally drained in every other respect, he decided to go back to the Club, read some of the novel about a coup d'etat in Washington that he was in the middle of, rustle up a little supper, and probably turn in early.

It was after five o'clock now. The lifeguards, Tim Flannery among them, were conducting a drill under Dale Hummer's supervision, swimming the lifeline that was kept on a huge wooden spool out to a designated "victim" (another guard) beyond the break. The beach was otherwise emptying. Many of the grown-ups with jobs in the city had ferries and then trains to catch. Andy loved the idea that it was Sunday evening and he didn't have to go back to the city. Standing there in the still-warm sunshine, watching Hughie Donovan pretend to drown, the even more wonderful thought occurred to him that, if he made certain arrangements in his life, he might never have to go back to the city again.

The dead sea turtle lay alone in the sand when he passed it on his way back to the club. At this hour, no one was standing around gawking at it, no children poking it with sticks. The expression on its upside-down beaked face appeared to be one of stoical resignation, as though now it were only waiting for the sea to reclaim it and so end the postmortem indignities it had been subjected to. Andy tried to shove it back toward the water, but it weighed over two hundred pounds and he could barely budge it a few inches through the unyielding sand. Then, seeing it was hopeless, he gave up and went down to the water's edge to wash its stink off his hands.

There was only one person left on the stretch of beach up along the Club—Tim Flannery's sister Franny. She was sitting straight up with a drawing tablet on her bare knees, glancing at the ocean and back down at her tablet repeatedly, as though trying to figure out a puzzle. Every so often she laid down a tentative stroke with the drawing pencil in her left hand. Her right hand was used alternately to hold down the pages of her tablet and drag the windblown hair out of her face. She was sitting directly in his path to the stairs that led over the dunes, and she watched Andy as he trudged up the deep sand toward her.

"Hi," she said with the cockeyed smile that might have been a Flannery family patent. Its resemblance to Tim's had the eerie effect of first putting Andy at ease and then disconcerting him in a rapid sequence of contradictory emotions. The wind kept blowing her buttery brown hair across her face, no matter how often she removed it, and when she spoke several billowing strands flew across her open mouth. Watching her struggle with it, Andy couldn't help but notice her lips and how so many freckles extended to the edge of them. He felt a sudden and reckless desire to kiss those lips. The strange impulse embarrassed and bewildered him. He wondered whether the LSD had left him permanently a little crazy.

"Hi," he said, trying to return a smile.

"I guess you and Tim ironed things out, huh?" she asked. Andy just stared back, not comprehending. "Since Friday in the Club," she explained. "When they were being so snotty."

It seemed to Andy like eons since the Flannerys had first invaded the Club, though it was less than three days ago.

"Oh, yeah," he replied. "I realize now that Tim was just clowning around. We're like old buddies now."

"People sometimes take him the wrong way. They think his sense of humor's warped."

"It's just highly developed," Andy said. "Most people don't get it."

"Well, I'm glad you think so. He needs a friend. Last summer he was drunk practically all the time."

"Oh?"

"I probably shouldn't be telling you this," Franny said.

"It's okay," Andy reassured her, but in a tone that suggested he wasn't entirely comfortable hearing all the Flannery family secrets. "Anyway, I'm sort of an odd-man-out around here myself, not knowing anybody and all. What are you working on?" he asked, though he could see for himself. It was a drawing of the ocean. Brian Flannery, now alone out there, still sat out the swells beyond the break on his surfboard.

"Just a dumb drawing," Franny said, embarrassed.

"Do you want a couple of pointers?"

"Sure," she said and searched his face expectantly.

Andy sat down beside her. She angled her tablet toward him so he could see it better. In so doing, her shoulders brushed his bare arm. She was wearing a bleached-out old blue work shirt but he could feel the warmth of her skin through it.

"First of all," Andy said, "when you're drawing, it's a good idea to think in terms of dark and light areas."

"Uh-huh."

"You're using mainly lines here. Lines are good for technical drawings, but for art you're better off breaking up the page into masses of dark and light shapes. Watch."

He took the tablet off her knees and rested it on his own. She handed him her pencil. In a few deft broad strokes Andy depicted the tubular shape of a wave.

"That's amazing," Franny said.

"You see what I'm doing that's different from you?"

"Well, you really know how to draw, for starters."

"I just have a little more experience than you. What I'm doing different is that I'm using the side of the pencil lead,

69

not just the point. That's the main difference. Another trick of the trade is to think in terms of three values of tone: dark, medium, and light. That's what makes a good drawing, just a bunch of interesting shapes done in different shades of dark and light. Oh, and here's one more pointer. If you're having trouble making out what the major shapes are in some scene you're looking at, try squinting." He showed her how.

"Like this?"

"That's right. See how when you squint it eliminates a lot of the distracting little details?"

"Yeah. That's neat. I never knew that."

With a few more quick, sure-handed strokes, Andy depicted the foamy slop and then the beach in the foreground with its pocked irregularities, and the stacked stratus clouds above the horizon.

"That's really incredible," Franny said as the scene took shape on the tablet. "It really looks like what's in front of us. But it's funny. You don't really seem like the arty type."

Andy laughed. "What's that type supposed to be like?"

"I don't know. A wild, slobby sort of person. Where did you learn all that?"

"At school," Andy said, and he told her a little bit about the High School of Music and Art, without mentioning how much he loathed the place.

"I'd give anything to go to a school like that," Franny said with a wistful sigh.

"Believe me, it's not as groovy as you think," Andy assured her, standing up and brushing the sand off his cutoffs. "You can get just as good at drawing in any normal school. Just keep practicing the way I showed you: using shapes and values, not lines."

"Thanks for the pointers," Franny said, shielding her

eyes from the westering sun behind Andy. "I guess I'll see you around, huh?"

"Oh, sure," Andy said, "I'll be around." He thrust his hands into his pockets and departed the beach marveling at how in the space of a single afternoon he had been with two girls, each quite different, who he liked so much. He considered what Tim had said about Franny trying to seduce him. Older brothers were naturally protective, Andy thought. She was pretty and sexy, in a completely innocent way, but—hell, she was only fourteen, for godsake. No, fooling around with Tim's kid sister was totally out of the question, Andy decided. Besides, there was Kathy Craig—godalmighty!—an incredibly beautiful creature who had all but agreed to go out on a date with him! For drinks, no less—!

Soon he reached the Club's Midway walk, which was once again disappearing under ankle-deep dunes of wind-blown sand and would have to be shoveled again in a day or two. Listening to the ocean pound in the distance, Andy wondered exactly how many times that summer he'd have to shovel off the damn thing.

CHAPTER SIX

You couldn't go anywhere on Thunder Island that summer without hearing the Beatles' new record album, *Sgt. Pepper's Lonely Hearts Club Band*. Songs from it blared out of radios on the beach, out of the bars downtown, and sometimes it seemed that every other household in Ocean Breeze owned a copy of the album and played it around the clock. It became a part of the landscape, as natural as the ceaseless pounding of the surf.

Ted Bass owned a copy of it, but around the Club Bob Dylan was more likely to be heard over the P.A. system on those weekday mornings when only Bass and Andy were around the big old place. Bass played the early Dylan albums with the songs about prejudice and injustice. Andy liked *Highway 61 Revisited* and *Blonde on Blonde*, with their eliptical lyrics about love and revenge and the fiercely beautiful rock 'n' roll music behind them. He practically wore out the grooves listening to the haunting fifteen-minute ballad "Sad-Eyed Lady of the Lowlands" when Bass wasn't around.

At the Flannerys' house just on the leeward side of the dunes—an architect's nightmare that looked like a colossal packing crate on stilts—the casual visitor was more apt to hear the first album by the Doors. Their songs were sexy, poetic, and rather sinister.

Andy became a drop-in at the Flannerys', but mainly just to get Tim, not to stick around. Tim's parents were nice enough in a detached, boozy way. The never-ending uproar between Tim's younger brothers—Shawn, sixteen, Brian, fifteen, and Matt, twelve—was hard to take for someone not used to sibling rivalry, and it made Andy nervous to be around Franny in the setting of the family stronghold, especially with Tim there.

So Andy and Tim spent their time together downtown in the bars at night—late on weekend nights, after Andy got off work—usually at McCauley's, which indeed became the gathering place for the younger crowd that summer, but sometimes at the Sea Witch where there was live music and a dance floor rigged with strobe lights. They drank beer, and though they tried to pick up girls, what came to be considered their "warped sense of humor" virtually always derailed the enterprise and they would stagger home at three in the morning, each headed for a solitary bed.

After that first grueling weekend, Andy's job settled into a more predictable pattern of hard work and idleness as regular as the tides. Fridays and Saturdays in the Club kitchen with Anatole were sheer hell, but Andy was off duty practically all the rest of the week—except for waxing the floors, meeting the freight boat with the hand-truck, and, of course, shoveling off the Club walk—so the job had its advantages.

Weekdays he was invariably up at the beach, often in the company of Kathy Craig, who would be excused from her babysitting duties for a couple of hours each afternoon while the terrible Jason napped. (Andy's high school classmate, Debbie Klinger, left the island for a summer in France after the Fourth of July weekend.)

It wasn't until a Tuesday evening in the second week of July that he finally managed to get Kathy out on a date. The occasion had evolved into something more elaborate than the original idea of "a drink." But their relationship had evolved into something more complicated than a boy trying to woo a girl. Somehow he had become her confidant. Perhaps it was because he didn't put any heavy moves on her from the start. Maybe he wasn't her type physically. Maybe he was too much the friend. Whatever the reason, she did not take him seriously as a suitor, and he didn't press the issue, at least not directly. Rather, in their hours on the beach together he became a sympathetic listener, and what he most often listened to was how crazy she was about Jeff Blum.

Jeff Blum, lifeguard and lead singer with the Molten Heads, Thunder Island's only *resident* rock band, was a freak in more ways than one. Genetically he was an aberration. Somehow this great-grandson of a slope-shouldered butter-and-egg peddler from the Lithuanian city of Vilna had grown up to be a Teutonic demigod—possible proof that Darwin was wrong and Lamarck was right (though Jeff's younger brother Seth looked like a rabbinical student with a good suntan). At age nineteen, Jeff Blum was six feet three inches tall with pectoral muscles like sirloin steaks, arms like Smithfield hams, and a brain like a walnut. He got into the University of Wisconsin because he could swim the two-hundred-meter butterfly at 2:07.06. Like many college sports stars of the era, he showed a marked weakness for the novelty of psychedelic drugs, and in his sophomore year (preceding this summer of 1967) he had turned into a bona fide acid freak. He grew his streaky brown-blond hair down to his I-beam shoulders. He joined a Sufi dancing group on campus. He played his guitar to Jimi Hendrix records for days on end and never did manage to get the riffs down right. He veered into vegetarianism as a religion.

Kathy Craig thought he was the most magnificent thing that a billion years of terrestrial life had produced, the summation of what God might have intended when he started the whole business. The way Jeff sat up in the lifeguard chair, leaning slightly forward as though contemplating the curvature of the earth, he looked like a statue of all the classical virtues embodied in bronze. He was strength, beauty, courage, wisdom, truth. It helped that Jeff had barely said two words to Kathy since the summer began, for had they conversed at any length Andy was sure that Blum would reveal himself as the egocentric dimwit that Tim Flannery said he was.

Slightly more puzzling to Andy, at least at first, was why Blum didn't fall for Kathy Craig, who after all was an exceedingly creamy young cookie, and who had taken some pains to get the lifeguard's attention. She had even considered—she confessed to Andy—faking a drowning while Blum was on duty in order to be "saved" by him.

Andy thought Tim put his finger on it when he said, "Blum's in love with himself. He doesn't have time for anyone else." Though no doubt true up to a point, the explanation didn't completely satisfy, for even if Blum was a self-centered lunkhead he presumably felt the same hormonal promptings any nineteen-year-old male feels. Moreover, he was often seen downtown at night, sometimes in McCauley's, with one girl or another, or sometimes two at a time—so there was proof that he had an interest in the opposite sex. But they were college girls.

While Andy willingly played confidant to Kathy Craig, he was too infatuated with her himself to share certain tidbits of information that might have explained Blum's lack of interest in her—for example, the time when he and Flannery were standing out on McCauley's back deck overlooking the bay with a lot of the O.B. collegiate crowd watching the Fourth of July fireworks, and Blum was among them, and one of the guys mentioned this "hot little blonde" (Kathy Craig) who was crazy about him, and Blum replied (in his oxlike voice), "Her? Get outta here. She's a kid."

But Andy did not want her to know it was as simple as that. Given the chance, she might easily convince Blum otherwise. Nor did he really want her to give up on Jeff Blum and set her sights on someone else, say another one of the guards, Hughie Donovan, Robbie Kugel, or even Duff Perleman, someone less choosy than Blum when it came to a girl's age, someone who might actually take her on a five-day fling before dumping her on the scrapheap of love.

It was therefore to Andy's advantage for her to remain infatuated with Jeff Blum. For as long as she did (and Blum failed to respond), he, Andy, could continue to lend a sympathetic ear. And he was sure that, given enough time, Kathy would eventually realize that he, Andy, was the one truly worthy of her love.

What Andy decided to do was take her out to dinner at Dixie's, which boasted far and away the best cuisine in town, even if it wasn't a hip place for younger people to hang out. Under the guise of being her friend and confidant, Andy thought, he would wine and dine her, he would wow her with gallantry. Where Blum ignored her, *disdained* her, Andy would pamper her, give her his complete attention. It was a strategy almost certainly doomed to fail, he realized, but he figured it was worth a try, since the alternative was to declare his feelings outright and probably blow the whole deal right there.

He picked her up at the Lillienthal house on Holly

Street at eight. The execrable Jason had a tantrum as they prepared to leave. In the soft twilight she looked particularly beautiful. She wore a white cotton blouse with puffy off-the-shoulder sleeves and her perfectly suntanned skin looked so golden and buttery against the paler fabric that Andy felt an ache in his belly akin to hunger pangs just looking at her. A necklace of turquoise beads dramatized the azure of her eyes. Her jeans were bleached to perfection and the suntanned tops of her slender bare feet were pretty against them.

Andy was especially nervous about ordering drinks in Dixie's, where he had not tried to get served before, but when he asked for a Beefeater martini the waiter just scribbled it on his checkpad without so much as a second glance. Kathy didn't know what she wanted, so Andy ordered a scotch sour for her because that was what his mother usually had when they went to a restaurant. This cocktail seemed to have an aphrodisical effect on Kathy, for she paused a moment while relating the latest installment in the never-ending saga of her love for Jeff Blum and said, as though she was surprised to have realized it, "You know something, Andy, you're really a great listener."

"It's just real interesting," he replied, embarrassed to have her point it out so boldly. He'd have preferred it if the realization bloomed in her brain, like a flower, some moonstruck night when she was alone in her bedroom at the Lillienthals, thinking about the various boys in her life.

"No it's not," she disagreed, wrinkling her nose. "It must be boring."

He did not want to have to go to dishonorable lengths to convince her that nothing in this world was more important to him than her feelings for this repulsive brute of a lifeguard.

"I just like listening to you talk," he said. "You could

recite the baseball box scores and I'd enjoy it," he added, coming dangerously close to a declaration of love. "Oh, waiter, would you bring us two more drinks?"

For dinner, Kathy ordered a steak with french fries. Andy ordered broiled filet of sole because he didn't like fish all that much and he reasoned that it must therefore be a more sophisticated dish. Kathy, he noticed, was not concerned about appearing sophisticated. She dumped a big blob of ketchup in the middle of her steak, and another on her french fries, and if there was one thing Andy felt was a sign of being grown up it was knowing not to ruin a good cut of beef with ketchup. Still, he forgave her completely because she looked so beautiful eating, even with two strong drinks under her belt.

After dinner they had more drinks—cognac for him and Irish coffee for her—and Andy revealed his plan for getting through college by selling sandwiches. He'd avoided mentioning it before because he hadn't wanted her to know that he came from such a screwed-up family that they wouldn't send him to college. Kathy thought it was a great idea and suggested that he sell brownies too.

"People love brownies, and they're real easy to make. You could probably make enough money to buy a car too."

"God, a car," Andy said, marveling at her ingenuity. "That would be great. I could come up and visit you."

"Where are you going to college, anyway?"

"Oh, well, probably the University of Tennessee," he told her, as though it were all but settled. "I applied there last week. But I also applied to these four schools in New York."

"Which ones?"

"You never heard of them, believe me," he said, growing momentarily gloomier. "To tell you the truth, I never heard of them myself until two weeks ago. Anyway," he said, brightening again, "wherever I end up, I'll drive into the city and we'll go out somewhere groovy. Do you like foreign food?"

"I adore Chinese."

"We'll go to Chinatown, then."

"That'll be great."

That settled, they were about to depart Dixie's to go to the Sea Witch and dance under the strobes—Kathy had never been in the nightspot—when Tim Flannery appeared in the doorway. He didn't look altogether steady on his feet. Then, spying Andy and Kathy, he wove through the dining room to their table and sat down. As he did, he pulled a Millers bottle out from under his windbreaker. Andy saw the waiter watching.

"Hey, I been lookin' all over for you," Tim said.

"We were here," Andy told him.

"Hey, I was just over in McCauley's," Tim turned to Kathy, "having a brew with some of the guards—you know, Kugel, Hughie, Blum. Your name came up."

"It did?" Kathy responded brightly. "You sure it was my name?"

"You're Kathy Craig, right?"

"Uh, we were just on our way out of here," Andy said, reaching for his wallet.

The waiter suddenly materialized, saying to Tim, "Hey, buddy, you can't bring beers in here off the street like that."

Tim chug-a-lugged it, set it down on the red-and-white-checked tablecloth, and said with a big smile, "I'll have another, thank you."

"How did my name come up?" Kathy asked excitedly.

"It was silly, really," Tim said.

"Sure, but what was it?"

"He's making this up," Andy interposed. "You're making this up, right? Uh, waiter. Could we have the check?"

"Why would I make up something like this?" Tim said.

"Why would you make up something like this?" Andy echoed him irritably.

"Well, what was it?" Kathy pressed him.

"They were rating the girls on the beach. You know, in terms of most attractive in a bikini and everything. And your name came up."

"Really?"

"Yeah. I think it was Blum who nominated you."

"Jeff Blum?"

"Yeah," Tim went on. "He's the older one of the two brothers. Kind of large—"

"I know! I know!" she said. "What'd he say, exactly?"

By this time, Andy had pretty much resigned himself to letting Tim play out the stupid game, and he sat there with his chin cupped in his hand and his eyelids drooping, watching his friend ruin a whole night of expensive courtship.

"They just said you were one of the better-looking girls on the beach."

"Jeff said that?"

"Well, he mentioned your name and then they all agreed."

"They?" Andy said. "You didn't have a vote?"

"Oh, sure, I had a vote."

"Who'd you vote for?"

"Kelly Donovan. But that was a loyalty thing. You know, the Club and all."

The waiter delivered the check and Tim's beer. Andy had already removed a ten and a twenty from his wallet, and handed it to the waiter saying, "Keep the change."

"Hey, thanks," the waiter said. His tip was more than twenty-five percent of the tab.

"What do you say we go over to the Sea Witch now?" Andy suggested to Kathy.

"Am I invited along?" Tim said.

"Let's go to McCauley's instead," Kathy suggested.

"Ten minutes ago you were dying to go to the Sea Witch," Andy pointed out, a little peevishly.

"I know," she admitted, "but I really don't think I could take the lights and the loud music and all. My head's spinning."

"Okay, let's go to McCauley's," Andy said, giving in and wanting to avoid a quarrel. He figured that if they went there and Blum was still inside and Kathy somehow ended up with Blum, that he, Andy, would then attempt to beat the shit out of Blum, even if it was suicidal to try it.

It was less than a five-minute walk. Downtown was quiet, almost gloomy. It was only Tuesday night. Few teenagers sat out on the concrete wall around the village square. There was no line outside the Sea Witch. McCauley's was lively compared to many of the other bars, though, and Robbie Kugel was there with his girl, Kelly Donovan, but there was no sign of Jeff Blum.

"He must have hit the road," Tim said. "You know old Blum: early to rise, early to bed. An intellect like his really needs a lot of rest. Winters he must hibernate. Can I get you two lovebirds a cocktail?"

Apparently Kathy didn't hear the potshots at her beloved. She was busy craning her neck around, searching the back room for him. But Andy kicked Tim hard on his shinbone with the instep of his bare foot. Flannery limped up to the bar. Andy steered Kathy toward a booth in the front room and got her to sit in the inside seat. He felt a lot more secure with her sitting between himself and the wall.

"The thing I don't understand," Kathy said, "is if he likes me, then how come he's so aloof?"

"Good question," Andy said distractedly.

"Maybe he's painfully shy?"

"That's probably it, all right."

"Are you okay?" she asked Andy, but before he could even think up an answer Tim reappeared with a plastic tray containing six tumblers of beer. "Is someone going to join us?" Kathy asked expectantly.

Andy rolled his eyes. Tim explained how they always gave you two beers when you ordered one at McSorley's in the city. Kathy appeared disappointed.

"Hey, did you guys hear about the big rescue today?" Tim asked, changing the subject.

"What rescue?"

"Just before we shut down at five o'clock. This dork got sucked into a mammoth sea-puss—"

"What's a sea-puss?" Kathy asked.

"A riptide," Tim explained. "His whole family got caught in it. The wife. Two kids. The dog. They were halfway to the Canary Islands when Blum chugged out and pulled them back in."

"Jeff Blum did that!"

"You should have seen him," Tim said. "He was magnificent."

"God, I wish I'd been there," Kathy groaned.

"He's really an example for us all."

"Tim's in love with him," Andy said.

"And Blum's in love with me. We're moving out to Piney Grove next week and opening a head shop. Jeff's going to model the waterpipes. You know, just sit in the window and suck all day long."

Kathy's suntanned face grew suddenly ashen and she set down her beer glass as though she had just realized it was poisoned.

"Can we go, Andy? I don't feel so well."

"The thing is, we can't decide on the decor," Tim blathered on. "Jeff wants black lights and posters and I want paisley wallpaper—"

"Why don't you just zipper it up, Tim?" Andy said, standing and allowing Kathy to push past him out of the booth.

"But wait," Tim said, "what about all these beers?"

Andy watched helplessly as Kathy hurried down the bar and out the door.

"Drink them yourself, fuckhead," Andy said and took off after her.

Kathy was still running when Andy caught up with her on Holly Street just short of the Midway. He tried to take hold of her arm, but she shook him off, saying, "Leave me alone." He continued to follow her up the narrow concrete walk toward the Lillienthals' house near the ocean. Once they reached the beginning of the wooden gangway that led up to the entrance of the dramatically modern house (which had been featured in *Architectural Digest* the year before), Kathy stopped, turned abruptly, and flung herself against Andy, weeping.

"Don't cry," Andy said, trying to console her but hoping actually that she might never stop, and stroking her head where her blonde hair dangled warmly behind her small ears.

"He's so cruel," she blubbered. "How can he be your friend?"

"He's probably just jealous," Andy said.

"Jealous? What is he? A queer for real?"

"Now, that's a mean thing for you to say."

"Well, he deserves it."

"Maybe he's crazy about you?" Andy deviously suggested.

"It certainly isn't the way to show it."

"Come on, let's go for a walk on the beach," Andy said. "You can't go inside like that. They'll think I did something nasty to you."

She didn't reply, but she let him slide his arm around her shoulder and he managed to steer her off the gangway back onto the walk and up the stairway over the dunes. A half moon was a pearly blob behind a bank of thin clouds high above the ocean. The lifeguard chair towered emptily against this backdrop.

"Let's sit down here."

He guided her down beside a wood and wire snow fence that helped hold the dunes together against the relentless assaults of the tides. The sand there was very fine, clean, and cool. Kathy shivered. Andy opened his windbreaker and tried to enfold her in it. The warmth of her body made his head swim. She smelled like shampoo and tears. Once they sat down, she began to cry again, quietly, undemonstrably, as though her grief was inconsolable.

Andy held her closer to him, more tightly, as a series of sobs shook her. His nose was in her hair and the smell intoxicated him. He reached up with his free hand and stroked her smooth cheek. His heart raced. He kissed the little hollow at the top of her throat. She stopped sobbing. His kisses made a purposeful incursion across her cheek to her lips. He was astonished that she allowed him to kiss her, and was even more amazed when her sweet, muscular lips responded hungrily, as though she could no longer bear to be deprived of putting them to some use.

The rickety snow fence yielded to their combined weight and they collapsed against the steep dune. Soon Andy's right hand began exploring the curve of her hip, her slender waist, then up underneath the cotton blouse to the silky bra. No longer crying at all, she made little moaning sounds as he touched the cleft between her breasts. He slid his hand behind her and found her bra clasp. With a deft movement that thrilled him, he managed to unhook the bra. "No," she moaned after he had already accomplished it, and she permitted his hand to return to her bared breasts.

"I'm a virgin," he whispered to her, as though he were revealing his membership in a special society for the sexually accursed.

"I am too," she said.

"I guess we better stop," he suggested breathlessly, still gently massaging her creamy breast.

"Okay," she agreed, pulling a strand of blonde hair out of her mouth and looking somewhat bewildered. He kissed her once more on the lips, a quick, hungry, but essentially chaste kiss. He liked the gallant feeling of putting an end to their kissing, as though it proved his superiority to the brutal animal appetites that undoubtedly ruled a lummox like Jeff Blum.

"You're shivering," he observed.

"It's cold out here."

"Give me your hand. I'll help you up."

"Wait." She reached behind her back and struggled briefly to snap her bra together, then adjusted the cups. "Okay."

Andy walked her back over the dunes to the Lillienthal house with his arm around her. They said nothing the whole way. At the gangway he spun Kathy gently around, but she gazed down at their bare feet as though she were ashamed to look at him. He had to urge her chin up with his fingers, and then the expression on her face was like nothing so much as childlike confusion. She looked fifteen.

"I hope this doesn't hurt your feelings," she said. "But I was pretending you were him, you know, Jeff."

As a matter of fact it did hurt his feelings. It offended him rather deeply. But he was still sufficiently intoxicated by her that he refused to acknowledge the injury or to show it.

"You can practice on me all you want," he told her with a rueful smile, only half believing what he had said. But it still appealed to his sense of the heroic. He felt a little like an actor playing the role of a doomed young lover with a fatal disease that would soon end his life. What could be more gallant than not to mention it to his beloved, he thought, so as to spare her the heartache of knowing. He bid her goodnight, kissed her even more chastely on the cheek this time, and left her standing on the gangway before the beautiful house.

"Look at yourself, you're drunk as a skunk," Andy told Tim. He had returned to McCauley's to give Flannery a piece of his mind, and found him sitting goggle-eyed in the booth where he had left him an hour ago. There were six empty tumblers on the table.

"So I am," Tim agreed with a cracked smile. "So I am."

"Well, thanks for almost wrecking my chances."

"Whadja get, lucky?"

"Maybe."

"Wuzzat mean?"

"I'm not going to give you the play-by-play."

"Well, goddam, I wish you would," Tim maundered, fumbling with his pack of cigarettes. "Gimme something to jerk off about."

"That's sick," Andy said, helping Tim put all the spilled cigarettes back into the pack and then lighting a match for him.

"Thanks," Tim said. "Hey, didn' I tell you this island was a sick goddam place?"

"How are you going to get home?"

"Beats the shit outta me."

"Come on. I'll help you."

Andy lent him a hand. Tim extracted himself from the booth and stood on his own for a moment, weaving back and forth.

"Hey, pal," a friendly voice called across the now-empty barroom. It was Tommy Oldfield, wiping down the taps.

"Hi, Tommy," Andy replied as a thud resounded behind him. He wheeled around to see Tim laying flat out on his back on the floor. Oldfield hurried out from behind the bar. He and Andy looked down in horror at Flannery, whose eyes were wide open and unnaturally glazed. The lit cigarette even remained between his lips. He looked like a corpse in a play by Noel Coward.

"I seem to be indisposed," Tim mumbled.

"I'll say," Oldfield agreed. Then he looked at Andy. "Can you get him home if I help you get him out the door?"

"I don't know. I'll try."

"Thattaboy," Tim said.

Each taking one arm, Tommy and Andy helped Tim back to his feet. Andy then draped Tim's right arm over his shoulder like a soldier helping his wounded buddy away from the battlefield.

"Too bad you can't call a cab out here," Oldfield observed, helping them to the door. "Well, good luck."

"Show me the way to the next whiskey bar," Tim sang, attempting the lyrics from a Doors song as he and Andy struggled up Juniper Street. "Oh, don't ask why." Somewhere in the distance a song from the Beatles's *Sgt. Pepper's* album floated on the breeze.

"Come on. Left, right, left, right," Andy said as Tim dragged his feet.

"What is this, the fuckin' Army?"

"You want to get home, don't you?"

"Wanna find the next whiskey bar."

"They're all closed."

"Aw, hell. Hey, wanna drop a little acid?"

"No! And don't you go doing it either."

"Wait."

"What?"

"Gotta stop."

"You okay?"

"No. Hey, do me a favor. Don't let me fall inna this goddam holly bush. Leaves are all prickly."

"All right."

While Andy held on to Tim's windbreaker, Tim emptied the contents of his stomach in a front yard expensively landscaped to look like a Japanese garden. Tim heaved half a dozen times and remained hunched over awhile longer, quietly spitting into the sand, when a screen door slapped somewhere beyond the dense shrubbery and soft footfalls could be heard on wood decking.

"That was wonderful, Mike," said a hidden female voice. It was the voice of an older woman, husky with sex and cigarettes. "You're wonderful."

"You're pretty fine yourself, Myra," a male voice said.

"How about next week?" the woman asked with a trace of urgency.

"I don't know."

"Here, take this, buy yourself some groceries."

"Gee, thanks, Myra."

"You'll come back next week, won't you?"

"Sure. I guess."

There was a wet slurpy sound like a kiss and the woman's husky voice saying, "Mmmmmm."

"Bye."

"Bye, darling."

Panic rose in Andy as the footfalls came closer. Then a lean, long-haired man appeared from out of a slot in the shrubbery. He had on cutoff khaki shorts and a Hawaiian shirt and was walking a beat-up, old-fashioned bicycle, a silly-looking thing with a streamlined false gas tank and a huge rusty basket hung on the handlebars. It was hard to make out his face in the darkness. The man saw Andy and Tim right away, and came forward toward them. Before Andy could apologize for his friend throwing up in the shrubbery, the man asked, "Is he all right?"

Tim looked to the side and up slightly, recognizing Mike Lovett, the surfer.

"That you, Flannery?"

"Yeah. Just tossing my cookies, Mike. No problem."

"Oh. Say, what do you hear from Terry?"

"Married life is great, California's great."

"Hey, that's great. Think he'll make it out at all this summer?"

"Nope."

"Gosh, that's too bad. Well, take 'er easy."

"Hey, Mike, gonna go catch some midnight heavies?" Tim asked, referring to waves in surfer lingo.

"I don't think so. Onshore breeze. Sloppy break."

"Maybe I'll see you out there one of these nights."

"Sure," Mike Lovett said, as though he truly looked forward to the prospect. "Well, got to go bag some Z's. Hang ten." Then he got on his bicycle and rode away.

CHAPTER SEVEN

The letter Andy got from his mother was short and yet replete with the sort of high-handed histrionics that made her an up-and-coming power to be reckoned with in the New York art world—and such a difficult woman to be the son of.

"Dear Andy," it began. "Since neither you nor anyone else ever seems to be around that place where you work to answer the phone when I call, this note is to tell you that I'll be out at Uncle Jack's for a long weekend starting Wednesday, July 24th. I will be accompanied by a gentleman named Leonard Kropotkin. Leonard is the art critic for *Newsweek* magazine and is a very nice man for someone in his position. For one thing, mirabile dictu, he is not a fairy. I'm sure you will absolutely adore him. Please call me at Jack's on Wednesday evening. I would love to take you out to dinner, if you can arrange your schedule accordingly."

When that Wednesday came, it was the beginning of what the islanders would call a three-day blow. Stiff winds out of the Atlantic brought raking rains that drove all the sun worshippers indoors to play board games, smoke pot, and listen to the Beatles, while huge waves carved a four-foot-high sandy cliff along the beach and tossed huge, strange flotsam up on dry land—among it, the aft end of a broken-up weathered dory, a dead dolphin marked with propeller cuts about its head, and several thousand ping-pong balls (thought at first to be some kind of dried-out bird eggs), the origin of which was never discovered.

Andy phoned his mother at his Uncle Jack's house at five o'clock that afternoon and she suggested they meet downtown at Dixie's at seven. She was an hour and fifteen minutes late. Andy sat at the bar nursing beers and nibbling handfuls of dusty little oyster crackers left in bowls on the bar to make the customers thirsty, all the while wondering why his mother was incapable of showing up somewhere on time. It was one of the "stupid little things that drive you crazy" that his father mentioned on one of the few times he had ever spoken of his ex-wife. Andy began to understand what his father meant. Finally, at quarter after eight, she appeared in the entrance struggling with her companion, Leonard Kropotkin, to close up a dripping red and green golf umbrella. For a moment or two it looked as though they were tussling over it.

Barbara Newmark was a trim, handsome, short-haired brunette, forty-three years old, with what people of her mother's generation would have called "good bone structure." In the city she favored Chanel suits. Here, under a yellow storm slicker, she wore a blue and white French boatman's shirt and baggy khaki trousers, rolled up to mid-calf because of the rain. Familiar with the island's customs, she was barefoot like the other middle-aged folk dining in Dixie's.

Andy was amazed at how exactly Leonard Kropotkin's actual looks complied with the image of a Kropotkin his mind had conjured up since receiving his mother's letter: a man about fifty, rather short in stature, with frizzy gray hair, a gray mustache and goatee, and thick-rimmed black eyeglasses. He was dressed in the white painter's pants and faded blue workshirt that had been the uniform of Greenwich Village bohemianism since the forties. He also wore a small, peaked Greek fisherman's cap that to Andy was emblematic of a certain nautical nincompoopery branding its wearer as someone who had never sailed on so much as a Circle Line cruise around Manhattan Island. He had brand-new tennis sneakers on his feet and they were so soaked from walking downtown that water squirted out of the ventilation holes on the sides even as he stood in place, shifting his weight from one foot to the other.

"Sorry we're so awfully late, sweetie," Andy's mother apologized disarmingly, fluffing up her dampened hair with her fingers. "You should have called and I would have asked you to come up to Jack's."

"You could have called me here if you knew you were going to be over an hour late."

"Well, let's not argue about it now. I'm famished. This salt air certainly gives one an appetite."

"It sure does," Kropotkin agreed, helping her off with her slicker. When he was done, he offered his hand to Andy, saying, "Call me Lenny."

They were shown a table beneath a stuffed sailfish. Dixie Meyers, the eatery's proprietor, had just sat down at the piano across the room. Meyers's skin was so brown from almost fifty summers of tanning that, with his white hair, he looked like the picture of the Negro on the hot cereal box, though in fact he was a Jew from Beylorussia who landed on Ellis Island at age five. He began by playing Gershwin's "Someone to Watch Over Me" in a style heavy with arpeggios.

"Isn't this divine?" Barbara Newmark said, rubbing her hands together. The waiter appeared. "Scotch sour, please," she said.

"Beefeater martini on the rocks with a twist," Andy said.

"This is not an invitation to get bombed, young man."

"Oh, let the kid have a drink, Barbara," Kropotkin said.

"Just one," Andy's mother said, giving in.

"It could be worse," Kropotkin said, shooting a grin at Andy. "He could be taking this LSD shit."

"Quite true," Andy said. "It's gotten to be all the rage out here."

"Well you don't have to follow the herd," his mother said.

Their drinks arrived shortly. "Isn't this truly divine?" his mother said again, sipping her cocktail. "There's nothing like a rainy night out at the seashore."

"Give me a sunny day anytime," Andy said.

"It makes you feel so . . . so . . ."

"Damp?" Kropotkin ventured.

"No, cozy. As though the whole world were drenched but you were safe and warm inside."

"A close-up sense of the elements," Kropotkin mused over his scotch. "Of mankind's never-ending struggle against Mother Nature's unrelenting forces, all but lost in the sterile hurly-burly of modern city life."

Andy was impressed at how much Kropotkin sounded like a *Newsweek* magazine article. That anyone could speak like that off the top of his head seemed a trick worthy of some admiration, like pulling colored scarves out of your sleeves.

"Shall I tell you why I'm here?" Andy's mother asked, leaning forward conspiratorially.

"Sure," Andy said, though he assumed the basic idea was to get away from town for a few days off at the beach with this new boyfriend of hers.

"Have you ever heard of a painter named Lee Koenigsburg, who drowned out here a couple of years ago?"

94

Andy's interest was suddenly piqued. He too now leaned forward, replying, "Of course I've heard of him. And guess what: he's got a sixteen-year-old daughter out here on the island."

"Really?" Andy's mother said. "Do you know her?"

"No. But I see her around. She goes out with this thirty-year-old artist guy named Max Something-or-other who makes giant hot dogs and hamburgers out of fiberglass."

Andy's mother and Kropotkin shared a glance.

"Max Pap," Kropotkin said authoritatively. "He's from downtown. Promising. American kitsch on the monumental scale. But sixteen-year-old girls . . . I don't know." Kropotkin shook his head, deploring the idea.

"Anyway, Koenigsburg's widow has a place out here," Barbara Newmark continued. "I want her to let me represent her late husband's work."

"He's going to be big. Very big," Kropotkin said, holding up his empty glass as the waiter glided by.

"And she's just sitting on all of it," Barbara said.

The waiter returned with a fresh drink for Kropotkin and took their dinner orders. Andy's mother tried to convince him to order the softshell crabs, which she described as "lovely, simply heavenly," but the idea of eating a crab, shell and all, seemed repulsive to Andy, so he asked for the southern fried chicken. Kropotkin, making a dyspeptic face, ordered "a piece of fish, whatever you've got, baked plain, no butter, no sauce." It was while they were waiting for their food to arrive that Andy, feeling the effects of his martini, disclosed his plan to pay for college by selling sandwiches.

"Your father should pay for it," his mother said frigidly, buttering a chunk of warm bread. "Have you been in touch with him, by the way?"

"No," Andy said.

"The sonofabitch won't pay for his child's education," Andy's mother explained to Kropotkin.

"Which college are you planning to go to, by the way," Kropotkin asked.

"I'm not sure yet. Probably the University of Tennessee."

"Tennessee!" his mother exclaimed, as though he had said the University of Bulgaria. "Where on earth did you come up with that one?"

"Some friends of mine go there."

"Who?"

"Some guys I know out here."

"Have you been accepted there?" Kropotkin inquired.

"Well, not exactly. I only sent in the application two weeks ago."

"It's pretty late in the year to be applying for the fall semester, isn't it, Andy?" Kropotkin said, glancing at the boy's mother as though to emphasize his concern.

"He applied *everywhere* this winter," Barbara said somewhat defensively, and then turned to her son. "But what happened?"

"I didn't get in," Andy admitted.

"He didn't get in," she said, as though he had proven her point. "Of course, his father couldn't have been less helpful," she added.

"Neither one of you were any help whatsoever," Andy declared brazenly. Then he turned to Kropotkin. "All the two of them ever do is argue through lawyers about who's supposed to pay for it."

"He's *supposed* to pay for it," Andy's mother said, her face turning red and her voice rising. "He's your *father*."

"Great. You two keep arguing about it until I'm thirty years old. In the meantime, I'm going to work my way through selling sandwiches. Okay?"

"Okay. Sure. Fine," his mother said. "First, get in somewhere."

"Did you, uh, ever consider going to City College, Andy?" Kropotkin tried to insert diplomatically, as Barbara tore open a fresh pack of filtered cigarettes and lit one. "I went to CCNY and got a hell of an education. You have access to all the city's great cultural institutions! And best of all, it's free! There's no tuition charge for residents of New York City."

"Lenny," Andy said, as the waiter set down their plates. "I wouldn't spend another year of my life in that goddam rat hole of a city if they paid me ten thousand bucks to go to college there."

"Oh, look at these crabs," Andy's mother exclaimed as the waiter rematerialized. "Aren't they divine!"

It was around eleven o'clock over in McCauley's—after Andy bid good-night to his mother and Lenny Kropotkin—that Tim Flannery, who was drinking beers with Hughie Donovan, proposed the idea of going into New York the next day to see a famous movie about surfing called *The Endless Summer*. Thursday was his and Hughie's regular day off, but with the forecast of more rain they would not be able to spend it surfing and making time with girls on the beach as they usually did, so a trip into the city seemed the obvious alternative. Tim naturally asked Andy if he wanted to come along with them, and Andy, of course, said yes.

Much as he loathed and detested the city, especially in the summer, the idea of going back for a day had some appeal. He was all but certain that he would never have to live there again, and though it was a little premature he could regard the place with a feeling akin to nostalgia. Lately, he had begun to think of Tim and even Hughie Donovan as his future college buddies at the University of Tennessee, and so this excursion would be just the first of many exciting road trips they would make together.

"Hey, we can stop and have a few beers at McSorley's too," Tim suggested excitedly. "It'll be great."

The next morning Andy woke up hungover, as usual, only with Tim Flannery standing at the foot of his bed shaking his foot. Tim wore a freshly ironed blue oxford dress shirt with his jeans.

"There's been a slight change of plans," Tim said.

"Whu . . . ?" Andy said, rubbing the sleep from his eyes. The rain continued to natter on his windowpanes as noisily as it had for the past twenty-four hours.

"Hummer's let everybody off for the day except Duff Perleman. They're going to stick around as a skeleton crew, but the beach'll be officially closed. We're all going into New York together, all the guards. The ocean guards, that is."

"Uh-oh. Am I still allowed to come along?"

"Sure you are. Only get yourself moving. We're supposed to try and make the ten-fifteen boat."

It was nine-thirty. Andy showered in about five minutes and put on jeans and one of his alligator shirts.

"Aren't you hungover?" he asked Tim, who sat in the room reading an old copy of *Newsweek* while Andy threaded his belt through the loops.

"We Irish don't know the meaning of the word 'hangover.' "

"My brain's starting to get fried."

"There's a cure for that," Tim said.

"What?"

"More beer."

"Can't handle it at this hour. I'd throw up."

"Then how about some of this?" Tim pulled a neatly rolled reefer out of his shirt pocket and dandled it in his fingers.

"Can't hurt, I guess," Andy said after some indecision. "Thataboy."

Minutes later, as they made to depart for the ferry, Andy had started down the stairs when Tim said, "Do you plan on walking around New York City barefoot? It'll be awfully rough on the soles of your feet."

It had been so long since he had worn any kind of shoes that Andy had totally forgotten they were standard gear in most places except Thunder Island. He rushed back upstairs, grabbed the sneakers he had worn to the island weeks ago, jammed them under his arm inside his olive-green slicker, and carried them down to the ferry landing.

" 'Negroes in Detroit Defy Curfew and Loot Wide Area, 43 Dead.' " Tim read the headline from *The New York Times* aloud to everybody as the otherwise empty ten-fifteen inbound ferryboat chugged through the heavy swells that the storm had whipped up in South Fork Bay. Jeff Blum said he felt like blowing his breakfast, but the rest of the guards appeared to enjoy the rough ride, and Andy, who had entirely missed the comaraderie of a normal high school, was delighted to be part of the gang. They had the whole passenger section below decks to themselves.

"I hope they don't go batshit in New York, too," Hughie Donovan said.

"At least not while we're there," Robbie Kugel added.

"You can't have a race riot in a three-day blow," Van Donovan sagely pointed out.

" 'Governor George Romney ordered fifteen hundred national guardsmen backed up by tanks to quell the riot,' " Tim read on.

"It's Vietnam right here in America," Hughie said.

"That's Amerika with a 'k,' " Seth Blum said.

" 'Destructive fury swept over four-mile sections of streets criss-crossing the heart of Detroit and ranging outward to the city limits,' " Tim read.

"Hey, how'd the Jewish Giant do yesterday?" Robbie Kugel asked. The Jewish Giant was their nickname for the Washington Senators's first baseman, Mike Epstein. He was distantly related to the Kugels by marriage and was therefore a great favorite among the Ocean Breeze lifeguard crew, who adopted the hapless Senators as their pet team.

"The Giant got a big goose-egg, zero for four," Tim announced after quickly rifling forward to the sports section. A chorus of raspberries and rude noises accompanied his report. "They got shut out by Kansas City, five to nothing. The Senators are in sixth place, eight and a half out." Assorted groans. "The Chi Sox remain in first, Boston only a half game back."

"I'm bummed," Jeff Blum muttered, gray with nausea.

"The Yanks finally crawled out of the cellar."

"Who let 'em out?"

Tim rifled back to the news section as the ferry rose and fell in some enormous troughs and the guards applauded the wildest ones as salt spray and rain lashed the windows.

"Hey, listen to this one," Tim said. " 'Tonga Crowns King in Colorful Rite. Taufaahau Tupou IV was crowned today in a Methodist ceremony in a small wooden chapel on the grounds of his palace here.' "

"Wicked groovy," Robbie Kugel observed.

"Does he surf?" Jeff Blum asked.

"I doubt it. Check out the picture." A wire service photo accompanying the story showed a man the size of a sumo wrestler emerging from a limousine.

"It would take a board as big as this boat to hold him up," Hughie said.

"What I'd like to know is what a Methodist coronation ceremony is," Tim said. "How many Methodist countries have kings?"

No one was able to answer that.

"Beats the hell out of me," Van Donovan admitted, and he spoke for all of them.

Before much longer the ferry pulled into the protected harbor at Weekapauk and soon it was tied up fast in its berth. The guards and Andy filed out onto the mainland. After more than a month on Thunder Island, the mainland had a distinct smell to it—the combined aromas of grass and automobile exhaust—and Andy, for one, was struck by how huge the elm and maple trees looked compared to the scrub hollies and stunted pines he had grown used to out at the beach.

Both Van Donovan and Robbie Kugel had cars, but rather than drive all the way into the city and hassle with parking, they decided to ride the train.

Here on the mainland, without the drama of gale winds lashing the water and the danger of the tides gone wild, the storm only made for an unusually rainy day. It was hotter here too, eighty-five degrees at eleven-fifteen in the morning, and they sweated in their jeans on the train. As it raced closer to the city and the older, quieter, more agricultural east end of Long Island gave way to the suburban sprawl of Nassau County, Andy felt a nausea other than the type that might be produced by a hangover or boat ride. It was more like a nausea of the heart.

"Did you ever read Walt Whitman, the poet, in high school?" he asked Tim as they gazed out the grimy window at a vista of tract houses that spread clear to the gray horizon.

"I don't remember," Tim admitted.

"He was from Long Island, back in the eighteen hundreds. He'd commit suicide if he saw what they've done to it."

"It's a good thing he's already dead then, huh?" Tim said.

The train arrived in Penn Station at one-thirty. *The Endless Summer* was playing at only one theater in the city, the York Cinema over on 1st Avenue and 64th Street. The show had just begun, but another afternoon matinee was scheduled for quarter to four, so it was decided by consensus that everybody would go over to McSorley's saloon down near the Bowery and then walk around the East Village awhile to check out the hippies if there was still time before the movie.

If Charles Dickens's Miss Havisham had been a saloon-keeper, McSorley's on East Third Street would have been her kind of establishment. Every effort was made to ensure that nothing ever changed. The elaborately carved mahogany back-bar dated from the eighteen eighties. The brass rail and the cuspidors were all turn-of-the-century vintage, as were the etched glass windows and the black and white tile floor. The round tables had so many initials carved into them that in some spots a beer mug would not stand upright. The bartender and waiters all wore white aprons.

Not that the place was maintained as a museum, like a tourist tavern in colonial Williamsburg. Far from it. The saloon was actually quite seedy. Even the dust was old, like the cobwebs in the fictional Miss Havisham's bridal chamber. For instance, hanging overhead from the turn-of-the-century chandeliers were hundreds of decades-old chicken wishbones sucked clean from the free lunch counter of yesteryear and put on display for no reason Andy could figure out. (In fact, of all the old-fashioned customs so strenuously maintained, it was interesting to note that the free lunch was no longer served. In a neighborhood over-run with half-starved hippies, this would've been impossible.)

The six lifeguards plus Andy sat at a big table in the rear of the saloon and began taking turns buying rounds. Tim Flannery had been quite correct: It was another of the saloon's strange policies that two mugs of beer were served for each beer ordered. Granted, the mugs were made of extremely thick glass. But by the time everyone at the table had paid for a round, each had quaffed fourteen mugs of beer, and Andy, for one, was quite bombed.

They took advantage of a lull in the rainstorm to stroll over to St. Mark's Place, which was being transformed from a neighborhood of Polish immigrants to the hippie center of the universe. The humid air out on the sidewalk was full of incense and marijuana. Jeff Blum bought a waterpipe with six drawstems on it in the first head shop they passed. Tim bought rolling papers in licorice and banana flavors. Robbie Kugel bought a poster of Grace Slick. (They were playing the Jefferson Airplane's "Somebody to Love" next door in the poster shop at the time.) Seth Blum bought another strobe light unit to add to his light show and a pair of eyeglasses with prismatic facets on the lenses that made the whole world look fractured. Hughie Donovan bought a second-hand blue and red military tunic with brass buttons in a shop called My Granny's Trunk. Andy bought a string of blue beads to wear around his neck. And Van Donovan, who had one foot each in the older and the younger generations, didn't buy anything, but he was panhandled by a grubby teenager with a guitar strung around his back on a length of twine and Van told the kid to "go get a job."

At quarter after three they headed up Third Avenue on a

bus and made it over to the York Cinema just in time to load up on snacks at the refreshment stand before the movie. Andy was starving, having eaten nothing all day besides a few morsels from the platter of cheese and crackers they had ordered for the table at McSorley's.

The theater was practically empty at that hour on a weekday. The air-conditioning felt delicious after spending a day in the gluey city air, the seats were very plush, and the buttered popcorn was delectable. Soon the lights dimmed and the legendary movie began.

It was a documentary about two young surfers and their worldwide quest to find "the perfect wave." They traveled from Southern California to Hawaii, where the waves were the size of a four-story building, to Australia, where the surf was too much like California only with more sharks. There was no shortage of critical commentary from the audience as, chiefly, Robbie Kugel and Hughie Donovan loudly berated the stars' surfing abilities and tactics. "Get off the nose, asshole!" "Paddle, shithead!" Finally the two surfers ventured to Africa, where on a desolate stretch of beach along the Indian Ocean they found their holy grail, the perfect wave.

It wasn't a very big wave, like the gargantuan rollers of Wiamea Bay, or a fearsome, watery tube, like the Banzai Pipeline. It was just perfectly suited to the two surfers' style of surfing, affording long, even rides during which many neat stunts might be performed for the cameras. Van Donovan summed it up for all of them when he pronounced the so-called perfect wave to be "a fucking bore," and said that he'd take Hawaii any day, since it was obvious that there was no place within a hundred miles of this African beach to buy a cold beer.

When they got out it was raining again. Seth Blum said he was so hungry he could eat meat. The others were also starved. They huddled for a while outside the theater trying to figure out which train to catch in order to get on a late outbound ferry, when Tim Flannery happened to say, "You know our buddy Andy the Slave lives right here in the neighborhood."

"You do!" several of them said excitedly.

Andy hadn't especially wanted it known because all the rest of the guys came from very large homes in the suburbs with their mothers *and* fathers and siblings and dogs— that is, from "normal" households—and he was embarrassed about having grown up in an apartment in the city, alone with his mother. It seemed unspeakably dreary.

"You live around here?" Van Donovan now asked, as though speaking for all of them.

"Well, yes. A few blocks up on Seventieth Street."

"Then we can stay in the city overnight and flop there, right?"

It wasn't possible, Andy thought to himself. There was barely room for one guest to sleep on the convertible sofa in the living room, let alone seven of them. It was out of the question. His mother would kill him.

"Sure," Andy said. "You can all flop at my place."

CHAPTER EIGHT

Once it was decided to stay in town overnight, they had a debate under the theater marquee about where to get some dinner. The Blum brothers and the Donovans reached an angry stalemate. Jeff Blum had a notion about looking for a macrobiotic restaurant that he had "heard about from this chick," and the Donovans said that was a stupid idea and argued for steaks, or at least Italian. Robbie Kugel suggested they just grab some burgers any old place. At this point Andy mentioned a chop suey house in Chinatown that was "excellent," he said, "and incredibly cheap," and that broke the impasse. And Tim Flannery said he didn't give a damn what international cuisine the rest of them picked as long as it wasn't seafood.

They subwayed down to Sun Wah Do on the second floor of a tenement on Mott Street and had a feast fit for seven warlords, plum wine, fortune cookies, and all, with the bill coming in at just over $40 including the tip. Even the Blums found it dietetically acceptable. After dinner it was still raining out and they took another subway ride over to the West Village to catch Slim Harpo playing the blues at the Cafe au Go Go. When they got out of the show at midnight there was a general mood among them to try and pick up some girls. Once again at Andy's suggestion they headed back uptown to try the watering holes of the upper East Side where, he assured them, hundreds of lovelorn females waited, ripe for the picking, in the singles bars of First and Second Avenues.

He took them to Maxwell's Plum on 65th Street, which even on a midsummer weekday night was swarming with working girls of the better sort and an equal number of young button-down bachelors trying to pick them up. The Ocean Breeze guards, with their bronze tans, long, sun-bleached locks, and collegiate swaggers did turn a few pretty heads when they stepped inside the vast air-conditioned saloon. But Andy for one had run low on money, and being exhausted and not a little worried about six guys flopping at his mother's apartment, he decided to leave Maxwell's Plum shortly after they arrived and to go home ahead of them—giving the address to Tim written on the inside of a matchbook.

When Andy entered the familiar lobby of the high rise on 70th Street, Omar the ever-smiling Moroccan night doorman was at his post and Andy had to borrow the passkey from him because he hadn't thought to bring his own housekey. The fourteenth-floor apartment had that just-cleaned smell of furniture polish. In the past he had always found it comforting, but now it made him uneasy. He switched on the light in the foyer. His mother had left the apartment immaculate. He cautiously entered the living room, with its elegantly severe modern furnishings. The many paintings on the walls were lit by track lights, as though the apartment were an annex of his mother's art gallery, which indeed it was, for she often entertained her best clients at home.

He briefly looked into his own bedroom, where the

sight of all his accumulated childhood belongings made
his stomach hurt—the model planes hung from the ceiling
on fishing line; the desk where he had failed to complete
so many homework assignments and instead spent his
time trying to formulate homemade gunpowder using salt-
peter from the drugstore mixed with ground-up artist's
charcoal and the carefully scraped-off heads of kitchen
matches; behind his bed, the wall papered with blown-up
posters of silent film stars. Even his bedroom—which had
always been a mess while he lived there—was immaculate, and he got the strong, sad impression of it belonging
to a child who had departed forever, whose effects were
preserved as a memorial by a grieving parent. The thought
made him feel sorry that he did not treat his mother
better. He turned off the light and returned to the living
room. There he carefully took a seat on the sofa as though
he were at the office of some exalted personage, nervously waiting for a momentous appointment. In a few
minutes, he toppled over on the cushions, fast asleep.

He was awakened by the shrill buzz of the housephone.
For several moments he blundered around the living room
in total confusion, not knowing quite who he was, or
where he was, or what was making the terrible noise.
Finally it all came back to him and he lurched for the
housephone in the foyer.

" 'lo?"

"It is I, Omar. You have many friends down here, yes,
who want to come up and see you, yes?"

"Yes."

"All right," Omar said in a tone of voice that suggested it
would be somebody's funeral.

Andy paced nervously in the dining room, awaiting
their arrival. All the alcohol he consumed over the long
day and night had worn off and he was now quite sober.

In fact his head ached. Through the door he heard the elevator stop and then the sound of voices, including some in the higher registers. Girls! he realized, with a twinge of panic. Girls, they've all got girls! Then the doorbell rang. For a moment he considered not answering it, but then someone—Hughie Donovan, it sounded like— pounded on the door with his fist, crying, "Open up in there," in an obviously drunken drawl, and rather than have them wake up the entire fourteenth floor, Andy let them in.

They had girls with them, all right, but only two. The Donovans had one each, and fairly good-looking ones too. Both wore miniskirts. One was a blonde with ironed hair and bangs and rather heavy eye make-up. Van Donovan had his arm around her. Hughie's girl wore no make-up and had dark hair parted in the middle like a folksinger. She had on a sheer lavender camisole worn without a bra that very nicely outlined the shape of her breasts.

"Hey, ole buddy," Tim slurred in a greeting. "Iss us."

Then, like a wave breaking on a beach, they were all flooding into the apartment, going every which way.

"Party time," Hughie said.

"Where'za 'frigerator?" Jeff Blum asked.

"Hey, look, drinks!" Robbie Kugel said, pointing to the lowboy in the dining room that served as Barbara Newmark's bar. Then the stereo in the living room came on with a crackle. Someone soon found a radio station and the song "I'm a Believer" blasted out of the speakers.

"Jesus! Not so loud!" Andy cried and rushed in to find Seth Blum rummaging through the records.

"Got any better sounds than Frank Sinatra?" he asked drunkenly.

"We can't listen to the goddam Monkees all night," Robbie Kugel elaborated.

"I've got some more records in my room," Andy told him, worried but still trying to please.

"Could you go get 'em?"

"Uh, sure."

When Andy returned with his Beatles and Byrds albums, Kugel was pouring twelve-year-old scotch into the best etched crystal tumblers Andy's mother owned. Tim Flannery emerged from the kitchen with an immense salami sandwich leaking mustard from one end. Jeff Blum was still in there boiling water for rice. The Donovans had their girls on the sofa in the living room. The blonde one was soul-kissing Van and the dark-haired one was giggling as Hughie ran his hand up and down her sleek exposed thigh.

"Great, you got *Rubber Soul,*" Seth Blum said, grabbing the records from Andy.

Meanwhile, the elder Blum had emerged from the kitchen and set about filling his new waterpipe on the coffee table in the living room. Robbie Kugel handed out the drinks. Andy was horrified to see that the scotch bottle he had put back on the lowboy was empty. Then Van Donovan was suddenly looming over him with his arm around the blonde, saying, "S'there some place me and Mimi can, you know, go for awhile?"

"Go . . . ?"

"You know," Van said. The girl, Mimi, giggled and buried her face in Van's shirt. "Like with a bed," Van pretended to whisper, smiling suavely.

"Sure," Andy said and directed him down the hall to his room.

By this time, Andy was so frazzled that he grabbed a vodka bottle off the lowboy and glugged down several swallows just to calm his nerves.

"Thattaboy," Tim said.

The Beatles were singing "I've Just Seen A Face."

"Wanna smoke some?" Jeff Blum bellowed in from the other room.

Before too long Andy's brain was tintinnabulating again. His anxiety had magically evaporated. It began to seem quite a splendid thing that he was actually having a *party with the guys* at his own home. It was precisely the kind of thing his high school career had been devoid of—just sitting around with a bunch of friends and getting a buzz on. Even Jeff Blum began to seem okay as someone to associate with. After all it was his weed, and he was generously sharing it with everybody. Maybe Andy had been wrong about the guy.

"Is something burning?" Hughie's girl, Liz, the one who looked like Joan Baez the folksinger, asked, surfacing from a kiss.

"Yeah, something's burning," Seth Blum said, giggling as he held a lighted match over the bowl of the waterpipe.

"No, I mean like something else," Liz said.

"I smell it too," Tim said.

"Holy shit," Jeff Blum said. "My rice!"

"Your rice?"

Andy and Jeff Blum both raced into the kitchen, which was filling with a fog of acrid gray smoke. Andy fought his way over to the range, where the smoke was pouring out of a saucepan. The burner under it was turned up to high.

"Shit, this always happens," Blum said.

"Is this some kind of party trick you do?" Andy asked, gagging.

"No, I always forget to turn it down low after the water boils."

The smoke finally drove them out of the kitchen. Andy could tell that the saucepan—a nice copper-bottomed Revere Ware two-quart model—was hopelessly ruined.

So he carried it, still smoldering, to the hall outside the apartment and into the little room where the incinerator chute was, and tossed it down into the abyss, wondering whether his mother would notice it was missing.

"Gee, I'm sorry about that," Blum said when Andy reentered, and since the lummox essentially had apologized, there was no way Andy could holler at him, so he said it was all right, that his mother could always get another pot, and they returned to the living room.

As soon as they did, Andy noticed that Hughie and his girl were no longer there, or anywhere else to be seen. He understood in a flash that they had stolen off somewhere to make love. Since Van and Mimi were already going at it in his bedroom, Andy quickly deduced that Hughie and Liz had gone into his mother's bedroom. By this time he realized—with the sort of crystalline insight marijuana affords—that the chances of his mother not finding out about this little wing-ding were dwindling away to zero. He might even have to tell her that one of his friends ruined her Revere Ware—"*making rice, for godsake?*" he could just hear her ask acidly—but he'd simply offer to replace it and that would be the end of it. He'd straighten up the apartment before they left in the morning. Besides, he rationalized, he was going away to college in the fall. He was never going to live here with her again anyway.

After reasoning through all that—which took less time than it appears—Andy felt perfectly at ease and happy. The burnt saucepan was forgotten. He smoked another bowl of weed with Tim, Robbie Kugel, and the Blums, and they had a fine time rapping about girls and surfing and listening to the Byrds' *Turn, Turn, Turn* album before, one by one, they dropped off to sleep around the coffee table.

———

Andy woke up to what sounded like the whooping of a gigantic bird. His head pounded, his throat was raw, and his bones ached from sleeping on something hard. Several moments passed before he understood where he was: on the living room floor of the apartment in the city. The Blums, Tim Flannery, and Robbie Kugel were all sprawled out on the carpet and the sofa. Andy heard the weird whooping sound again, then a male voice saying, "For chrissake, do it in the bathroom, will ya." A door opened down the hall. There were hurried footsteps, then more whooping. By now Andy realized that someone was throwing up.

He stumbled out of the living room. Hughie Donovan was standing in the hall outside Andy's mother's bedroom while the whooping continued from behind the door of the adjoining bath.

"She had an accident," Hughie said sheepishly.

"An accident?"

Andy squeezed past him into his mother's bedroom. The air-conditioner hummed. On the flowery bed-linen was an evil-smelling splash of vomit. Andy walked gingerly around the bed, as though keeping the terrible sight at bay. There was more of the foul stuff on the headboard and the carpet below.

"I'm really sorry," Hughie said from the door.

"Do you think she might clean it up?" Andy asked timidly.

"I don't know. I'll ask."

Then, suddenly, Robbie Kugel was in the hall saying, "Come on, we've got to make the first possible train."

"What's it doing out?" Seth Blum asked.

"Clearing up."

"Aw shit."

"There's a seven-fifteen. We could make the noon ferry."

114

"Well, hell, we better shake a leg," Hughie said, and he went back into Andy's mother's room to put on his clothes. Meanwhile, Robbie Kugel rapped on Andy's bedroom door calling for Van, who soon opened it a crack. The blonde Mimi was on the bed behind him with the sheet pulled up only to her waist and her face bleary from sex. In the midst of this, the dark-haired Liz emerged from Andy's mother's bathroom smelling of toothpaste, sex, and vomit. She was completely naked also, acting very upset and preoccupied, and immediately commenced putting on her clothes. Andy did not know how to ask her to clean up the mess. She appeared to have no intention of doing it.

"Uh, Hughie, could you ask her about cleaning up?"

"How can I do that?" he whispered back helplessly.

There were only her panties, miniskirt, camisole, and sandals, and in a minute she was dressed. Then, sniffling and unable to look anyone in the eyes, she grabbed her leather sack purse and hurried out of the room past Andy and Hughie. Back down the hall the others were stirring.

"You mind if we have some of this orange juice?" Jeff Blum bellowed.

Liz waited impatiently at the door of Andy's room for her friend Mimi to get dressed, and in a few minutes they were both headed out the front door.

"You'll have to clean it up," Andy told Hughie.

"Me?" Hughie said. "I don't know how."

"But—"

"Come on, Hughie," Robbie Kugel hollered from the foyer. "We gotta make that train."

"If I don't get back, Hummer's going to have my ass," Hughie explained, cinching his belt.

Just then his brother, Van, came into the room and strode around the bed, surveying the damage.

115

"She was pretty bummed," he remarked, referring to Liz.

"I'm bummed," Andy said. "My mother's going to kill me."

"I'll stick around and help you clean up."

"You will?" Andy said, greatly relieved. Then, out of misguided politeness, he said, "You don't have to."

"No," Van said. "I do."

Tim Flannery, looking puffy and hungover, with eyes like slits, stuck his head in the room and made a sour face when his nose detected the rancid odor.

"You got this under control?" he inquired.

"Nothing to worry about," Van said. "You guys go ahead and make that train. We'll catch the next one."

"We'll make it up to you, buddy," Tim said, shaking Andy by the shoulder. "Hey, what's a little vomit between friends, anyway?"

Van Donovan did indeed clean up the mess his brother's girl had made, and he did it virtually himself with a pail of hot water and strong soap, while Andy straightened up the other rooms. Eventually Van came down the hall with the sheets all balled up.

"I turned over the mattress so the damp spot's underneath," he explained unemotionally, as though this was a situation he had met with before. "You'd probably be better off deep-sixing these," he said, indicating the sheets. Andy took them out to the incinerator chute, then found a clean set and made his mother's bed. "It's not too bad," Van said, sniffing the air when they had finished.

"Maybe she'll never find out," Andy said, not really believing it himself. His whole head seemed filled with the bad smell, whether it was still there or not. It was the kind of smell you couldn't get out of your brain for a long time.

"She'll never have a clue," Van said. "Well, what do you say we go make that train?"

"Okay."

Together they rode several subways to Penn Station and caught an eight-ten train to Weekapauk. Between them they bought two magazines and a newspaper. Van didn't talk much the whole way, being famously taciturn by nature, but at one point he said, "I hear you've applied to Tennessee?"

"Yes, I have," Andy said.

"You'll like it there. It's fun."

"That's what I'm hoping."

"You could pledge our fraternity."

"I could?"

"Sure. We'll both sponser you, me and Hughie."

"God," Andy said, "that would be great."

College fraternities—whatever their shortcomings as modern social institutions—were another item from that broad category of mainstream Americana that Andy longed to be a part of. He had very little idea of what being in a fraternity was about, beyond the continual party atmosphere, and he did not even know that some fraternities discriminated against Jews, Negroes, and people whose names ended in vowels.

They got to Weekapauk in time for the one o'clock ferry, which was crowded with weekenders trying to get a jump on the other weekenders who would follow in greater droves as the day progressed. It had stopped raining and the boat ride was much smoother than the trip to the mainland the day before. To the west, the clouds were breaking up and here and there a swath of blue showed through. The three-day blow was over.

When they got into Ocean Breeze, the dockmaster, Tom Pendergast, spotted Andy disembarking and signaled him over.

"You know you've got about a hundred pounds of meat rotting in the freight house, pal," Pendergast said.

"Omigod," Andy groaned. Between all the excitement and drinking of the past two days he had entirely forgotten about the Thursday freight boat, which had delivered the Club's weekend supply of food. "I'll come right back down and get it," he promised Pendergast and practically ran the mile to the Club to get the hand-truck.

CHAPTER NINE

"I don't think Anatole is feeling very well," Bass observed as the chef sat slumped in the chair where he customarily retired in an alcoholic stupor after the arduous job of preparing the Friday night meal—except now it was only three-thirty in the afternoon. Anatole's eyes were open, if somewhat crossed, his tongue lolled in an expression of congenital idiocy, and his plump, hamlike arms with their sausagelike fingers hung limply at his sides.

"Is he all right?" Andy asked, meaning in the sense of major organ function.

"Yeah, sure, basically," Bass said, trying to appear confident. "That is, I think so. I'm afraid he's just, uh . . ."

"Plastered?"

"Well, yes."

"Great. What are we going to do?"

"That's sort of what I wanted to talk to you about," Bass said, sliding an arm around Andy's shoulder and steering him away from the pathetic sight of Anatole. "You've been here, what, five, six weeks now?"

"Uh-huh."

"You've been watching the old guy do his thing, correct?"

"Uh-huh."

"I mean, it's not that complicated, what he does," Bass more or less asserted before his voice veered up to a more dubious note. "Is it?"

"It's just baked fish and stuff."

"Exactly. You could do it. Right?"

Andy was first stunned, then thrilled, then terrified.

"You want me to cook the whole dinner and everything?"

"Andy, we've got a situation here. Know what I mean? Our asses are really on the line. My ass. Your ass. These Club members, they're not like ordinary people, you understand?"

Andy wasn't quite sure what Bass meant by that. "No," he said.

"Well," Bass patiently explained. "They're not like you and me, for example. They're not Jewish. They don't adapt so easily. They expect to come over here and have their fish supper just like every Friday since Jesus Christ was crucified. Frankly, I'm a little worried that they might freak out if they don't get that fish supper."

"Freak out?"

"Yes. Do something rash. For instance, fire me. And Andy, if I go, you go. We're in this together, my friend."

"Why don't you go hire some other cook?"

"Andy, Andy," Bass said, desperation creeping into his voice. "Be realistic. This is Thunder Island, a little speck of sand miles out in the ocean. Where am I going to find another chef two and a half hours before suppertime? You've got to do it. For us."

"But what about the dishes?"

"The dishes? The dishes?" Bass asked, getting a little shrill. "What dishes?"

"The dirty dishes."

"What about them?"

"You expect me to do the cooking and wash all the dishes too?"

"Of course not. Did I say that?"

"No. I just—"

"I'll find someone to help you."

"Oh. Great."

"And Andy, need I say that there will be a special reward in this for you. A cash bonus. When this night is over, I'm going to give you twenty-five bucks right out of my own pocket, no taxes taken out or anything."

"Jeez. Twenty-five bucks!" Andy said, thinking that it was indeed a great sum of money, more than he'd ever made in one night before. "Hey, that's great."

"Then you'll do it?"

"I'll give it a whack," Andy said.

"That's the spirit. Only one more thing," Bass added, putting on one of his most dazzling smiles. "If you get drunk too, I'll kill you myself."

Having returned from the city rather late to begin with, Andy was already behind on the many little chores that would have comprised his usual kitchen slave duties— chopping parsley, mincing garlic, washing lettuce, et cetera—and he just didn't see any possibility of getting the meal together for one hundred thirty-four people by six o'clock. All Anatole had managed to accomplish before his collapse was to make a tray of the vile little anchovy-paste hors d'oeuvres that were his specialty. Andy was about to break it to Bass that it just wasn't going to work out when Franny Flannery breezed in the swinging door, all freckles and eagerness.

"Hi," she said. "Bass sent me in to help."

"He did?" Andy reacted dubiously, trying to think of a way to tell her it was hopeless but thanks anyway. But she asked if he wanted her to start by making the muffins or stringing the wax beans, and it struck him that perhaps Franny actually knew what she was doing. "You can cook?" he said, as though he were remarking on a miracle.

"Of course," she said, tying on an apron.

Soon she was bustling around, making the corn muffin batter in a very organized manner. Andy watched her for a minute or so with some admiration and decided that the venture might just be worth a try after all. So he went and got the fish out of the walk-in refrigerator and began arranging the sole filets into turbans on several oiled baking sheets. Before long, a spirit of efficiency and teamwork such as Andy had never seen before in the Club kitchen began to establish itself. Bass was right: Andy had learned Anatole's job just by watching him for five weeks. And as he and Franny moved from one task to the next, Andy began to realize that he, not Anatole, had really been doing most of the work all along, without ever knowing it. And having Franny helping made it come together in half the usual time.

By five o'clock—when the screen door started to slap, when the buzz of conversation and the *chinka-chinka-chinka* of Bass's cocktail shaker and the golden (if scratchily played) voice of Vaughn Monroe could be heard from the Club bar—Andy and Franny were all caught up. The muffins were done, the potatoes were baking, the fish was ready for the oven, the salad was made, and they were just about to frost the sheet cake.

The whole time, Anatole remained slumped asleep in his chair in the corner beside the pantry door. They knew that he was not dead because he snored away musically hour after hour. Bass had decided to leave him in place rather than remove him to his room upstairs, lest one of the Club members discover that the entire Friday night supper was being prepared by the dishwasher and a fourteen-year-old girl with no supervision.

During the actual mealtime crunch, some unfortunate problems did crop up. Andy burned a big patch of his palm and several fingers when he saved a teetering sheet pan full of baked sole turbans from falling off the prep table by grabbing it without a potholder. It took about five minutes before it really started to hurt like hell, and by the time he got ice on it a big water blister the size of a plum had bubbled up. Franny dropped a glass cruet of french dressing on the floor. Though she mopped it up, a greasy spot remained and one of the waitresses went down with a tray full of salads as though she had stepped on a banana peel. They had put the wrong number of eggs in the sheet cake, and when they got around to portioning it out, they discovered it was leaden, like floor tile. But none of the members complained, and the dessert plates came back to the kitchen empty.

When the horror of mealtime was over, Franny helped Andy tackle the towers of dirty dishes and pans. His burned hand hurt too much to stick in a sink full of hot water, so he dried and stacked the dishes while Franny washed. Anatole continued to snooze through it all. Around ten o'clock, he was even visited by Charlie Dern—husband of Club president Edna Dern—who complimented the sleeping chef on "the great spread," and who was so drunk himself that he failed to notice the chef was totally unconscious.

Finally, a little after eleven o'clock, they took out the garbage and mopped the floor, and the ordeal was over. Andy and Franny went out to the rickety back porch overlooking a sandy expanse of rustling dune reeds to have a cigarette.

"How much did Bass say he was going to pay you, by the way?" Andy asked.

"Fifteen dollars," Franny said cheerfully and bent to the match Andy held cupped in his hands.

"Fifteen dollars! The cheap bastard."

"I usually only make ten waitressing," Franny said. "We pool tips, and all the parents have this idea that it's only their kids, you know, like we're only pretending to be waitresses, so they give us these tiny little tips. It's stupid."

Andy was impressed at how much she sounded like her brother Tim. It was the attitude more than the voice or the midwestern inflection. "Here," he said, fishing his wallet from the back pocket of his cutoffs and handing Franny a five-dollar bill. "He's giving me twenty-five, and as far as I'm concerned you did as much work in there tonight as I did. This'll even it up."

"Thanks," she said, taking the five. "That's really nice of you."

"I'm a real gallant guy," Andy quipped, thinking at once of that night on the beach with Kathy Craig, and what an idiot he had been not to take advantage of the situation. Franny took a deep drag off her cigarette and leaned on the weathered rail. The surf pounded crisply in the distance. A night breeze blew strands of amber hair into her face, just as the wind had that other day up on the beach. Andy leaned against the rail beside her, enjoying the closeness.

"You did great tonight," he said. "If you hadn't helped, we would have been sunk. Bass might have got fired, and me with him."

"They'd never fire Bass," Franny said. "The mothers are all in love with him."

"The fathers aren't."

"Yeah, but the mothers really run the show around here. Look at old Mrs. Dern."

"Well, anyway, they wouldn't have been too happy without their Friday night fish supper."

"I suppose not."

"I sure feel filthy."

"Me too," Franny said.

"I have to take a shower and wash this crud off me," Andy said, adding, "Guess me and Tim'll head into town."

Still, he remained leaning at the rail beside Franny, liking her so much and feeling so grateful to her that he wanted to kiss her, even though he was afraid to.

"Hey, you know what?" she said, sculpting the cigarette's red-hot tip to a point against the wooden rail.

"What?"

"I've been doing a whole lot more drawing since that day. And painting too. Just watercolors—"

"Watercolors are goddam difficult," Andy said. "They're harder than oils, in my opinion."

"Anyway, I've been doing a lot more."

"You'll have to let me see them."

"Would you look them over? And tell me what you think?"

"Sure."

"That'd be great."

She turned her face to him and even in the stark glow of the outdoor porch light her eyes were radiant. She smiled self-consciously. He touched her cheek with his left hand, the unburned one. Her eyelids closed expectantly. He leaned forward and kissed her on the lips. A strand of hair had blown across them. Though the kiss thrilled him, Andy could not help thinking that the girl he was kissing was Tim Flannery's sister, and only fourteen years old.

Indeed, he worried whether he had crossed a dangerous frontier from which there was no turning back.

"I have to go now," he told her.

"All right," she said, a little breathlessly. Something seemed caught in her throat.

"Thanks for everything." He touched her cheek with his fingertips and, leaving her there on the rickety back porch in the night breeze and the weird light, went back inside.

"Get this," Tim said as they hurried down the dark walks away from the Club toward town. "Hummer's demoted me and Hughie down to the goddam bay for a week."

"For coming in late today?"

"Yeah."

"Why only you two guys?"

"Why us?" Tim echoed Andy sardonically and snorted.

"Why not Kugel or the Blums?"

"Pure discrimination," Tim said.

"Hummer's not Jewish. He's a Club member."

"But that's it exactly, don't you see? He doesn't dare punish them. Instead, he's making an example out of us. Those are his words, by the way, 'an example.' I'm a member of an oppressed minority group."

"Well, that stinks," Andy said. "What about Van Donovan? He must have gotten up to the beach much later than you guys even."

"Hummer's afraid to breathe the wrong way around Van."

"Then how come he punished Hughie?"

"Van's Van and Hughie's Hughie," Tim said.

As they crossed into the village of Ocean Breeze and turned down Juniper, they could hear the Beatles' *Sgt.*

Pepper album playing in a house somewhere. The song was the one with the creepy circus music:

> *For the benefit of Mr. Kite*
> *There will be a show tonight*
> *On trampoline*

The village was as crowded as Andy had ever seen it on a Friday night. It was balmy and clear after the spell of rotten weather, the very peak of summer. The cement wall around the square was packed with pubescents, girls and long-haired boys, all wearing beads, all stoned. *Barefoot in the Park* with Robert Redford and Jane Fonda was playing that week at the Community Center, a poster advertised. The boutiques were open late, taking advantage of the crowds. The ice cream shop, the fudge stand, and the spin-art parlor were packed with vacationers. More promenaded on the sidewalks around the square, which looked like a moat of denim. There was a long line outside the Sea Witch. The Bayside was jammed. Only a few customers sat in the ill-fated Sandpiper, out of which blasted a lugubrious song with a lot of organ in it called "A Whiter Shade of Pale," by the band Procol Harum.

After an obligatory circuit of the square, "just to check things out," as Tim put it, they went over to McCauley's, which was also jammed with the usual crowd that had made the place its hangout this year, along with a lot of assorted weekenders. "You Can't Hurry Love" by the Supremes bopped out of the jukebox. Andy ordered four large beers and then had to search Flannery out. He found him standing beside a booth occupied by the Blums, who were with a couple of girls. When Andy came over with the beers, neither of the Blums said much more to him than "Hey, Slave, how's it going?" which rather annoyed

Andy, considering all the trouble they'd put him through the night before, not to mention the fact that he didn't appreciate the moniker "Slave." They might at least have asked how he and Van made out cleaning up the mess they made of his mother's apartment, Andy thought. He decided that he had been correct to despise Jeff Blum in the first place, and that he wasn't too keen on Seth either. The brothers appeared to be discussing the pros and cons of short-grain versus long-grain brown rice. Flannery was trying to make time with one of the girls, but she was rolling her eyes in boredom as he cracked jokes. Eventually Andy steered Tim away from the booth and into the back room, where they found a table in the rear and settled in to watch girls and make pithy observations about the guys they were with.

By midnight they had put away four rounds—eight beers each—and were working on the fifth.

"Looka this asshole," Tim remarked about an off-islander who was doing the monkey with his girl to a tune called "Hanky Panky" by Tommy James. "Looka those stupid pants." The object of his ridicule was wearing garish red and green striped jeans with widely flared bell-bottoms. "Man, you are so groovy," Tim said loudly.

"Hey, Tim, ssshhh," Andy said, beginning to worry that Tim might take out his frustration about being demoted by starting a fight. "Be cool."

"I don't have to be cool," Tim retorted. "That asshole's cool enough for both of us. Hey, if he twirled around, you s'pose his ankles would show?"

Fortunately, the song ended and a slower Dylan song took its place. The guy in the flaring bell-bottoms retired to a table with his girl.

"It's assholes like that who are ruining this island," Tim said, reaching for his ninth beer.

"Do you think Dylan's got brain damage, or what?"
Andy said.

"You keep on asking me that. I think *you've* got brain
damage."

"No, really."

"Oh, I don't know," Tim finally answered morosely. "I
just hope he's all right."

"I heard he was a vegetable."

"Do we have to keep talking about him? It's depressing."

"Sorry."

"This place is depressing. Especially with guys like Joe
Groovy over there. C'mon. Let's get out of this stupid
place," Tim said, chugging down the remainder of his
ninth beer and then at least half of the tenth, which had
come with it. Andy drained one of his, but couldn't even
begin the other. Tim lurched out of the back room, muttering "assholes," and Andy followed him. Outside they
paused a moment at the west end of the village square.

"Air feels good," Andy said.

"We gotta go claim a new bar," Tim declared and then
belched. "This goddam place has gotten too goddam
popular. That's the problem out here. You find a perfectly
good bar and then before you know it half the groovy
assholes from the mainland are cluttering it up."

"Where do you want to go?"

"Who cares?"

"Wanna to to the Sea Witch?"

"If you wanna. I don't give a damn."

"Okay, we'll go there."

They started around the square. Even after midnight
there was quite a crowd in town. It was still mild out and
many teenagers remained along the concrete wall. Tim
took a joint out of his cigarette pack and lit it. Andy didn't

catch on until he smelled the marijuana, and then he snatched it out of Tim's mouth.

"Are you nuts?" he reproached the swaying Flannery.

"Hey, gimme it back."

"You want to get arrested?"

"I'm gonna complain to the cops about you stealin' my—"

"Andy, darling?"

"Whu . . . ?"

Barbara Newmark and Leonard Kropotkin stood directly in front of Tim and Andy. Her arm was looped inside Kropotkin's as middle-aged married folk do when they go out for a stroll. Bumping into his mother was upsetting enough, considering what had gone on in her apartment the night before, but this intimacy with Kropotkin—who was wearing both his Greek fisherman's cap and a dopey smile—added a layer of anger over Andy's anxiety.

" 'lo, Mom," he mumbled, not even trying to sound sober.

"Aren't you going to say hello to Lenny?" his mother asked. "Where are your manners?"

"Oh. 'lo, Lenny."

"Hey, this your Mom?" Tim asked.

Andy introduced Tim.

"Let me tell you something, ma'am," Tim began in a folksy manner. "This boy of yours here is about the most crackerjack dishwasher we've ever had at the Thunder Island Club. I know because I'm a member. Believe me when I say you should be proud. His future's all ahead of him."

"I should hope so," Kropotkin quipped, looking to Andy's mother for a corroborative laugh that she failed to return.

Instead, Barbara Newmark just glared at her son, and at

Tim, and back at her son, and with the kind of bluntness that was her trademark back in the Manhattan art world she declared, "You two are both bombed."

"We are," Tim agreed, switching into an Irish brogue. "But we couldn't help ourselves. The testimonials went on for hours, ma'am, and at each one we were obliged to drink another toast. But then it's not every day a fellow wins the Nobel Prize for dishwashing—is it, me boy?" He turned to Andy.

"You did say this was a friend of yours?" Barbara Newmark asked her son, looking the grinning Flannery up and down as though he was a freak on exhibit in a sideshow.

"We have to get going now, Mom," Andy said.

"Just a second. I tried to get hold of you all day yesterday."

"I was off."

"Off on a lark," Tim added, and Andy jabbed him with an elbow.

"We're having a brunch on Sunday at your Uncle Jack's," his mother went on. "I'd like you to come. Lee Koenigsburg's widow and daughter are going to be there and—"

"May I come too?" Tim asked.

"Absolutely not," Barbara told him plainly.

"How come?"

"Because you're drunk, young man, and I have reason to believe that you'd get drunk again and embarrass me."

"Probably right," Tim agreed. "But don't worry, I won't take it personally."

"That's noon Sunday," Andy's mother told her son, ignoring Tim. "Now, how do you suppose you'll remember this?"

"Oh, I'll remember, Mom," Andy assured her. "Have you had a nice time out here?"

"Divine," she said. "But I could do with seeing you drunk less often."

"Today's youngsters behaving the way they do, you're lucky it's only booze and not these new mind-altering drugs," Kropotkin inserted in the boys' defense, in his ineffable news magazine manner.

"Spoken like a true American," Tim said. "Here, I'd like you to have this as a little token of appreciation from today's youth." He fished in his cigarette pack and produced another joint, which he gave to Kropotkin, who held it in his hand and gawked at it as though it were a tiny bomb about to blow up in his face. "We must be going," Tim said, looping his arm through Andy's, much as Barbara Newmark had hers looped through Kropotkin's. "Toodle-loo," he said, and he began dragging Andy up the still-crowded sidewalk.

"Don't forget, Sunday at noon," his mother called after him.

"I won't," Andy said.

"Jesus, did you have to give him that joint, for godsake?"

"It was worth it. It blew his mind," Tim said. "Did you see the look on his face?"

"I'm the one who's got to live with her," Andy said.

"Hey, you don't have to live with her. You're leaving home in the fall, you cluck. You're gonna be far, far away, down in good ole Tennessee. Hey, what's this about Karen Koenigsburg and her old lady?"

Andy explained about how his mother was seeking to become the exclusive dealer for Lee Koenigsburg's unsold paintings.

"You ought to try and weasel your way into Karen's heart while you've got the chance," Tim suggested. "Such a cute little thing."

"She'll probably show up with that asshole who makes the giant plastic hamburgers."

"I forgot about him. Well, maybe you can find a way to quietly kill him before brunch is over."

At one A.M. there was no longer a line outside the Sea Witch and so Tim and Andy decided to go in. They had just stepped inside the vestibule entrance where a bouncer was taking dollar cover charges when a commotion erupted toward the rear of the establishment. For a while the band played through it—they were murdering Wilson Pickett's song "In the Midnight Hour"—but eventually, with tables crashing over, and glasses shattering, and women's screams filling the room, the music stopped. The psychedelic lights kept swirling and blinking, though, and it was hard to make out what sort of disturbance was going on. A few seconds after it started, the bouncer at the door rushed from his post into the fray and so Tim and Andy walked in free.

There was still a good crowd in the Sea Witch, and many of them now formed a ring around the combatants. Shortly, a pair of uniformed Ocean Breeze policemen hurried in the entrance and forced their way past the gawking spectators. Meanwhile, a breech opened in the crowd and two very large bouncers—both linemen on the Hofstra football team—dragged a man out. The man, his face a bloody, pulpy mess, appeared not to resist. His feet dragged.

"Christ almighty," Tim whispered to Andy, "that was Duff Perleman."

A minute later the two police officers emerged from the crowd flanking Van Donovan and escorted him toward the door. Tim and Andy exchanged an astonished glance. Van Donovan had a cut lip, but was far less bloody than Perleman and walked under his own power.

"Hey, Van," Tim greeted him abashedly as Donovan passed within a few feet of him.

"Hey, guys," Van replied without emotion as the cops led him toward the exit.

The band tuned their guitars and made a plea about the need for world peace while the crowd buzzed excitedly as they always do in the exhilarating aftermath of a brawl. Among those who had been in the back, and now following Van Donovan to the exit, was Robbie Kugel. Tim grabbed him by the sleeve as Kugel tried to squeeze past the other patrons returning to their places at the bar.

"What the hell was that all about?" Tim asked.

"Van punched Duff's lights out."

"Because of Hughie getting sent down?"

"Yeah, but that was only an excuse," Kugel said. "One of his old fraternity brothers got it over in Vietnam and he just was told about it this afternoon."

"You mean killed?"

"That's right. Dead."

"Jeez," Tim said.

"What was one of his fraternity brothers doing over in Vietnam?" Andy asked.

"He was in the Army," Kugel said, as though it were an extremely dumb question. "He flunked out and they drafted him."

CHAPTER TEN

On Saturday Anatole was back in service, foul-tempered as usual. He drove Andy wickedly through the long, hot afternoon—hottest of the summer, with the mercury creeping above one hundred degrees at three P.M.—as though to reassert through sheer meanness that he was in charge again. Unfortunately there was something wrong with the meat, the steamship roasts that Andy had left overnight in the ferry company freight office on Thursday. He could smell it as soon as Anatole sent him to fetch them from the walk-in cooler. It was a pungent, oppressive, funky odor as of something squashed on the roadside and left to rot. It was almost as bad as the enormous stinking sea turtle that had washed up on the beach at the end of June.

Anatole appeared not to notice it, but went right ahead and roasted them all up. The result was that within ten minutes of the dinner plates being sent out of the kitchen that evening, there was a stampede to the restrooms that evoked one of those mass evacuation scenes in a horror movie, as though radioactive beasties from the ocean's briny depths had crawled through the dining room's windows.

When the dust settled and casualties were counted (there were two medical doctors and a podiatrist on hand), roughly half the members were pronounced victims of severe food poisoning, and many of the others were feeling none too swell, if not actually gagging in sympathy with their loved ones. Anatole was cashiered on the spot by Ted Bass, who was acting on orders from the furious president Edna Dern, as soon as she emerged unsteadily from the ladies' room. "Tell him to pack his bag and get out at once," she snarled, before her husband, Charles—an alcoholic who rarely sampled solid food and was therefore unaffected—helped her stagger back to their nearby cottage.

Anatole took the news stolidly. But then he was drunk again. Bass found him in his regular chair in the corner near the pantry with the usual postprandial glazed expression of boozy exhaustion on his sad Greco-Parisian face. In fact, he didn't appear even to understand what had happened, or what Bass was telling him, and so Bass went upstairs to gather the old man's few things in the cheap plaid vinyl bag that he traveled with and then proceeded to show him the rear door.

Much as he hated the old idiot, and much as Bass tried to dispatch him gently, Andy felt sorry and not a little guilty to see Anatole kicked out of the place so ignominiously, like an old dog who has peed on a carpet one too many times. Of course he did not volunteer the information that the beef spoiled because he had failed to meet the freight boat on Thursday. Rather, he tried to rationalize his guilt away, telling himself that Anatole *should have known* the meat was bad and that he, Andy, had just followed orders. This made him no better than a *good Nazi*, Andy thought, disgusted with himself.

Still, he had his duties to get on with, all the plates and

pots and pans to wash, and then the puked-in bathrooms to clean out—a task so vile that his burden of guilt was lightened somewhat—and it was midnight before he was all done. Only a handful of hard-drinking members remained out at the bar. Tim Flannery, who had escaped poisoning, was with them. He had dined on frozen pizza at home earlier with his brothers Shawn and Brian and had only come over at eleven to wait for Andy to get off work so they could go carousing over in Ocean Breeze.

When they got downtown, the scene had a sinister air to it. The lurid lights of the honky-tonks, the rock 'n' roll blaring from them, the sickening smells of fried food, fudge, caramel corn, and here and there a whiff of marijuana, the red, sunstroked faces of all the weekenders— everything seemed relentlessly harsh to Andy, and then they saw Anatole sitting huddled and dazed in his filthy cooking whites on the bench between Karp's Superette and the ferry terminal.

"Jesus, where's he going to spend the night?" Andy wondered out loud. "There aren't any more ferries until morning."

"Cops'll probably lock him up if he tries to sleep there or up on the beach. Don't worry, he'll be better off overnight in the jail."

The Ocean Breeze town jail was a two-cell cinderblock bunker in the middle of the town dump. Being cramped for space on the narrow island, the civic authorities had to make optimum use of their limited facilities.

"C'mon," Tim tried to urge Andy, "let's go have a few."

Tim bought a round at McCauley's, but the beers did not improve Andy's state of mind. Then all of a sudden Meg Marvin—Tim's burnt-out old flame from the summer before—was standing beside their table. Tim immediately invited her to join them, and she did. Inside of five minutes Tim had his arm around her. Andy could see what was developing and was overcome by a profound desire to be somewhere else. Saying that he didn't feel well, he bid goodnight to Tim and Meg and left the bar. He found Anatole on the same bench near the ferry terminal where he had been an hour before.

"Come on back to the Club," he told the old man. "You can't stay here all night."

"I wait for boat," he muttered.

"There are no boats until morning. C'mon. You can sleep in your room. Nobody will notice. I'll wake you up in time for an early boat tomorrow."

Anatole finally looked at him. His chin twitched as though he were trying to resist a tide of emotion.

"You are good boy," he said, and with some difficulty stood up. Andy picked up his vinyl bag. The old man seemed not altogether steady on his feet. He took Anatole's arm and helped him up a side street, away from downtown, toward the Midway. They were silent all the way back to the Club, except when Anatole wanted to stop and rest awhile, saying, "I walk all over hell today."

Andy was dreaming that he was back in Maine surrounded by tall, aromatic pine trees and laughing children when someone threw the light switch and woke him up. Squinting in the glare, he peered from his narrow bed and saw two faces grinning in the doorway: Tim and Meg Marvin.

"Hey, Andy ol' buddy," Tim said.

Meg giggled.

"What do you want?"

"You know if anyone's stayin' inna gues' suite?"

"No."

138

"No you dunno, or no nobody?" Tim asked.

"It's vacant."

"Hey, great," Tim said, turning to grin at Meg. "Whereza key?"

"Down in Bass's office."

"Be a buddy and go get it for us."

"Aw, for godsake—"

"Come on."

"Oh, all right. But get out of here a minute and let me put some pants on, huh?"

Meg giggled again and hiccuped. She and Tim withdrew from the room.

Andy put on his shorts and with his hands cupped over the face of a flashlight he stole downstairs to Bass's office. From Bass's adjoining bedroom came the unmistakable moans and grunts of passion and the squeak of bedsprings. The strange notion seized Andy that he was prowling through a whorehouse. He returned upstairs with the key in a state of great agitation. Tim had Meg up against the wall and was rummaging under her shirt. They both broke into giggles when Andy had to clear his throat to get their attention, as though they knew he was standing there waiting.

"Ssshhh," Andy said, as he unlocked the guest suite. Inside were a king-sized bed and various articles of furniture in the motel moderne style. Meg flew across the room and flung herself on the huge bed, squealing with anticipation. It was easy for Andy to imagine her as a mental patient.

"Why don't you both stay," she suggested, peering up behind a pillow she had liberated from under the cheap blue bedspread. "We could have a threesome."

"Uh, no thanks," Andy said while Tim rolled his eyes at the suggestion.

"Hippie girl," Tim said, as though explaining. "If it feels good, do it."

Meg giggled again, then got up, kneeling on the bed, and whipped her shirt off. Andy felt the blood drain from his head.

"Well, we'll see you in the morning," Tim said, now more or less shoving Andy out of the room.

Even through two closed doors—his own and the one on the guest suite—Andy could hear Meg Marvin emitting little shrieks of ecstasy for quite awhile afterward. He put a pillow over his head, and eventually the noise stopped, but he could not go to sleep, his bloodstream racing with hormones and piquant yearnings. He considered self-abuse as a soporific, and would have done it, but he half expected Meg Marvin to barge in and rape him sometime after Tim fell asleep and he didn't want her to discover him in the loathsome act.

She never did barge in on him, and to a certain degree Andy was relieved, for apart from her overt sexiness, he didn't find her especially appealing, and he was sure that the vivacious personality she had revealed this night was mostly a product of alcohol and marijuana.

He drifted into a turbulent sleep sometime after the window began to glow pink with sunrise. But another torrid day was gathering outside. By nine o'clock his little dormer room was filled with dry, stifling heat, like a sauna, and he woke up again for good. Only then did he remember that Anatole was back in his room and had to be evacuated before anyone found out he was there. Aching with fatigue and nausea, he made himself get up and went down the hall to rouse the old chef. Anatole had slept in his clothes, as usual, and sat up almost at once like a prisoner of war who has been moved innu-

merable times from one place of internment to another
and is used to rude awakenings.

"Time to catch your boat," Andy told him.

Anatole grunted, nodded, and patted Andy on the arm.
"Good boy," he said.

Next, Andy went to the guest suite to wake up Tim and
get him out of there. He didn't want anyone, not even
Bass, to know that he had let Tim use the apartment.
Andy hesitated at the door, listening for signs of activity
within, but all was quiet. He tried knocking lightly, but
there was no response. He didn't want to knock any
harder and risk waking up Bass below, so he took a deep
breath, turned the knob, and went inside.

They were both asleep, their backs to each other, a
sheet drawn up only to their waists in the heat. Andy
paused a moment to gaze at Meg Marvin. She had a
peaceful expression on her face that was very different
from the usual pinched, anxiety-driven look she wore
when awake. Here she appeared serene, rather lovely.
Her little breasts lay compressed against each other like
two creamy cones, lacking even a tan line. Indeed, her
skin was strikingly pale, as though she never ventured up
to the beach—Andy couldn't remember ever actually seeing
her there—especially compared to Tim's freckly deep tan.
Andy cleared his throat and reached down to shake Tim's
ankle.

"Whuzzit?" Tim said, looking up pained and bewildered. Meg, too, stirred and awoke, and Andy was amazed
how rapidly the serene look on her face was replaced by
the fearful, driven one.

"It's after nine," Andy said. "You've got to get out of
here and go be a lifeguard."

"Oh, God . . ." Tim groaned, knowing Andy was right.
In an act of sheer will he dragged himself out of bed and

began putting on his clothes. It quickly became evident to Andy that Tim would just as soon have left Meg there— she had drawn the sheet over her head, as though to shut out reality—and in fact he did. Andy followed Tim out into the hall, peeved.

"Hey, you can't leave her in there."

"She likes you," Tim said, implying possible favors. "Let her stick around."

"You've got to get her out of here right now," Andy insisted. "If anyone finds out you two were in there all night, I'm history."

"Oh, all right."

They went back into the guest suite.

"Rise and shine, my little beach plum," Tim cooed to the dome-shaped object under the sheet that was theoretically Meg's head.

She threw back the sheet and, snarling between clenched teeth, said, "You bastard."

"What could possibly be the matter?" Tim asked.

"I feel like such . . . garbage!"

"You're a dear, sweet girl and I adore you," Tim lied to her suavely, despite a sudden headache. "Only please get dressed and come with me."

"Why do I let you do this to me?"

"Do what?" Tim said, but she wouldn't answer. "What?"

"What if I committed suicide?" she snarled. "You'd be sorry then, wouldn't you?"

"I'd be crushed," Tim agreed, sitting down beside her on the bed, "and what's worse, you wouldn't be around to enjoy it."

"Bastard!" she screeched and began hitting him about the head. "Bastard! Bastard!"

Andy and Tim were forced to resort to physical restraint. Tim clamped his hand over her mouth and asked Andy to hold her arms so she would stop flailing at him.

"Now lookit, Meg," he told her coolly, rather like a hospital attendant trying to deal with an hysterical patient. "My buddy Andy here was nice enough to let us use this shack last night. It is time for us to vacate the premises. Otherwise he will get in trouble for doing us this favor. Do you understand?"

She nodded her head.

"Good," Tim said. "Now we're going to let go of you. I expect you to act like a mature adult, okay?"

Andy left the room so that Meg could put her clothes on. Through the door he could hear her mutter the word "bastard" several times. But soon the door opened and the couple emerged, Tim all smiles and Meg glowering darkly.

"Well, here we are," Tim said with a sigh of relief. "I'll come back after work and straighten up the place, okay? Change the sheets and all."

"Bastard," Meg muttered.

"Fine," Andy said.

Then Tim led her downstairs, to Andy's great relief. Meanwhile, he hadn't heard a thing from down the hall, and returning to check on Anatole, he found the old chef laying on his bed again with his face to the wall. At first Andy was afraid that Anatole had died, but a few moments of observation confirmed that he was breathing, so Andy roused him again. Once more Anatole quickly sat up, as though ready to be moved to another prisoner-of-war camp. This time Andy helped him to his feet. Anatole was cooperative but groggy.

"We're going to the ferry," Andy said, picking up Anatole's bag and leading him out of the room.

They were crossing the Club barroom to the exit when the door to Bass's room opened with a creak. Andy froze in his tracks (Anatole did too) and waited in terror to be

143

discovered by Bass. But instead they were greeted by the sight of Kelly Donovan, Van and Hughie's blonde-haired eighteen-year-old sister (and Robbie Kugel's steady girl), emerging from Bass's quarters. Seeing them, Kelly turned a shade of red rather deeper than her excellent tan. In an inspired gesture at once both perfectly apt and absurd, Andy put his index finger across his lips and said, "Ssshh," as though all three of them were suddenly party to the same conspiracy, and the mortified Kelly nodded her head as though everything was understood.

Andy steered Anatole the rest of the way out the door. They had gotten perhaps a hundred yards up the walk toward the Midway when, unbeknownst to Andy, Edna Dern looked over a rugosa hedge in her garden, clippers in hand, and with eyes slitted against the morning sun, watched Andy help the limping, grubby figure in white toward town. Two minutes later, she saw Kelly Donovan debouch from the Club and wondered to herself: Just what in hell is going on around here?

Andy put Anatole on the nine-forty-five boat—wondering what the old man's destination was, and whether he'd get there all right—and with the ferry cutting a white wake back toward the hazy mainland, Andy went over to the bay swimming area where Tim and Hughie were doing their punishment duty. He had two hours to kill before going over to his Uncle Jack's house for brunch, and there was no sense in returning to the Club, which was a mile in the opposite direction.

"I read the news today, oh boy," Tim sang from atop the high guard chair. At this hour on a Sunday there were no children in the water yet and Tim had the whole Sunday *New York Times* piled up on the seat beside him.

Andy looked up, shielding his eyes from the sun. "What's

going on in the world?" he asked. "It feels like I don't really live in it anymore."

"You'll love this: 'Lindsey Heckled at Harlem Cafe.' "

"What was he doing up there?"

" 'Black nationalists angrily interrupted Mayor Lindsey last night as he spoke at an opening ceremony for Harlem's first sidewalk cafe. "We don't want Paris in Harlem," three hecklers kept shouting, "we want Africa!" ' Great, huh?" Tim laughed.

"Maybe they should let loose some lions and tigers from the Central Park Zoo up there."

"That would bring a little bit of Africa uptown, wouldn't it? Oh wow, listen to this one: 'Nine are Killed in Head-on Collision.' "

"Jesus. Where?"

"Mississippi. Hey, it says five of them were members of the same family. Goddam."

"Being out here all summer you almost forget there's such a thing as cars."

"I know. I hate goddam cars," Tim said, turning more pages. "They're wrecking this country, cars."

Just then, a lone F-104 jet out of Snell Air Force base veered off the bay and transected the island at about one thousand feet. The thunderous noise of the engines lagged several seconds behind and then filled the air long after the plane was out of sight over the Atlantic. At the sound of it, Hughie Donovan emerged from the guard shack—a dinkier version of the one up at the ocean—and searched the empty sky where it had been. Then, seeing Andy beside the guard chair, he ambled over.

"I meant to apologize about that girl, you know, barfing on your Mom's bed and all," he said. He was wearing a T-shirt tucked into a Yankee baseball cap like a foreign legionnaire's headgear.

"It's all right," Andy told him. "Your brother cleaned it all up. And besides, I won't be living there anymore anyway."

"Yeah. I hear you applied to Tennessee."

"I did."

"Great. We'll have another guy to help pay for gas driving back home on vacations."

"I might get my own car," Andy said, realizing at once how unfriendly that sounded, and then thinking that getting such a car was predicated on the success of his sandwich-selling scheme, which suddenly struck him as a lot less plausible than it had seemed a few weeks ago. "I mean, maybe you could ride up with me sometime."

"Sure," Hughie said. "Whatever."

"I hate cars," Tim reiterated from above.

"Did you know this friend of your brother's who got killed over in Vietnam?" Andy asked Hughie.

"Sure. We were all in the same fraternity together."

"What happened to him?"

"He got blown up by a street bomb in Saigon."

"No, what happened to him in college—how come he flunked out? Was it hard?"

Hughie sighed and puffed out his cheeks. "He was a Tennessee country boy from a little place called Turtletown, way down near the Georgia state line. He wasn't dumb, but he just couldn't hack it academically, know what I mean?"

"Was he in the Army long?"

"Long enough," Hughie said ruefully.

CHAPTER ELEVEN

It was well over ninety degrees when Andy arrived at his Uncle Jack's house overlooking the beach at the far end of town close to Holly Wood, the WASP enclave. The first thing his mother said to him, in a fiercely controlled tone of voice, was, "I cannot believe the way you are dressed. Look at yourself!"

Andy looked down at his cutoffs and yellow T-shirt, which happened to be clean, and asked, "What's the matter with how I'm dressed?"

"If you don't know, you must be retarded." She herself wore a plain rose-colored cotton sleeveless shift, but with a full complement of her customary jade and gold jewelry and makeup.

"This is Thunder Island, for godsake, Mom."

"And this is a rather important occasion," she went on, fussing angrily with the platter of smoked salmon, capers, and lemon slices that she was rearranging on the table out on the deck facing the ocean. "The least you could do is make an effort to look presentable."

"Mom, I don't even have any nice clothes out here," he said, trying to reason with her as Kropotkin emerged gingerly through the sliding doors with an ice bucket and a large ceramic pitcher.

"Don't you look lovely, Lenny," Andy's mother said. Kropotkin was wearing pressed khakis, a blue blazer, a white button-down shirt, and a paisley tie. He was, of course, also wearing shoes: oxblood loafers. For the first time, he was not sporting his Greek fisherman's cap and Andy noticed that Kropotkin was bald. He had figured as much but he tried not to hold it against Kropotkin. Beads of sweat were forming on Kropotkin's bare head, and Andy felt that the art critic's outfit was, at least, impractical.

"Bloody Mary, anyone?" Kropotkin asked cheerfully.

"Sure," Andy said.

"One more thing, young man," his mother said, brandishing the salmon knife. "If you take advantage of the situation and get bombed, I will cut your throat."

"Don't worry, I won't embarrass you."

"Oh, where are they, for crying out loud."

"It's only twenty after twelve, Barbara," Kropotkin pointed out.

"My lovely salmon is going to spoil in this heat."

Andy's Uncle Jack and Jack's third wife, Deanna, emerged from inside the modernist cube of a house that Jack had built with the profits from his business, which was syndicating old television shows. Two years older than his sister, Barbara, Jack had gone to Dartmouth with her ex-husband, Alex Newmark, Andy's father. In fact, he had fixed up his buddy Alex with Barbara on a blind date. Romance, marriage, Andy, and divorce court followed.

Deanna was a stately and intelligent Nebraskan in her late twenties with a flair for comedy who worked regularly on the Broadway stage. She had a generous and confiding nature and was Andy's favorite relative. She was now six months pregnant and had on a billowy caftan that concealed it, except when she sat down. Jack wore a white blousey Indian wedding shirt (popular with hippies), which looked a little odd with his dark slacks and shiny Italian loafers.

"They're not coming, they're not coming," Andy's mother fretted as she sat tensely in a director's chair with her drink. "My gorgeous salmon is going to absolutely rot in this heat."

"Put it back in the fridge, Babs," said Jack, the only person on earth who ever called her by that name. Then, having picked up the Sunday *Times* crossword puzzle, he announced to all present: "I need a seven-letter word for salivary gland."

"There is no other word for it," Kropotkin said, "The salivary gland *is* the salivary gland."

"Maybe they want the scientific name for it?"

"That *is* the scientific name for it."

"Maybe they want Latin or Greek," Jack said. "How the hell do I know?"

"Have you got any letters for it yet?"

"No, it's one across. Spittle? Could that be it?"

"I've never seen the salivary gland referred to anywhere as the spittle gland," Kropotkin said eruditely.

"Spittle, slobber, it's got to be something like that," Jack said, shrugging in exasperation. Andy noticed his mother cutting an irritated glance at both of them.

Just then the Koenigsburgs suddenly appeared on the wooden gangway that led around the side of the house from front to rear.

"Ah, there you are," Barbara Newmark cried and fairly flew out of her seat, sweeping across the deck the way Loretta Young used to sweep into America's living rooms on her TV show.

For a mother and daughter who shared so many physical traits, Karen and Katya Koenigsburg presented a marked contrast in appearance. Katya, in her fifties, was a Pole who had escaped the Nazis by living in a farmer's root cellar for two years. Though diminutive—just five feet tall—she was as sturdy and solid as a wooden barrel, and this impression was reinforced by the dull grayish brown shift she wore. Her hair was a similar grayish brown. Makeup and jewelry she dispensed with entirely. She had no suntan, but rather an ashen pallor, as of someone who has sustained a terrible personal catastrophe—which she certainly had in the loss of her husband. Only her strong chin, fine lips, and delicate, bladelike nose suggested that she had once been a tiny, pretty maiden in the Baltic village of Elblag, and even so, the expression on her face was austere, unsmiling, grim.

Karen, on the other hand, while equally small in stature, was a slender brushstroke of a girl in a white sundress that accentuated her deep tan and glossy long black hair. She had her mother's fine facial features, and something more: an inner light, a glow of spirit burning inside that seemed to have been extinguished in her mother by the harshness of life. Altogether, Karen's beauty was so striking that just seeing her left Andy feeling a little lightheaded in the heat. That she had been carrying on a romance with a sculptor twice her age implied to him that she was a girl with awesome powers to excite men.

"Please come in and sit down," Barbara Newmark said, taking Katya's hand like a foreign dignitary's and leading her to one of the deck chairs. "Drink?"

"Tea, thank you," Katya said with a hard-edged accent.

Barbara's smile wilted slightly. There was a big pot of fresh-brewed coffee inside on the stove, but she had not thought about tea.

"I'll get it," Deanna sensitively volunteered.

"What would you like, Karen, dear?" Barbara asked.

"One of those would be fine," she answered, pointing

to the bloody mary Andy was holding. She had a smooth, wry voice, deeper than one would have expected in a girl so physically slight.

Kropotkin fixed Karen a drink and brought it over to her with a napkin. The goblet seemed enormous in her little hand. As he gave it to her, he said, "I was vaguely aware that Lee Koenigsburg had a little girl, but not of drinking age." It was meant to be both a quip and a compliment.

"Why? Are you checking I.D.s?" Karen replied coolly, and sampled the concoction.

Andy got a kick out of her easy insolence and chuckled. He noticed that his mother was grinning very uncomfortably. Deanna reappeared with a mug of tea.

"Come everybody," Barbara said. "Let's have a bite to eat."

An awkward silence oppressed the small group like the steadily rising heat while they consumed their salmon, bagels, cream cheese, stuffed cherry tomatoes, chicken liver, melon slices, and the miniature Danish pastries from the terrific bakery on 80th and Madison.

While her mother sat stiffly in her director's chair with a plate on her lap, Karen, occupying a chaise lounge, put her barely picked-at plate down on the wooden deck, and in a sudden, deft, and rather startling motion, pulled her white sundress off over her head. Under it, she had on an olive-green bikini. Andy noticed both Kropotkin's and his Uncle Jack's eyes bug out as they discovered that the little black-haired girl in a sundress actually possessed an adult's sexual equipment. She adjusted the back of the chaise to afford optimum exposure to the sun and reclined.

Andy took the opportunity to remove his T-shirt. It was obvious to him that his mother disapproved, but she didn't dare hassle him about it with Karen lying almost naked on the chaise like an odalisque. Andy sensed that Karen was actually looking at him for the first time since she arrived. Kropotkin fiddled with his shirt collar as though it was making him miserable.

"Perhaps you two kids would like to go up to the beach?" Andy's mother suggested.

Andy didn't answer one way or the other before Karen spoke. He most definitely wanted to be wherever she was.

"Sure, that's fine with me," Karen said in an almost flippant tone of voice, as though to show she knew the question was part of a delicate charade meant to disguise the fact that this brunch was essentially a business meeting. "Want to go for a swim?" she asked Andy, making it sound like a challenge.

"Love to," he replied, thinking his ardor made him ridiculous.

Karen planted her little feet on either side of the chaise and lifted herself up. As she leaned forward doing so, both Andy and Kropotkin were treated to a glimpse down her bikini top at the paler flesh cupped within. Andy felt a ringing in one ear. The heat was so ferocious on the deck that little waves of light danced over the buffet spread.

"Take this home for me please, Mama," Karen said, handing her mother the white sundress. She kissed her mother on the forehead, bid a lofty good-bye to the others, and then glanced at Andy to follow her. Walking behind her down the wooden gangway, he couldn't take his eyes off the twin dimples above her small, flared, finely sculpted rear end in its triangular scrap of clothing.

The surf was still rough from the lingering effects of the three-day blow. Karen waded brashly into the teeth of the foamy slop—the waves appearing gigantic behind her the further out she ventured—until finally she dove through the green-black glassy wall of a surging breaker and disappeared. Andy fought his way out in pursuit, the instincts of a Red Cross certified swim instructor vying with his seventeen-year-old hormones to drive him against the scary waves.

The official O.B. swimming area with its lifeguards and green flags was a mile up the beach. Over here there were no lifeguards. People swam at their own risk, and while Andy wasn't exactly terrified, he did feel a little insecure about it. He dove late under a huge wave that had already broken and even underneath it the turbulence twisted him around like a sneaker in a washing machine. He came up gasping just as another one crashed down over his head with the weight of a Buick. This one dragged him helplessly back toward shore. Karen was nowhere to be seen. Growing a little frantic now, Andy fought his way out all over again. This time he plunged through the soaring glassy wall of a giant breaker and emerged on the far side, where Karen could be found swimming a graceful six-point crawl parallel to the shore over the rising and falling swells.

Andy didn't know what to do now. To swim beside her as though they were a pair of frolicking porpoises seemed overly familiar. He didn't want to appear to be competing with her, either. His idea of swimming in the ocean was to try to catch waves body-surfing, but he wanted to be with her. Ultimately, he could think of nothing better to do than to tread water, fearing that finny monsters lurked below, licking their chops over the sight of his dangling legs.

In a little while, however, Karen stopped swimming the crawl back and forth.

"I love the water this time of year, don't you?" she cried, seeing him close by, treading water.

"It's real nice," he agreed, failing to think of a more scintillating reply. *Nice*, he thought. *You jerk!* "I mean, it's nice and rough," he said.

"I like it rough," Karen said, and she flipped over on her stomach to swim again, this time toward shore. She shot forward on one huge swell and vanished as she rode it in. Andy was left alone, treading water beyond the break. He wasn't quite sure, but he thought that one of his feet had bumped against something hard and rounded—a shark's nose!—and as panic seized him, he started windmilling toward the beach. An enormous wave sucked him into its crest and hammered him back down so hard that his head filled with stars and static. Then he was gasping in the slop, feeling the shifting bottom of smashed clam shells and sand on his hands and knees, and literally crawling out of the ocean like a shipwrecked sailor.

Karen was sitting Indian-style about midway up the beach, demurely combing her long hair with her fingers. Andy joined her, short of breath and feeling as though a pile-driver had pounded his head into the ground. He sat on the hot sand beside her.

"I got kind of bashed up on that last one," he admitted, in case it was not obvious to her.

"Those waves'll do it to you," she said.

"Oh, goddam!"

"What?"

He reached into the pocket of his cutoffs and withdrew a sopping red and white pack of Winston cigarettes. "I totally forgot."

Karen glanced back at the house looming over the dunes two hundred feet away. "We can always get some back there."

"I guess so."

"This thing about choosing a gallery has got my mama all freaked out."

"Has she been talking to a lot of dealers?"

"They come to her, mainly," Karen said. "Some of them are incredibly rude."

Andy worried for a moment whether his mother was included in that category. He knew she could be very aggressive when she wanted something. What he didn't quite appreciate was how meteoric her rise had actually been in the art world. Starting off as little more than a clerk in Karl Adler's estimable 57th Street gallery the year of her divorce, Barbara Newmark had become a major player with her own gallery in less than a decade.

"We used to study your father's paintings in school," Andy said.

"Oh, yeah?" Karen brightened, really for the first time. "Where do you go?"

"Music and Art. Only I graduated this year, thank God. I'm going to be a freshman down at Tennessee this fall," he said. It was the first time he had had occasion to speak of his future with such assurance, and he loved the way it felt. The word *Tennessee* itself was so musical and so drenched with American history: slavery, the Civil War, Davey Crockett. It was the *real* America, the *true* America, a whole other world, really—

"Where in Tennessee?" Karen asked, bringing him back to the here and now.

"The University of. In Knoxville."

"Never heard of it."

"You never heard of the University of Tennessee?"

"No, I never heard of Knoxville."

"It's a big town," Andy said. "That is, it's a small town compared to someplace like New York. But it's a big small town. It might even be the capital—I'm not sure."

"Oh," Karen said.

"A bunch of the guys from out here already go there.

155

Van and Hughie Donovan. Tim Flannery's starting this year too."

"Tim Flannery," Karen said with a snort and a sardonic smile on her small, beautifully shaped lips.

"You don't like him, I take it."

"He's *always* so loaded."

"Not always. At night, maybe, in the bars. You should catch him in the day sometime. He's perfectly normal."

"Whenever I see him he's loaded. It's unattractive."

"Anyway, all those guys go there," Andy said, not wanting to keep defending Tim. "Where do you go?"

"Riply," she said.

"Riply?" Andy couldn't help echoing her, it seemed such an odd school for her. Riply was a very anglo-style private academy on 79th and Madison. He had often passed by its elegant Beaux Arts building on his way to the Metropolitan Museum. The building had once been the mansion of a railroad tycoon in the eighteen nineties. The fresh-faced girls who swarmed outside it at mid-afternoon on fall days all looked like budding socialites. It was hard to imagine Karen fitting in. Her father had been one of the original *beatniks*.

"Riply's all right," Karen said. "They give you a good education there, at least. I think I'll go get us those cigarettes now, okay?"

Andy decided to let her go up to the deck by herself, thinking that if he tried to grub smokes it would only aggravate his mom. Andy watched Karen the whole time, the way she rubbed the sand off her thighs, the graceful way she walked across the beach, her lovely tanned shoulders, her fine little back. She lingered up there awhile, apparently bantering with Kropotkin, and finally returned with several filter-tipped cigarettes clutched in her hand and a pack of matches.

"Here," she said, falling to her knees on the soft, hot sand and giving Andy three of them. "One's for now. Stick the other two behind your ears for later." She demonstrated. Her ears were so small and beautiful. Her hair had virtually dried since they had gotten out of the water, the air was so hot. Andy was thrilled at the suggestion that they would be together at least for two more cigarettes. "Mmmm," Karen said, exhaling, "menthol. It feels nice on a day like this."

Andy generally hated menthol cigarettes, but the way the long white cigarette looked in Karen's small sun-bronzed hand was so beautiful, as was the plume of smoke blowing out of her lovely mouth, that he could only agree. "Yeah, it's real cool and minty."

"I think they were getting down to the nitty-gritty up there," Karen remarked.

"Oh, yeah?"

"No matter how this thing comes out, we're going to make a fortune," she declared, laying back and shielding her eyes from the sun.

"No kidding?" Andy said, not sure if he understood her correctly. She sounded so coldly crass and commerical.

"Yeah, Daddy left tons of paintings. Hundreds. They could sell out a show a year for the next twenty-five years and there'd still be plenty of stuff left over for the museums."

"Gee," Andy said guardedly, because he was beginning to grasp that Karen was indeed speaking in cold commercial terms, and it occurred to him that if the Koenigsburgs made a fortune, then his mother was liable to make a fortune too as the deceased artist's exclusive dealer, and that if indeed she did cinch the deal then perhaps he, Andy, wouldn't have to sell sandwiches to get through college. All the tension that his mother had been under finally began to make sense. "He was a great artist, your dad," Andy said, though he had never cared for Lee Koenigsburg's work, or even thought about it very much, before coming out to Thunder Island.

"Right near here is where he drowned," Karen said. "About a hundred yards over to the right."

Andy found her cool precision eerie.

"They took Daddy over to the firehouse and tried to get him breathing again but it was no use." She looked at Andy with a rueful smile—but a smile nonetheless—on her face, and he didn't know quite what to make of it.

Just then they heard Katya calling for her daughter from the deck. "Karen, Karen," she called, waving.

"What, Mama?"

"Come."

"I'm with somebody," Karen called back, and Andy was flattered to think that he was actually a somebody in her scheme of things.

"Come now," Katya insisted.

"Oh, all right," Karen said. She got up and Andy did too. "Want to stop over later?" she asked.

"Over?"

"Yeah, to my house."

"When later?" Andy asked, amazed and a little intimidated.

"In the evening. Seven-thirty, eight. After dinner."

"Okay, yeah, sure. I'd love to." His eagerness embarrassed him.

"It's seventy-two Hawthorne. I'll see you then."

Andy repeated seventy-two Hawthorne over and over again to himself so he wouldn't forget it as he watched her traverse the beach to the house on the dunes. He lit another menthol cigarette, and when he was sure that the Koenigsburgs had departed, he went back to his Uncle Jack's.

The whole gang sat scattered around the deck like victims of sunstroke. Kropotkin had his blazer, tie, shoes, and socks off and was lounging with his khakis rolled up. Deanna lay on a chaise, drowsing. Barbara Newmark remained fidgeting in her chair, holding a glass with nothing in it but some melted ice cubes and a squashed lime. Jack had resumed doing the crossword puzzle. Altogether, they looked like a demoralized group of adults.

"How'd it go?" Andy asked his mother cautiously.

"She's a rough customer," Barbara said as though exhausted. "She drives a hard bargain."

"Did she go for it or not?"

"She didn't commit herself. She said she's going to make up her mind tonight."

"Gee, really?" Andy said. "Karen invited me over to her house this evening."

A gray stricken look came over Barbara Newmark's sunburned face. Jack put down his puzzle. Deanna opened one eye.

"Well," Kropotkin said, glancing at Andy's mother. "That ought to be interesting."

CHAPTER TWELVE

On his way back to the Club late that afternoon, Andy stopped off again at the bay swimming area. Hughie Donovan was up on the chair watching a crew of four-year-olds splash in the knee-deep water of "the crib," as the swimming area between the two town piers was called. Tim Flannery lay on a bench inside the guard shack reading a battered copy of *Catch-22* with his head propped up on a wad of towels.

"Isn't this the life?" he said, not even looking up. "There's no jerks trying to sneak picnic coolers onto the beach, no sea-pusses to suck lousy swimmers out into the Gulf Stream, and best of all no Dale Hummer to bust your chops."

"Guess what?"

"What?"

"I've got a date with Karen Koenigsburg tonight."

Tim finally set the book down on his stomach.

"Hey, nice goin'," he said. "Only where's the guy she hangs out with who makes the giant fiberglass hot dogs?"

"Who knows? He wasn't there today."

"Maybe she dumped him," Tim said.

"Maybe," Andy agreed. "She's a weird chick, though.

We were sitting down on the beach and she pointed to the spot where they pulled her father out like it was just some geographical point of interest."

"They didn't pull her father out," Tim said. "He drowned at night. They found him washed up on the beach the next morning."

Andy flinched, wondering if he'd heard Karen correctly.

"She said they pulled him out of the surf and took him to the firehouse to try and get him breathing again," Andy said, recounting her version.

"They took him to the firehouse all right, but I seriously doubt anybody attempted mouth-to-mouth on him. He'd been dead for hours. You know what's down at the firehouse, don't you?"

"No," Andy said. "What?"

"The O.B. morgue. Cute little refrigerator unit with two roll-out slabs. That's what they took Lee Koenigsburg to the firehouse for."

"Oh. I wonder why she told me they pulled him out of the surf?"

"Beats the hell out of me," Tim said. "Maybe nobody ever told her the truth. Want to know something else?"

"Sure. What?"

"They did an autopsy on her dad and found out that the guy was practically pickled."

"He was drunk when he drowned?"

"He was totally blotto."

"Jeez."

"But he was always a big boozer. You'd see him down at Clausen's practically every night the last few summers when that was the 'in' spot. He liked young girls. And they liked him pretty well too. Believe me, he made out okay. He was a drinker but he wasn't that old, and he was still a pretty handsome guy in that Greenwich Village way right up to the end. He used to wear these paint-splattered white overalls and always a baseball hat. He was so all-American—which was funny because he still had a slight German accent—''

"Polish," Andy said.

"Is that what it was? Anyhow, he used to play on one of the town softball teams. He could play real good for a guy who grew up in Europe. Karen used to come down to the ballfield out by the dump and root for him. She looked about nine years old even when she was fourteen, but she used to smoke cigarettes. It cracked you up to see it, this little stringbean lighting up. Her father was a very liberal guy that way. Everybody knew that he was a big hot-shot artist, but he didn't act like a celebrity. He'd talk to anyone. I probably talked to him two or three times myself back when I was sixteen, seventeen. Real conversations, too, about life and all. To tell you the truth, I was real sorry to hear that the guy drowned. He sort of represented the spirit of Thunder Island. Without him around, something's definitely missing.''

Andy returned to the Club by five. The place was empty, not even Bass was around, and the sound of crickets chirping in the reeds outside the old Coast Guard station in the still-ferocious heat was so loud that it almost drowned out the distant muffled crash of the surf.

He pulled a can of corned beef hash from the pantry, fried it up in a pan on the big professional-sized stove until it was brown and crusty on the bottom, smothered it in ketchup, and wolfed it down in five minutes flat. His cutoffs were loose at the waist. Despite all the beer drinking, he had lost weight over the summer. His eating had been extremely haphazard. He wondered whether the

163

fraternity that Van and Hughie belonged to provided its members with square meals.

The crickets and the stillness, the glaring late afternoon light, and the terrible heat all combined to imbue this hour with intimations of summer's end. Andy had always dreaded the coming of autumn, of his return to the prisonlike public schools of Manhattan. Now, sitting in the large, quiet, hot kitchen, he felt an unaccustomed yearning for the coming fall. He pictured himself at a University of Tennessee football game, the band playing and his fraternity brothers all around drinking beers. He imagined the campus, the many old red-brick buildings with white columns in front, the town with its peaceful tree-lined streets of pretty nineteenth century houses where the people kept their doors unlocked and rocked on the porch on warm September nights waving paper fans, as he'd seen in the movies.

It was a little harder trying to imagine his career as a sandwich tycoon. He wasn't sure exactly how or where he would sell them. He first pictured himself wearing a tray rather like a cigarette girl's, with shoulder straps, making the rounds of the dormitories and other frat houses. But sandwiches, he reasoned, were a lot heavier than cigarettes and such a rig probably wouldn't do. He'd have to build himself some kind of pushcart. Wouldn't it be embarrassing? Pushing a cart around the campus like one of those grimy hot dog vendors on the streets of New York? He could solve that problem. He'd wear a suit and tie. What a thought! It even gave him an idea for a name to dub the enterprise: Upper Crust Eats. That way he could pretend that it was all just a lark—a way to meet girls. Only Tim Flannery would know the truth. And if the business really took off, he'd plow back some of his earnings, build a second pushcart, and hire another person. By the end of his freshman year, he'd probably have a whole fleet of pushcarts with a dozen vendors working for him.

And tonight he actually had a date with the exquisite Karen Koenigsburg. What could she possibly see in him? he wondered. He hadn't done anything so far in his life, had not even built a giant-sized figerglass hot dog. Maybe it was a schmucky thing to do, Andy thought, but it was at least *something,* to build a giant fiberglass hot dog. It probably took a lot of hours of labor just to mold the stupid thing. What had he himself accomplished? Better not make any cracks about her old boyfried, he silently warned himself.

And what did she have in mind for the evening, anyway? Not dinner, obviously, because she had made a point of telling him to come over *after* dinner. She probably expected him to take her out somewhere—to McCauley's for a drink, or for ice cream cones, or maybe a movie. What was playing? *Barefoot in the Park?* Ycchhh. Perhaps he'd suggest a stroll. They could go down to the ferry dock and watch the boats turn on their running lights as night gathered out on the bay. No, she'd think that was corny and boring. They could go over to the beach to watch the sunset. Of course the beach faced due south toward Venezuela, so the sun could not be viewed sinking into the sea, but the evening light would still be pretty. And maybe he could get her to make out with him as he had gotten Kathy Craig to do. Wait a minute, he thought, stopping himself. The beach is where they found her dad washed up. How could he even think of trying to make out with her there?

He washed the frying pan and went upstairs to lie down for a while. But his room was like the metal torture box that the Japanese colonel put Alec Guinness into in *The*

Bridge On the River Kwai. It was still over ninety degrees up in the gable and a nap was impossible. Instead, he sat in the shower stall for half an hour with cool water pounding down on his skull. At seven o'clock he was headed nervously downstairs in a clean alligator shirt and jeans when he heard the screen door of the Club entrance creak open, followed by the sound of somebody taking a few cautious steps on the squeaky wooden floor. He stole down the last few stairs silently, on tip-toes, his heart in his throat, thinking that someone up to no good—a thief possibly!—had entered the apparently deserted establishment.

He waited at the bottom of the stairwell behind a wall that separated it from the Club barroom. The footsteps continued, slowly coming closer and closer. Finally a person came into view, and Andy was relieved to see that it was only Franny Flannery.

"Hi," he said without otherwise making his presence known. Franny let out a choked scream and wheeled around in terror.

"It's only me," Andy said, trying to reassure her.

"I thought you were—I don't know what."

"The Phantom of the Summer Club."

"My heart," she said. "It's pounding."

"I thought you were a robber."

"There's no robbers out here."

"Really?" he said, truly surprised that there wouldn't be.

"Where would you go with the loot? It's an island."

"I hadn't thought of that."

"Besides, what's there to steal here?"

"Liquor. It could've been your brothers snitching bottles."

"Tim and Shawn are allowed to drink beer at home

166

now," she said. "Brian and Matt are turning into drug snobs. They look down on booze drinkers."

"Your brother Matt does drugs already?"

"Oh, yeah."

"Isn't he just twelve?"

"He's a very advanced twelve," Franny said. "We're all advanced out here. You grow up fast. Besides, how are you going to stop them?"

"What drugs does he do?"

"He smokes pot. I think he's even taken acid and stuff."

"And stuff? What stuff?"

"You know, DMT, STP, whatever they come out with."

"Tim's right," Andy said conclusively. "This island is a sick place."

"It's not just here. Matt was doing it back in Shaker Heights."

"Well, I hope he doesn't fry his brain," Andy said, harking back to his one LSD trip at the beginning of the summer and recalling how scary it was. "Do you do drugs too?"

Franny hesitated. "I smoke some pot," she said.

"You ever do LSD?"

She shook her head.

"Why not?"

"It frightens me, I guess. I don't want to see God. I'm happier thinking that maybe he's not really there. It's the Catholic upbringing and all."

"I'm Jewish and I don't especially want to meet him either."

"I heard Tim tell Shawn about how you two dropped acid together, and you had a freak out," Franny said.

"I'd hardly call it a freak out," Andy said, a little galled

167

that Tim had mentioned it to anyone, even his brother. "I just saw some hallucinations."

"That's what God probably is, huh? A hallucination."

"Probably," Andy agreed. He glanced at his watch. It said seven-fifteen.

"I'm probably holding you up, huh?" Franny said.

"I do have to be somewhere."

"I brought over some of my paintings," she said, holding up a watercolor tablet that she had held clasped under her arm.

"Can I look at them?"

"Would you?"

"Bring them out here into the light."

They moved from the dark barroom into the dining room, which was filled with rich amber evening light.

Andy opened the tablet. The first painting was of the dock down at the ferry landing.

"Nice," Andy said. "Good shadows on the buildings. And the figures are great."

"They're just little blobs of color."

"That's okay. It's what the eye makes out that matters. If this little blob says *person* and my eye believes it, then that's all you need to do."

He turned the page to a scene of the town tennis courts near the bay.

"These are real good," Andy said with true admiration. "Watercolors are goddam difficult."

Franny glowed.

"I'm holding you up," she said, reaching for the tablet.

"No you're not."

The next page was a scene up at the beach. People laying on their blankets. A woman rubbing suntan lotion on.

"These are great," Andy said. "You're a much better artist than half the jerks I went to school with."

"When can I see some of your stuff?" she asked.

Andy was taken aback. He hesitated before saying, "I don't really have any stuff out here."

Franny looked bewildered.

"How come?" she asked, and then, as though sensing the gaucheness of the question, she added, "I'm sorry. It's none of my business."

"It's just that when you go to a school like I did, where they force you to draw or paint or play the goddam oboe every day—well, I guess you get sick of it," Andy tried to explain, not even to his own satisfaction, and finished with a regretful sigh. "The truth is, Franny, I haven't done a damn thing all summer. I haven't drawn so much as a single straight line between two points."

The Koenigsburg house was one of the larger old ones in Ocean Breeze that had survived the devastating hurricane of 1938. It was built just after the Civil War in the carpenter gothic style by a New York City broadcloth merchant who made a fortune furnishing uniforms to the Union Army. The exterior was in poor repair, almost dilapidated, its blue paint peeling in the salt air, much of the fancy wooden fretwork broken off or rotting under the eaves, the porch listing to starboard as the footings decayed. Yet a pretty cottage garden bloomed in the front yard, hollyhocks, orange lilies, and roses grew in untamed profusion, and a healthy wisteria vine as thick as a ferryboat's hawser twisted up a corner column and framed the porch with the mauve blossoms.

Katya Koenigsburg was the one who answered the doorbell. She stood there for what felt to Andy like an eternity, studying him as though he were an artifact in a museum:

mid–twentieth century teenager, male. Her face registered little emotion beyond a kind of clinical curiosity.

"Is Karen home?" he finally asked.

"Come in," she said icily.

The house was even gloomier inside, particularly at this time of day, with the natural light ebbing. The first floor was paneled with cherrywood wainscotting (brought over from the mainland one hundred years ago at great expense) which had turned reddish black with the years. And everywhere in sight on this dark background hung canvases by Lee Koenigsburg, many of them from his prolific last period. In these, each canvas was all but completely occupied by dark, gloomy square blobs of paint in the blue-purple range just faintly outlined in orange or dirty yellow. Sometimes there was a single blob, sometimes two, never more than two. To the art critics of America, like Leonard Kropotkin at *Newsweek*, and to Andy Newmark's teachers at the High School of Music and Art, Lee Koenigsburg's paintings represented the high-water mark of the aesthetic called Abstract Expressionism. To Andy, confronted here by dozens of them, they only looked like glimpses inside an unhappy man's brain. The darkness was booze. The orange or yellow outline was the rest of the world outside, barely apprehended. He wondered if the artist had left a suicide note.

"Karen," her mother sang musically up a stairwell at the house's center. Andy could hear a TV up there. Karen appeared above and leaned on the railing.

"Oh, hi," she said. "Come on up."

Andy glanced at Karen's mother, whose face remained inscrutable. Without a word she turned away and retreated down a hall to where Andy could see a kitchen. He mounted the stairway. The banister was loose. He watched Karen watching his every step. The upstairs of the large house was brighter. The walls were white-washed, at least, and a big bay window let in what remained of the daylight. As below, paintings by Lee Koenigsburg hung everywhere, but these mostly from his earlier years when his abstract subject matter was bold, slashing bright color on white fields. Karen watched Andy study them.

"Before too long, people will pay twenty-five thousand apiece for one of these," she said.

Once again, Andy was so amazed to hear her speak of her father's work in such cold monetary terms that he didn't know how to reply. He figured she had said it because his mother was an art dealer and thus supposedly he'd have an appreciation for the commercial aspect of the artist's struggle. But then, Lee Koenigsburg's struggle was over.

"Too bad he didn't live to enjoy it," Andy found himself saying, and was instantly embarrassed. He had meant to be sympathetic, but it came out sounding reproachful.

"Come in here," Karen said, unruffled by the remark.

He followed her into what was apparently her room. It was very large compared to his cramped quarters back at the Club. The room was filled with a blue haze of cigarette smoke and appeared quite messy. At the far end was a double bed with its sheets and blanket in disarray. A portable TV on a cheap aluminum rolling cart faced the bed, shedding lurid patterns of bluish light over the sheets. At the near end of the room stood a big table piled high with all manner of stuff—clothing, a camera, costume jewelry, magazines, glue pots, drawing tablets, a tray of pastels. An easel was set up nearby and on it, taped to a drawing board, was a collage of pasted cut-out photos from the magazines surrounded by pastel squiggle marks.

The cut-out photos were of celebrities: Jackie Kennedy, various Beatles, Jim Morrison of the Doors, Cassius Clay, Andy Warhol, the Maharishi, and Charles Whitman, the Texas Tower Sniper, a famous maniac who shot a dozen total strangers the previous summer.

"This one's a little closer to the average person's price range," Karen joked as she watched Andy examine her artwork.

"How much," Andy bantered back.

"For you, a hundred bucks."

Andy thought that was a little high, even for an early Karen Koenigsburg, but he didn't say so. Instead he said, "I didn't know you were an artist too."

"Someone's got to carry on the family tradition," she said, and for a moment all Andy could think about was the little girl watching her dad play softball, as Tim described it, and how much she must have missed him. "Want to smoke some?" she asked.

"Guh, sure," Andy said. Among city kids smoking marijuana had rapidly become a social formality, the way their parents offered drinks to company.

"It's over here."

She went over to her bed and lay down with her back propped against the wall. She kept her weed in a little brass box on the bedside table. Working with the expertise of a connoisseur, she cleaned off the screen in the bowl of a small brass pipe, filled it with the dull green marijuana, and then held it up for Andy, an enticement. He finally went over to the bed and stiffly sat down there beside her. She lit a match. They smoked the bowl. Andy was impressed at the amount of smoke Karen could exhale, for such a diminutive person. A warm tide of happy excitation welled within him. A chunk of time flew by— really only a couple of minutes—that he simply couldn't account for until he realized that he had been staring hypnotically at the television screen. The Ed Sullivan Show was being broadcast. An act called the Suzuki Violins (thirty oriental tots playing Bach on three-quarter-sized fiddles) had just concluded, and the famous master of ceremonies was introducing a soul music act called the Four Tops. Andy adored the music of the Four Tops, and hearing their name announced brought him instantly out of his trance.

"God, this is great," he said. "The Four Tops."

"Here. Relax," Karen said, giving him a pillow so he too could sit propped up against the wall. To wild applause, the curtain came up on the Four Tops dressed in conservative suits like investment bankers. Smiling shyly for a moment at the applause, they soon began snapping their fingers in unison and wailing a new song from their just-released fifth album: "Reach Out I'll Be There." Andy could not believe his good fortune to be practically lying beside Karen Koenigsburg, stoned, watching the Four Tops.

"Aren't they great," he said.

"They're all right," Karen replied. He glanced at her to see if she was putting him on, and her laconic smile told him that she was amused by his enthusiasm.

"I don't think you realize how good these guys are," he said.

"I'm crazy about them," she said.

At the end of the song, they segued directly into a second number, a tune called "Walk Away Renee." An earlier version by a flash-in-the-pan group named the Left Banke had made the charts the previous winter. It was a plaintive song and for Andy it piquantly evoked the old, sad, complicated feelings of being in high school in New York City. The way the Four Tops did it, however, was so much more powerful than the original version that it was no longer just a sad song about teenagers in love. It was a cry from the heart. And knowing that a new and better chapter in his life would soon commence in faraway Tennessee, Andy felt a surprising nostalgia for those wintry days, now gone forever, that he had spent in the High School of Music and Art.

He could feel the heat radiating off Karen's arm beside his and a desire to touch her rose within him. He couldn't quite bring himself to believe that she had invited him here—up to her own room, no less—to make out. But this conclusion began to seem inescapable. Karen's grass was very potent and Andy realized that he was extremely stoned. He glanced at her watching the tube. In concentration, her face had some of the same seriousness as her mother's. Then, before he had to even worry about how to make contact with her, Karen snuggled up next to him and rested her head in the little hollow just below his rib cage.

Andy's heart went wild. Then he realized that he had developed an erection and he desperately hoped that Karen would not notice the bulge in his jeans. He cautiously touched her shoulder, so tan and small. It was astonishing how soft her skin was. Her arm was so slender that he could practically close his thumb and middle finger around her bicep. Eventually his hand explored down to the crook of her hip and remained there, as though to be polite. Yet he couldn't believe how delightful the curve of it was. She was small, but she was most assuredly a woman. Before he was aware of it, the Four Tops had vanished from the TV screen. A commerical message for a laundry product that got whites whiter came and went, and Sergio Franchi was crooning to the nation in his dulcet baritone.

To Andy's further astonishment, Karen began to un-
buckle his belt. Panic gripped him. "What are you doing?"

"Nothing," she said, then craned her head back to look
at him. Turned upward like this, her face did not look so
severe as it usually did. A mischievous smile bloomed on
her lips. She laughed throatily, then reached upward,
rolled over, and climbed up him—rather as though he
were a hill to be scaled, a sand dune—until they were
face to face and she lay warmly pressed against him.

"You're cute," she said. "So shy."

"I'm a little nervous," he confessed.

"Are you afraid of girls?"

"No."

"Then it's just me."

"You're so beautiful," he said, as though that explained
it. She closed her eyes and her face came forward to
touch his. Her mouth was so small he was afraid to
suffocate her, so he tried not to cover it with his. He
reached around and held her close, still amazed at her
littleness. She wore a spicy perfume that was unlike any
other he was acquainted with. It was concentrated in the
hollow between her chin and her collarbone.

Kissing, they slid down from their position propped
against the pillows until they were lying side by side on
the bed. His hands roamed freely over her now and in a
little while he found the courage to touch her breasts
through her shirt. They were small like the rest of her but
fully formed. His fingers struggled with the buttons of her
cotton work shirt, but in time he had the whole front of it
open and she seemed to spill out of it, as though she were
made of warm liquids. She rolled onto her back, her torso
exposed, like so many figure drawings Andy had seen in
the galleries and museums of New York City. On her back
like this her breasts appeared to lose much of their sub-

175

stance, but the dark and surprising nipples riveted him like a pair of bull's-eyes. The playful smile was gone. In its place was an expression much like her mother had displayed at the door: profound curiosity. He propped himself up on one arm, half sitting, drinking her in. Again she reached for his belt buckle.

"What about your mother?" he asked in a dry voice.

"What about her?"

"She's here somewhere. Downstairs or something."

"It's all right," she said. "I'm allowed."

These words—*I'm allowed*—were as electrifying to Andy as anything that had happened to this point. They summarized so succinctly Karen Koenigsburg's unique privileges in life, as a beautiful female, as the daughter of a famous man, as a person assured of future riches. The peculiar notion struck Andy just then that he was somehow smaller than her, if not physically then spiritually.

"You're not going to believe this," he said. "But I—"

"Don't worry," she said. "I'm on the pill."

"You are? Gee. Great. But that wasn't what I wanted to tell you."

"What," she said, having unbuckled the belt and now struggling with the button and zipper of his blue jeans. "What did you want to tell me?"

"Nothing really," Andy said, his courage suddenly ebbing. "Just that, well, I've . . . I'm a virgin."

Karen stopped what she was doing, looked at him blankly a moment, fell back on the bed, and rocked with laughter, covering her mouth as she did.

"You think it's funny, but it's not," Andy said. "I've tried."

She continued to laugh but eventually stopped and reached for his hand. "It only makes it more exciting then, doesn't it?'' she said with a sudden gravity that made him shiver.

"I just don't want you to think I'm an oaf."

"You're a good kisser," she said. "You'll be fine."

With a look of self-assurance that frightened him a little, Karen sat up and unfastened her jeans. Andy fumbled with his polo shirt, catching his chin in the collar as he pulled it over his head. By the time he managed to get the shirt off, she was shedding her bikini briefs. And then they were naked together. Though Andy was the uninitiated one, the truth is that neither of them were old enough to have outgrown the wonder of their own burgeoning sexuality.

"I love doing it in front of the TV," Karen said as she stretched out catlike in the blue light. "It's so public and private at the same time, like art."

CHAPTER THIRTEEN

Andy had never spent the night in bed with another person. And though they made love several times with the kind of boundless energy that only teenagers have, kissing and clasping until well past midnight, he could not go to sleep when they were finished. He remained so astounded to find himself beside this beautiful creature that he really didn't want to go to sleep and miss a moment of his being there with her.

Unfortunately, it was one of those breezeless furnacelike summer nights when even being at the seashore doesn't ease the heat. And though he wanted to lay in the darkness holding her, she rolled over with her back to him and shrugged away his attempts to touch. Every so often he would reach for her again, and she would rebuff him ever more strenuously, until one last time, around five o'clock in the morning, he reached to put his hand on the extraordinary curve where her waist turned into a hip, and she wheeled around in sudden fury, saying, "If you can't keep your goddam paws off me, then leave."

He was stunned, not really at her anger so much as at his own feckless yearnings. It was obvious to him that the heat made sleeping in close contact impractical. It was equally obvious to him that she had more experience being in bed with other people and probably wanted to get some sleep. This was normal, he understood. His foolish desire to remain awake and cling to her was abnormal. He was therefore stunned by his own foolishness, not by her words, and lay carefully back, trying to be as inert as possible.

But this only increased his torment, for now he was afraid to move a muscle, in case he might wake her again. And so as the room began to swell with light, he wearily climbed out of her bed and put on his clothes, watching her sleep, with continued amazement that he had been there at all and that in this room he had encountered one of the milestones of his life.

He returned to the Club by way of the beach with the sun at his back, rising over faraway Montauk, and screaming seagulls strutting around feeding on the detritus of low tide. All the way home he wondered and worried about how he would manage his future relationship with Karen. Would they sleep together regularly? How many nights a week? Would they go out to McCauley's together in the evenings? And if so, what would Tim do? He got the distinct impression that Karen was not crazy about Tim. What if the three of them started hanging out together and she changed her mind about Tim—maybe even fell in love with him! It promised to be a very sticky situation. And what about her old boyfriend, Max Pap, the giant hot dog sculptor? Maybe he was just off somewhere else this weekend. What if he came back to the island and Karen pretended that this . . . this night had never happened? Anything was possible, he thought. But he hoped that she would be his girlfriend.

He stole quietly into the Club, and in spite of the rising sun beating hotly on the dormer roof above his little

180

room, he fell asleep almost at once. It seemed like virtually an instant later that he heard a voice calling to him through the void of a dreamless sleep.

"Andrew," Bass crooned to him. "Andrew, me boy."

"Huh . . . ?" Andy said, sitting up on his narrow bed, disoriented.

"Phone call," Bass informed him.

"What time is it?"

"Eleven."

"What day is it?"

"Monday," Bass said. "Are you okay?"

" 'Course I'm okay," he replied a little testily. His ears rang with exhaustion.

"I think it's your mother," Bass said before withdrawing from the doorway.

"Oh God . . ." Andy muttered to himself, worrying about the apartment. No doubt she had returned and detected that someone had been there, possibly even that someone had thrown up on her bed. What would he tell her? He located his cutoffs, put them on, and lurched downstairs to the phone in Bass's office.

"How come you didn't come back to say good-bye?" she began. He was surprised and relieved that she hadn't shrieked at him about someone vomiting on her bed. "You knew we were taking a Sunday night boat."

"Jeez, I guess I just forgot, Mom."

"You forgot," she echoed him sarcastically. "Your manners are simply atrocious."

"How'd your deal go with Mrs. Koenigsburg?" he inquired, to get off the subject of his manners.

"There's no deal," she said.

"What?"

"I just got off the phone with her. She's going with Leo Castelli."

"God, Mom. I'm sorry."

"The dreary old bitch," his mother added. There was an awkward pause. "Did her daughter—what's her name?"

"Karen."

"Karen—did she happen to say anything to you?"

"Say anything?"

"About this deal. Honestly Andy, you're being such a dim bulb this morning. Are you drunk again?"

"No, I'm not drunk, Mother, just tired."

"From what? Being drunk?"

He ignored her remark. "She said they expected to make a lot of money. 'A fortune' is how she put it, I believe."

"The little bitch."

"Well, after all, Mom, she's sixteen and she knows a lot about art. She goes out with this thirty-year-old sculptor guy."

"I know all about him," Barbara Newmark said, and Andy wondered what she could possibly have meant by that.

"What do you know about him?" he asked.

"Lenny filled me in. He's from downtown, this guy."

"Oh . . . ?"

"But this is beside the point. The point is I know that I offered her a better percentage than Castelli. Much better. I don't see how she could go with him. It doesn't make sense."

Andy's stomach turned sour as it began to occur to him that perhaps his presence overnight at the Koenigsburg house had scotched his mother's business deal. He could hear Karen's very words reverberating through his aching head—"*I'm allowed . . . I'm allowed . . . I'm allowed . . .*"—but at the same time he recalled Katya Koenigsburg

182

greeting him so coldly at the front door, and it seemed to him now that she had been scowling with disapproval.

"Maybe it's the prestige thing," he offered lamely.

"Oh come on, Andy, Leo Castelli isn't the only class act in town. I've got a reputation too, you know, and a damn good one, even if I am the new kid on the block. She didn't say anything else?"

"Who?"

"The daughter," Barbara Newmark said, growing shrill. "What's her name?"

"Karen."

"Karen—she didn't tell you anything else out there on the beach?"

"Not really," Andy said, thinking of how he remembered her not on the beach but naked in the blue light of her television. "She pointed out where her father drowned."

"She did that?"

"Yes."

"Poor little thing."

"They were real tight, I guess. She used to go watch him play softball down at the town dump."

"At the dump?"

"I mean at the ballfield next to the dump."

"Oh," Barbara Newmark said with a sigh that signified she was tiring of the conversation. "Then she must take after him. She certainly didn't get her looks from the dreary old bitch. My god, she looks like a Polish beetpicker. No wonder Lee drank."

"He drowned because of it," Andy said.

"Well, everybody knows that," his mother said. "Listen, I have to go now, pussycat. We may be out again in a couple of weeks. We're going up to the Vineyard on Thursday. Lenny's got friends there. But do me a favor, will you, darling?"

"Sure. What."

"Lighten up on the liquor."

"Sure, Mom."

"Who was that horrible boy you were with downtown?"

"My friend Tim."

"Well, in my opinion your friend Tim is on his way to becoming a drunk. He'll end up like Lee Koenigsburg, dead on the beach."

"No he won't. He's a lifeguard—"

"I really must go, darling. Have fun, but be good."

" 'Bye, Mom."

It wasn't until after he hung up that he realized she hadn't said a word about the condition of the apartment. Perhaps, by some miracle, the cleaning job had worked. But his sudden elation changed very quickly to dismay when he thought again about the Lee Koenigsburg deal and how he had possibly ruined it. Just then, Bass burst back into his quarters, all sunshine and good cheer in his baggy shorts and Hawaiian shirt.

"Mail call," Bass sang and gave Andy an official-looking letter in a cream-colored envelope. Andy had hardly received any mail all summer. This letter was from the University of Tennessee. Thrilled, he grabbed it and slowly drifted out of Bass's sunny quarters into the dimmer Club barroom while he took pains to open the envelope carefully and not tear the letter. Eventually he drew the cream-colored page out. It was folded in thirds. Atop the letter-head was an engraving of a university tower, an elegant old building he expected to stand in front of in a month or so.

"Dear Mr. Newmark," the letter began. "We regretfully inform you—"

Andy put the letter down and stared for a moment at the stuffed tarpon on the barroom wall. Many of the fish's huge silver scales had fallen off over the years. He had the peculiar sensation—much like his acid trip—that the floor was no longer solid beneath him, that somehow he might sink through it and be swallowed by the earth. He read on:

"We regretfully inform you that all places in the freshman class for out-of-state students in the coming academic year of 1967–68 have been filled. Thank you for considering the University of . . ."

There was another sentence about applying as a transfer student after establishing a "sound academic record" somewhere else—which he took to mean that his high school marks were indeed too abysmal to qualify him for admission anywhere but a fourth-rate trade school. By this time, without really being aware of it, he had stumbled to the Club door and had stepped outside into the broiling sun. He did not notice Edna Dern toiling in her sandy garden or even acknowledge her when she said good morning. He just kept drifting down the walk, the letter dangling from his hand and all his hopes and dreams for the coming year being shed in an invisible trail behind him.

What began to gall him above and beyond the ruination of all his hopes and dreams was this crap in the letter about out-of-state students. Why had the sonofabitches even accepted his $20 application fee if all the out-of-state slots were already filled when he had applied? They must have realized he was an out-of-stater, since they mailed the goddam application to him in New York State, the chiseling redneck bastards.

He crumpled the letter in his hands and was about to toss it in somebody's holly bush, but thought better of it when he imagined a stranger—or worse, an acquaintance—coming upon it by accident. Instead, he jammed it in his pocket and decided to throw it in the ocean later, for that was what he felt the faceless admissions officer at the University of Tennessee had done to his future—cast him hopelessly adrift.

At Hawthorne he hung a right toward the beach, his destination Karen Koenigsburg's house—though he was only half conscious of it. What he needed desperately at this dark hour of his life was consolation, and what better place to seek it than the place where he had so recently passed his brightest hour. He certainly couldn't go down to the bay and cry on Tim Flannery's shoulder because the rejection from Tennessee also meant that he would be banished from his new friends, Tim and Hughie, at summer's end, and he couldn't bear the humiliation of it.

The Koenigsburg house looked more forbidding in the stark noonday sun than it had in evening's half-light. He rang the bell and Katya Koenigsburg opened the front door immediately—as though she had been there waiting—and gave him a fright. She wore her usual somber mask of greeting and announced at once that her daughter wasn't at home. As to where she might be found, the widow said she had no idea, but that he might as well try the beach.

"Why did you decide to go with the Castelli gallery instead of my mother's?" he found himself asking her bluntly, as though his life was nearly over and he might as well gather all the truth he could find to answer the riddle of his brief existence on earth.

"More money," she answered just as bluntly, followed by a European-style shrug of the shoulders so as to suggest *why else?*

"But she offered you a better percentage," he persisted.

Katya Koenigsburg regarded him as though she found his impertinence a great curiosity. "I feel better with a man," she told him and then retreated inside the house, virtually shutting the door in Andy's face.

He departed the Koenigsburg porch with his heart in his belly, followed Hawthorne to the ocean, and hurried up the stairway over the dunes. The Ocean Breeze swimming area between the two green flags was moderately crowded at this noontime of a Monday, but mostly with children, their mothers, and knots of gabbing teenagers. Andy trudged among the blankets and the blaring radios searching for Karen but did not see her anywhere.

"Andy, I've got something great to tell you," came a voice from behind him. He stopped trudging in the hot sand a moment and turned to face Kathy Craig in her polka-dot bikini, a bubbling, creamy blonde antithesis to the darker, saturnine Karen. "Jeff asked me to go out with him."

Andy said nothing.

"On a date," Kathy explained.

"I don't give a fuck," Andy said brutally, and he did not even glance back to see the crestfallen look on her face as he trudged off to continue his search. Evidently Karen Koenigsburg was elsewhere.

"Hey, Slave, how's it goin'?" another voice called to him.

Andy looked up at the lifeguard's chair where Jeff Blum sat regally sprawled, his bronze pectorals and deltoids glistening with suntan lotion and his vacant eyes hidden behind a pair of dimestore sunglasses. How could a moron like him get into the University of Wisconsin, Andy was suddenly dying to know.

"Call me Slave one more time and I'll rip your fucking ears off, Blum," Andy told him brazenly and walked on without even checking the large boy's reaction.

He left the green flag area and proceeded east down the beach with no particular destination in mind, just a desire to leave Ocean Breeze and the rest of the known world

187

behind him. In a little while he passed his Uncle Jack's house and a half mile after that he came to the boundary of Holly Wood. There was no chain-link fence across the beach itself, of course, but the change in atmosphere between Ocean Breeze's mostly Jewish new-money community and Holly Wood's Protestant old-money culture was palpable. The people on the beach looked different. The young mothers and teenaged girls of Holly Wood did not wear skimpy bikinis, like the females of Ocean Breeze. Rather, they favored less revealing one-piece suits, and the older ladies wore bulky outfits that positively harked back to photographs of the twenties. Here, unlike Ocean Breeze, the beach was dotted with large striped umbrellas, for the Anglo-Saxons had a tendency to burn. Finally, looming over the dunes back of the beach stood the immense old Holly Wood Club building, a massive shingle-style monstrosity designed by an imitator of Stanford White in 1904, which had defied the surging storm tides of the Atlantic much as the WASP community it served had defied the rise of other ethnic groups into the social strata once reserved exclusively for its own breed.

Holly Wood was only half the size of Ocean Breeze and Andy soon traversed its mile of beach, reaching the town's eastern boundary where the U.S. government-owned slice of Thunder Island National Seashore began. Here, under federal protection, stood the curiosity of nature called the Sunken Forest, really a remnant of the natural vegetation that once covered the whole island before the coming of the white man with his brush cutters and weed killers. The Sunken Forest was not below sea level as its name suggested. Rather, it lay sunken in a trough just behind the high dunes. The forest was composed almost entirely of prickly holly trees and scrub pines, none of them over twenty feet tall. Yet they shut out a lot of sunlight. Therefore no shrubs cluttered up the understory, and so the Sunken Forest had an otherworldly look to it, like one of the tidy, spacious, fairy tale forests of a Disney movie where dwarves and other enchanted beings dwelled. The only catch was that the ground—a thin, sandy loam—was almost entirely carpeted with poison ivy.

The beach here was virtually devoid of human life and Andy began to notice the proportionately greater number of interesting seashells that lay scattered about from the withdrawing tide. There were quite a few whelks and giant scallop shells, which would have been quickly snatched up by collectors back in the populated settlements. He still fumed about what the University of Tennessee had done to him, but he no longer felt like killing someone—in particular a huge goon on the order of Jeff Blum—and he regretted speaking so cruelly to Kathy Craig.

He had picked up a handful of shells—thinking to bring them home—when three F-104 jets in a triangular formation skimmed overhead at eight hundred feet in an eerie silence that was soon shattered by the lagging roar of their mighty engines. The planes caught Andy unawares and frightened him so badly that he scurried up the beach to the dunes and clawed his way over the top, his mind reeling with images of war, death, and devastation. It was more than a minute before his nerves quieted down sufficiently for him even to notice what lay on the leeward side of the dunes.

Below, in a glade cleared from the surrounding Sunken Forest, stood a shanty made of driftwood and scraps of tar paper. In the small "yard" before the house stood a young blond-haired man working on a surfboard stretched between two makeshift sawhorses. The man was applying some sticky goop from a small can. He looked up to find

Andy atop the dune and Andy realized that he had stumbled on Mike Lovett's legendary hideaway.

"Hey, ho-dad." Lovett greeted Andy genially in surfer slang, apparently unperturbed by this invasion of his secret domain.

"Oh, sorry to barge in here like this," Andy said, embarrassed.

"You're Flannery's buddy, aren't you?" Lovett said.

"How did you know that?" Andy asked, amazed.

"Well, that was you with him a few weeks ago when he was tossing his cookies in the bushes, wasn't it?"

"Yes, it was."

"I thought so. You're a ways from home, aren't you?"

"I really didn't mean to barge in on you like—"

"Don't sweat it. The jets scare you?"

"Yeah, kind of," Andy admitted. He had the distinct impression that Lovett understood how he felt and that it was all right to be honest with him.

"They scare the shit out of me too," Lovett said. "Come on down. I like my privacy but I'm no hermit. It gets sort of lonely out here with no one to talk to. Want a cold drink?"

As a matter of fact Andy was terribly thirsty, but he hadn't been conscious of it until Lovett brought it to his attention. "I could really go for some water, if you have some to spare," he said.

"You got it, ho-dad," Lovett said and vanished for a moment inside his shack. While he was inside, Andy climbed down off the dune. He was just about to step on some vegetation when Lovett came back out carrying a green jerry can and said, "Better watch the poison ivy on your bare feet. It's a lousy place to catch the shit."

Andy glanced down. Except for a narrow path cleared

from the dune to the sandy circle where the shanty stood, the ground was completely covered with the nasty weed.

"Keeps busybodies out," Lovett explained with a lopsided smile. "Or at least it fucks up their feet pretty good when they leave."

He filled a plastic tumbler with water for Andy and one for himself.

"I feel guilty drinking your water," Andy said. "It must be hard to get the fresh stuff out here."

"Naw," Lovett said. "There's a lady over in Holly Wood lets me take all I need from her garden hose." He paused a moment and looked wistfully westward in the direction of the WASP enclave. "Sweet lady," he mused. "Well, ho-dad, you look like a guy with a lot on your mind."

Lovett was certainly correct, but how he knew baffled Andy.

"Sit down and tell me about it," the surfer said. "We've got all afternoon."

CHAPTER FOURTEEN

The young men of Ocean Breeze liked to brag about their "surfer's knots"—calcium deposits on the knees from kneeling on a surfboard—but Mike Lovett never talked about it and, as far as Andy could tell, he was the only one who really had them. They looked like a couple of marbles embedded under his skin.

In addition to the surfboard Lovett was working on, there were four others standing in the sand around the shack, their skegs, or rear keel blades, sticking out like sharks' fins.

"What's the matter with the board?" Andy inquired as Lovett pounded the lid back on his can of epoxy resin with a hammer.

"Just a little ding," he answered, meaning a dent. "Robbie had a brief encounter with a hunk of sea trash."

"Is this Robbie Kugel's board?"

"Yup."

"He's a pretty good surfer, huh?"

"One of the best on the island," Lovett said.

"I don't surf," Andy volunteered, as though there was no point trying to keep secrets from Mike Lovett.

"You would if you had a board," Lovett said.

"How do you know I don't have a board?"

"Well, if you did, you'd surf, wouldn't you?"

"I guess."

"Sure you would."

"It looks very difficult."

"It's challenging," Lovett agreed gravely, and then his face brightened, "but it sure is fun once you get the hang of it. You want to learn?"

"But I don't have a board," Andy said.

"You can use one of these. The tide's on its way out. We get a bar break out here at the forest at low tide. Nice six-foot curls. With a good offshore breeze like we've got today the tubes'll be glassy. Good for learning."

"That would be great," Andy said, and then sighed as he thought again of the rejection letter from the University of Tennessee.

"You get some bad news?" Lovett asked.

Again amazed at the surfer's prescience, Andy fished in the pocket of his cutoffs and handed Lovett the crumpled letter.

"Hmmm," Lovett said, reading. "Van and Hughie Donovan go to school down there."

"Tim Flannery too."

"Oh, yeah? His brother Terry and me go back a long ways."

"Tim's only a freshman. I was planning to go too. Until today."

"Kind of had your heart set on it, huh?"

"Yeah."

"Tough break."

"Did you ever go to college?" Andy asked, curious because he suspected that Lovett wasn't the type.

"A bunch of 'em. All around."

"Where did you finally end up?"

Lovett chuckled. "Nowhere."

"Nowhere?"

"Well, here. But this is kind of nowhere, know what I mean?"

Andy wasn't sure.

"What about the draft?"

"What about it?" Lovett echoed him.

"Are you four-F or something?" Andy asked staring at the knobs on Lovett's knees. Four-F was the classification for those medically unfit for service.

"I'm not four-F," Lovett told him. "Matter of fact I was called up. I'm supposed to report for induction in three weeks."

Andy was momentarily shocked. Lovett kept grinning.

"How could they call you up?"

"Easy. I'm twenty-three, single, not in school or anything. Man, I was prime."

"No, I mean how could they even get ahold of you way out here."

"Hey, I've got parents, you know, like anybody else. We stay in touch. My folks got the telegram."

"Jeez," Andy said, reflecting on the seriousness of it. "Where's your home?"

"Sag Harbor."

"What if they send you over to Vietnam?"

"They're not sending this boy to Vietnam," Lovett said as though the idea was ridiculous. "As Cassius Clay put it, 'I ain't got nothing against them Viet Congs.' "

"But they'll make you go. Or they'll throw you in jail, right? They can make you do anything they want."

"This boy's heading north in three weeks, ho-dad."

"North?"

"Canada. How about yourself?"

"I don't know," Andy said.

"Looks like you're not going to the University of Tennessee."

"I applied to some state schools too."

"Getting pretty late to get into any school."

"I know."

"I suppose you could always get married and have a kid," Lovett suggested tongue-in-cheek.

"I don't think my prospects for marriage are very bright right now," Andy said, watching Lovett sandpaper the epoxy patch on Kugel's board.

"Well, if you want to go north with me, I'll be leaving here in about two weeks. You can ride up with me in my truck."

"I won't turn eighteen until October."

"Oh, no sweat then. Look me up when you get there. I'll be in Toronto. Know where that is?"

"Vaguely. Somewhere near Buffalo?"

"That's right."

"How'll I get ahold of you?"

"There's a draft resisters' organization up there. They help you get settled and all. I'll be working for them."

Andy nodded his head. The idea of fleeing into exile was a lot less alluring to him than the idea of going to a normal American college where they had football games and fraternities and nice tree-lined streets. "There's no surfing in Canada," he blurted out incongruously, as though without it a person like Lovett might not have any reason to live. "What'll you do?"

"I don't know." Lovett stopped sandpapering for a moment and gazed over the top of the dunes. "Get a dog sled or something. Anyway, this stupid war is starting to take all the fun out of surfing."

For a while afterward, Andy just watched Lovett working on Kugel's board. The sound of the sandpaper was

196

similar to the rasp of the surf. Eventually Lovett stooped down and eyeballed the board from its back end.

"Looks clean," he declared with quiet satisfaction. "Come on, let's give her a test drive. You grab that nine-four Hobie over there with the red stripe."

Andy went over to where the four other boards stood stuck in the sand and located the one in question. It was heavier than he expected, and wider too—carrying it under his arm, he could barely hook his fingers under the bottom. Lovett climbed over the dune easily as though he were a breed of human especially evolved for life on a barrier beach. Andy took longer to follow, struggling up and over with the unwieldy board. By the time he made it, Lovett was waiting for him at the water's edge.

A thin white line stretched below the horizon several hundred yards out from the beach. This was the renowned bar break, a place where the weather and the currents had created a submerged sand bar. The bar caused the ocean swells to gather and crest far from shore, affording much longer surfboard rides than could be gotten in the shore break. Also, the waves on the bar were bigger than the ones at the shore break. A sand bar such as this might suddenly form during a June storm and then disappear just as suddenly after the hurricane season. The bar break at the Sunken Forest had been in existence for three summers, which was a long time. It would be gone the following year.

"Watch what I do," Lovett said loudly to Andy over the crash of the surf.

"Sure," Andy agreed, trying not to show the terror he felt.

Lovett waded out and dropped his board onto the foamy slop, bending to hold onto it. Andy did likewise, glad to be relieved of its weight. In the water, the fiberglass-coated styrofoam board floated like a big flat cork. Its surface was nubby where Lovett had dripped paraffin wax to provide a nonslip surface for the feet.

Andy watched as Lovett waded deeper and deeper out toward the shore break. The experienced surfer paused a moment in slop that was up to his hips, waiting for an opportunity to make his move. Then he hopped on the board, assumed a kneeling position, and began paddling furiously toward a cresting breaker. He paddled up the wave, at what looked like an impossibly oblique angle, and disappeared over the top just before it formed into a curl and broke. After the wave crashed down—with a hiss that seemed to taunt Andy—Lovett could be seen beyond the momentarily flattened break, beckoning with his arm.

Andy tried to imitate Lovett, but he found the kneeling position that Lovett had assumed with such natural grace to be very uncomfortable and paddling from it felt extremely awkward. Then, before he could prevent it, his board was sucked forward into the maw of a cresting breaker, which crashed down on him like a brick wall. Knocked off the board and separated from it, he was terrified that its knifelike skeg would cut him in half. But when he surfaced after tumbling in the rough slop, he saw the board safely washed up on the beach and went back to get it.

The second time, instead of kneeling he lay belly-down on the board and paddled out beyond the shore break successfully. Once past it, though, the distance out to the bar break looked vast and terrifying. Lovett was already there, a bronze speck riding the swells, waiting. Andy saw him signal to come. Still lying on his belly, he began paddling further out. He was certain that huge and voracious creatures lurked unseen beneath him, and on the way out he passed a pulsating jellyfish the size of a

Frisbee. Closing in on the bar break, he was shocked at the size of the waves. They looked at least twice as big as the shore break waves and he couldn't figure out how it might be possible to paddle over them. But before he was able to think about it further, his board was caught in the tow of a gathering crest, and the choice was either to paddle like hell or get wiped out and have to swim the three hundred yards back to shore without his board and risk getting entangled in giant jellyfish and devoured by sharks. So he paddled like hell, and to his amazement he made it over the top of a breaker to the quiet side where Lovett sat waiting.

"Way to go, ho-dad," the older surfer said.

Andy struggled to sit upright on the board. His shoulders ached from paddling. The shore seemed miles away. He felt a sense of cosmic insecurity similar to what he had experienced tripping on acid.

"Nervous?" Lovett said.

"Scared shitless," Andy admitted, sensing there was no point trying to hide the truth from Lovett, who seemed to read his every thought.

"I've had 'em all out here at one time or another. You made it out pretty quick compared to some. It took Duff Perleman practically a whole afternoon."

"Ever see sharks out here?"

"Not too often," Lovett said, which wasn't very reassuring. "Relax. I don't see any around today."

For a while they rode the swells silently. Lovett kept looking out to the open ocean as though waiting for a sign. Andy couldn't see anything except the hazy silhouette of a trawler miles away on the horizon.

"Okay, here comes a decent set," Lovett finally said and swung the nose of his board toward the beach. "Think of it as a hill. A hill that moves. You move with it, sliding down the glassy hill as long as it moves. Here goes. Watch."

Lovett leaped up to the kneeling position and started paddling hard. The way Lovett caught the wave and then rode in the curl, Andy could only see him from the waist up. One thing he noticed was that Lovett was riding the wave right to left, on a diagonal to the shore. He seemed to be staying just a few yards to the left of the wave's foaming crest. After a fine ride, he kicked out of the wave and paddled back to where Andy waited.

"You get the idea?"

"I suppose. In a general sort of way."

"Well, hang ten, ho-dad."

Andy let three swells pass by until he felt it was no longer possible to stall. Then he paddled hard as Lovett had done and to his considerable astonishment found himself sliding down a green hill of glass. He didn't even attempt to stand up, but rather rode the wave lying on his stomach, like a kid riding a Flexible Flyer sled. But he wasn't able to steer left as Lovett had done and soon the crest dumped him. He hung tenaciously onto the board, though, and climbed right back on to paddle out again in the vast quiet trough between the shore and the bar.

"That was pretty good," Lovett said, when Andy made it back out. "This time, I want you to stand up."

"But I don't think I can."

"Sure you can. Keep your knees bent. Get your arms out like a tightrope walker."

"Okay, I'll try."

"Don't try it, ho-dad. *Do* it. People are always trying too hard instead of just doing stuff. Something like surfing, it's much easier if you just *do* it, know what I mean?"

"I think so."

"All right. Go get 'er."

Andy took off with the next swell and paddled like hell until he caught it. The nose of the board cut through the rising wave like a knife through jelly. Thinking *don't think!* he grabbed the edge of his board. Then he was sliding down the glassy hill standing, at least for several seconds before the board shot out from under him like a banana peel. He swam after it halfway back to the shore break, but was so thrilled by his success that he didn't worry for a moment about sharks or jellyfish.

Lovett was right behind him anyway, crying, "Way to go!" and then waiting to paddle back out to the bar with him.

Everything after that was just a matter of refinement. Lovett taught Andy how to control a board by moving his weight from the back to the front. He showed him how to "turtle"—to hang onto the board upside down under water beneath a broken wave. He taught him how to kick out of a wave before the end of a ride so he wouldn't have to paddle through the break to catch another. When Lovett announced that they should ride the next one all the way in, Andy was disappointed, as though he had been awakened from a beautiful dream to a harsh and banal reality.

"You did real good," Lovett said once they were back on the beach.

"All I need now is a board," Andy said ruefully.

"You'll get a board."

"In Canada?"

For the first time all afternoon, Lovett hesitated, at a loss to reply. But then he sunnily said, "Sure, we'll all get wet suits and surf the banks of Newfoundland. Hey, do me a favor will you, ho-dad?"

"Sure, what?"

"Take this board back to O.B. and leave it up at the guard shack for Robbie."

Though it was a long way back to Ocean Breeze, Andy felt privileged to carry the surfboard, because it signified his membership in a very exclusive society. He even paused at Holly Wood to catch a few waves in the shore break and show his new stuff to all the blond-haired WASPS who dotted the beach. By the time he returned to Ocean Breeze, it was after five o'clock. The lifeguards were all gone for the day and the shack was locked. So he left the board leaning against the pilings under the shack and then left the beach at Hawthorne to go see Karen Koenigsburg. He hadn't thought about her most of the afternoon while he was out at the bar with Lovett, and it seemed like weeks since he had been with her that magical night, though it wasn't yet twenty-four hours. But he felt now that his transformation to a surfer was equally momentous, if not more momentous, than his sexual initiation, and he couldn't wait to tell her about his afternoon out at the Sunken Forest.

He was mentally prepared to deal with Karen's scowling mother again, but when Max Pap answered the doorbell Andy was thunderstruck. He simply stood there unable to speak while the sculptor glowered at him as though his suspicions were lethal.

"Waddaya want?" Pap finally said. His accent was strictly Brooklyn.

"Is Karen home?" Andy couldn't stop himself from asking. He felt he had to say something.

Just then Karen appeared in the hall behind Pap, a dark figure against the darker cherrywood interior. She didn't say anything, not even *hi*. Despite his own dismay and anxiety, Andy detected from the way Karen kept glancing at him and then down at the floor that she was in a jam. His showing up like that unannounced had put her into a jam, and he had to help her out.

"I . . . I just came over to . . . to ask Karen for a date."

"She don't date," Pap said.

"Oh," Andy said. "Are you her father?"

"No," Pap said and then leaned forward to whisper, "Her father's dead."

"Oh! Jeez. Well—"

Pap then closed the door in his face. Andy stood there dumbly a moment, then stumbled down from the decrepitating porch through the rank garden to Hawthorne Street. Why hadn't it occurred to him that she had been toying with him for one night, he asked himself? And all the way up the Midway, past the edge of town and out to the Club, he couldn't come up with a satisfactory answer. He must be a stupid chump, he thought. It was as simple as that. And then, to make things worse, he had to go and try to be gallant about it. *I just came over to ask Karen for a date.* Now, when it was too late, he thought of a dozen vicious things he could have said to Max Pap. *I just came over to screw your girlfriend again . . . I had such a great time with Karen last night that I came back for more. . . .* But thinking about all the interesting possibilities only made the whole rotten deal seem more depressing and futile, and by the time he got back to the Club, the larger futility of his predicament in life, of the rejection letter from Tennessee, and the likelihood of having to run away from America to escape the draft, descended on him like a killer wave, bigger than anything out at the Sunken Forest bar break.

CHAPTER FIFTEEN

Franny came up to his room when it was just starting to get dark. This time she didn't bring any drawings or watercolors but brashly came upstairs looking for Andy and sat down on the edge of the narrow bed where he lay staring up at the steeply pitched ceiling. His silence gave her permission to stay.

"Soon the summer'll be over and I might never see you again," Franny said, and she reached out to touch his hairline.

"You're so young," Andy said. "Too young for us to . . . to do anything. Why do you have to be so young?"

"I'll be fifteen in November."

"Your brother would kill me."

"It can be a secret."

"There's no secrets on this island. Everybody knows everything."

"Kelly Donovan's sleeping with Bass and nobody knows."

"You know. And I already knew 'cause I've seen her leaving his room early in the morning. So it's not such a secret, is it?"

"Sssshhh." She put her finger across his lips, then lay

down beside him. For a while he said nothing, just enjoyed the warmth of having her next to him and listening to her breathe. Then it was completely dark, except for the lights of the water taxis out on the bay, and Andy began to tell her about his day, about getting the letter from Tennessee, and chancing upon Mike Lovett's shack at the Sunken Forest, and learning how to surf, and about the idea of running away to Canada. He didn't tell her about Karen Koenigsburg and the disappointment she'd caused him, thinking that maybe Franny was right, that some things could be kept secret.

"I could visit you in Canada," she said. "Cleveland's right across Lake Erie from it."

"I wish I didn't have to go there. Goddam this goddam Vietnam War."

"Anyway, we have tonight," she said, and she kissed him. He felt that he was at the mercy of an irresistible force. "Tomorrow the war might be over."

The idea that the Vietnam War might actually come to an end had a certain novelty and appeal for him. It seemed to Andy as though the war had been going on as long as he could remember. But all wars end, he now realized, and this one would too someday. This meant that sooner or later he could return from Canada, and he was grateful to Franny for pointing out this fundamental fact, which he had somehow overlooked. His gratitude quickly translated into passion as he responded to her kisses. He didn't try to remove her clothing, and she didn't volunteer—which was some relief to Andy, who kept imagining the disapproving face of Tim Flannery floating in the darkness above them—but for the longest time they lay together kissing and touching until Franny came up for air and announced that she had better go, and Andy had to agree that she should.

She came to his room in the Club the next three nights—
after he had returned from town drinking beers with Tim—
and the third night, which was Thursday of that August
week, she took off her jeans and T-shirt and offered herself to him. Rationalizing that perhaps some secrets could
be kept after all, he descended willingly into her arms. He
was half drunk and more than half in love with her, and
much more than a little appalled with himself when he
woke up the next morning with a headache and she was
gone and he remembered what they had done together.

And when he saw Tim up at the guard shack the next
day, he had trouble looking at him straight in the face.
However, Tim was concentrating on that day's edition of
The New York Times and was not even looking at Andy,
who stood in the sand below.

"Hey, listen to this," Tim said. " 'Bears Kill Two Girls in
Glacier National Park. West Glacier, Montana. Bears, in
two separate incidents twenty miles apart killed two
nineteen-year-old girls in sleeping bags early today.' "

"That's terrible."

"Yeah, pretty disgusting. It says, 'The two girls were
the first persons killed by bears in Glacier National Park
since it was established in nineteen thirty-two.' And they
both got it the same night. What a strange coincidence. I
bet they were on the rag. It doesn't say, but I bet they
were. It drives bears crazy."

"Was it the same bear?"

"How could it be the same bear twenty miles apart?"

"It must be two bears then."

"It says here that park rangers with high-powered rifles
are searching for 'em. Now isn't that just like the goddam
human race? They're gonna execute the goddam bears for
acting like wild animals, which is what they're supposed

to be in the first place. Besides, how are they gonna even know they plugged the right bears?"

"Maybe they'll find body parts inside 'em."

"Okay, how are they gonna find human parts inside unless they kill 'em first?"

"I don't know."

"Well, they're not gonna pump their goddam stomachs, that's for sure. They'll have to shoot the goddam bear and then cut it open to find out. How many bears do you suppose they'll blow away and cut open before they find the right ones?"

"I don't know."

"Besides, nowhere in this story does it even say that the bears ate any part of the victims. Nowhere. It says they were 'slashed to death.' So how are they gonna prove it's the right goddam bears they're shooting?"

"I don't know, Tim."

"This kind of thing makes me sick. The human race is hopelessly stupid."

Andy had never seen Tim so mad before. Just as Tim angrily flipped the page, Dale Hummer swaggered out of the guard shack.

"You're on duty, Flannery," he said sourly.

"'Hold it a sec."

"Don't tell me to hold it, pal. When I say you're on, you better jump."

"Yessir, Dale, sir," Tim replied acidly and made as if he was going to hand the newspaper to Hummer, but then stopped and said, "Oh, I forgot, you don't know how to read."

"Keep busting my chops, asshole, and see where it gets you."

Tim ignored his boss, descended the steep stairway from the guard shack to the beach, and began trudging to the high chair.

"I didn't get into Tennessee," Andy said, trailing be-hind him.

Tim stopped.

"Well, that's great," he said sardonically.

"You sound like you're mad at me for not getting in."

"What'd you do, fuck up the application?"

"No, I filled it out just the way they wanted. No funny snapshots or anything. Totally straight. The whole thing was a raw deal. They said they weren't accepting any more out-of-staters. They took my money order for the application fee, of course. They accepted that—" Even though Tim was wearing sunglasses, Andy somehow sensed that his eyes were glazing over, and that he'd stopped listening to this drawn-out explanation. "Anyway, I may have to go up to Canada."

"What the hell's in Canada?" Tim asked, thinking Andy was referring to some other college.

"To keep from getting drafted and all."

"Oh," Tim said without enthusiasm, as though neither evading the draft nor getting drafted were really acceptable.

"Mike Lovett's heading up there in a couple of weeks," Andy quickly added, invoking a person he knew Tim respected.

"Really? How do you know that?"

"He told me so. He got called in to report to the Army."

"No shit?"

"No shit."

It took Tim a moment to absorb the news.

"Well, that's cool for him maybe, but what the hell are you going to do up in Canada?" Tim said derisively. "He's older than you. He's had some experience in the world. You're still a kid. You've never been away from home before or taken care of yourself or anything."

"What do you call what I've been doing out here all summer?"

"What? You mean your job at the Club?"

"Yeah. I'm living away from home, taking care of myself."

"Get serious," Tim said, making a face.

"Hey, Flannery?" came a voice from above them. It was Jeff Blum atop the guard chair. "You owe me ten minutes already."

"Cool your jets, man."

"Anyway, I'll sell sandwiches on the streets of Toronto if I have to," Andy said. "At least I know how to do that."

"Hey, that's a great idea," Tim said sarcastically as Blum climbed down and he went up to take his place. Then, as soon as he was up there, he had to blow his whistle and get a bunch of kids to move back inside the green flags. Down below, without saying anything more to him, Andy spun on his heels and headed back to the Club.

Friday afternoon at the Club was full of surprises. First, there was a new chef. This one was a fiery Cuban named Benito, who after the formalities of introduction would prove to be a worse tyrant than Anatole. For one thing, he was much younger—about fifty—and didn't fall asleep when he got drunk—which he was in the process of doing virtually since arrival. And for another thing, he didn't just yell when he had a tantrum, he threw objects around, often without regard to their breakability or lethality. For example, between the hours of one P.M. and four P.M. he hurled a coffee cup, a head of lettuce, and a steel spatula across the room at Andy because Andy had said that there were certain established ways of doing things around the Club, which Benito regarded as backtalk.

At four-thirty, Bass came into the kitchen with a rail-thin, long-haired blond teenage boy who was dressed in ragged khaki cutoffs belted with a length of nylon rope and a torn sweatshirt that had the word *Loomis* across it in red block letters.

"Andrew, this is John," Bass said, putting a hand on the boy's skinny shoulder. "John is going to be your new helper."

"Really," Andy said brightly. "Hey, that's great."

"Andrew's about the best dishwasher we've ever had here," Bass went on to say, which galled Andy a little since it was only a week ago that he had cooked Saturday night dinner for the whole club when Anatole was out of action, and Bass seemed to have forgotten. Moreover, Andy began to worry whether this really meant he wasn't doing his job well enough, and whether he might suffer any corresponding reduction in pay. He looked the new kid over again. The boy appeared bedraggled and underfed. "You'll show John here the ropes, won't you?" Bass added.

"You bet."

Grinning as ever, Bass went out to the bar.

"Ever scrub pots before?" Andy asked.

"Not really," said John, who had a strange look on his face—stoned or frightened, Andy wasn't sure.

"You'll love it. It's really character-building."

Andy got over his initial suspicions very quickly when he saw how pleasant it was to have a helper. The first job he put John on was to scrub all of Benito's prep pots. Between five-thirty and six-thirty both of them were fully occupied helping the chef pump out the dinners. For the next forty-five minutes, with the meal out and the dirty dishes yet to return, there was a lull. Andy was pleased to notice that Benito, though fairly plastered, was actually tidying up his cooking area, putting away his knives and wiping down the butcher block table—something Anatole had never done. Then he staggered out, leaving Andy and John alone.

"It's okay for us to eat now," Andy told him. "Grab whatever you want."

John heaped a plate with fish fillets, potatoes, and buttered rolls and commenced shoveling it in like someone who hadn't eaten for days. It occurred to Andy that indeed John was starved. He cleaned his plate in a matter of minutes and loaded it up again almost as fully. This time, though, he ate at a more normal pace.

"You from around here?" Andy asked.

"Nope."

"Where are you from?"

"Connecticut."

"Your family out here?"

"Nope."

"How long you been out here?"

"Few days."

"Where'd you come from?"

"A boat."

"Working on a boat?"

"Nope."

"Just on one."

"Uh-huh."

"What kind of boat?"

"Sailboat."

"How old are you?"

"Sixteen."

"Where do you stay out here?"

"Around."

"I hope you don't sleep on the beach. They arrest you if they catch you, you know?"

"I don't sleep on the beach."

"Well, you must stay somewhere," Andy said, trying to press him.

"I have a place," John said.

"Oh." Andy let it drop, frustrated with John's reticence.

By then the waitresses started bringing back the dirty dishes. Andy was delighted at how much easier the job was with a helper. They got a regular assembly line going at the sinks—John scraping the plates and washing, and Andy drying and stacking the clean ones back on the shelves where they belonged. They had finished with the dinner plates and were waiting for the cake plates when Franny came to the kitchen and invited Andy outside to have a cigarette.

"Who's the new guy?" she asked at once.

"I don't know. Mystery boy," Andy said. "He's about the most untalkative kid I ever met."

"He's weird-looking."

"You find him attractive?"

"I didn't say that. I said he looks weird."

"I think he's one of those hippie vagabond love-child creatures they've been writing about in *Time* magazine."

"It's strange, him being here," Franny said.

"Maybe when everything went crazy around here last week Bass realized it was too much for one guy."

"Maybe," Franny said.

There was a crash inside and they rushed back in to find John piling cake plates back on a dropped tray. The thick plates were practically indestructible.

"Anyway, maybe I'll see you later," Franny said.

"Maybe," Andy replied. It was his way of saying yes without having to feel responsible for her showing up late at night.

With a helper, the big kitchen was all cleaned and

213

mopped and squared away by ten o'clock. John slipped out the back with a giant slab of cake wrapped in a napkin. Tim was not in the Club bar, so Andy decided to go into town by himself and unwind with a few beers. Heading upstairs to shower and change first, he worried whether Tim was onto his secret romance with Franny. Tim certainly had been in a foul mood on the beach that morning, he thought. But then, when Andy came back downstairs all clean, Tim was sitting at his usual corner seat in the bar.

"Whaddya say we go out and tie one on?" he proposed. Andy could tell that Tim was already half loaded, but at the same time he was mighty glad to find him there at all. He wanted everything to be okay, like it was at the beginning of the summer.

"What's the occasion?" Andy asked.

"Does there have to be an occasion?"

"No. I just wondered."

"It's Herbert Hoover's birthday."

"No shit?"

"No shit. C'mon, let's get out of this ridiculous place."

With Martin Donovan playing "Someone To Watch Over Me" at the piano, Tim and Andy left the Club.

"You're in trouble," Tim said as soon as they were outside.

"Trouble?" Andy echoed him warily, thinking that Tim had just pretended to be friendly inside and was now going to jump all over him about Franny.

"That new kid's gonna get your job."

For a moment Andy was relieved. But then what Tim had said sunk in and he became worried all over again. It was chilly out so he zipped up his windbreaker.

"I've seen 'em do it before," Tim went on. "They bring some new kid in as a, quote, 'helper' and get the old kid to show him how everything's done, and then when the new kid understands how to do the job, they fire the old kid. That way they don't have to mess up the operation and everybody gets their little fish-wishy dinner.

It seemed to Andy that Tim might have the situation pegged pretty well. Still he felt the need to argue, saying, "Bass wouldn't do that to me."

"It's not Bass. It's the old bitch, Edna Dern. I saw her pull the same deal three years ago on this guy Arnie Schlossman."

"He must have done something to get them pissed off. Probably got sick of shoveling the goddam walk."

"No, it wasn't that. He was fooling around with Kelly Donovan."

Andy's heart flew into his throat. Could this possibly be Tim's extremely indirect way of making an accusation, he wondered?

"Oh?" was all he said.

"They're weird about it," Tim continued. "They think a little summer romance with a Jew-boy is a threat to the whole Irish race. To tell you the truth, I'm embarrassed that we even belong to this goddam club."

"Well, I'm not fooling around with Kelly Donovan," Andy declared boldly, practically daring Tim to come clean.

"No, but I bet you wish you could," Tim retorted, flashing a trademark lopsided Flannery smile which at once reassured Andy that Tim didn't know about him and Franny, but also gave Andy the willies because it looked so much like Franny's smile.

By now they reached Ocean Breeze. Inside a house they passed the Beatles were singing a song about fixing a hole.

"Are you pissed off at me for not getting into Tennessee?" Andy asked.

"I guess I was this morning. I realize it's stupid to blame you. I was just feeling so fed up with all the jerks I work with and being a guard and all."

"Some of them are supposed to be your friends."

"Not really."

"Come on. Not Hughie and Van? I thought you were going to Tennessee because of them."

"I'm going to Tennessee because my brother Terry went there. And who the hell knows why *he* went there? Probably some jerk on the guards talked him into it. No good reason. It's too stupid for words. As for the Donovans, Hughie's not interested in anything except surfing, and Van's not interested in anything, period. Underneath that big silent facade is a big empty space between his ears. I don't think I ever had more than a five-second conversation with the guy in my whole life. Why do you think I read the paper all the goddam day long?"

"He was pretty talkative on the train with me that day we came back from New York."

"Oh yeah? What'd he talk about? His fraternity, I bet."

"As a matter of fact, he did."

"It's the only thing he *ever* talks about. It's the only goddam thing he *knows* about. Hey, if these guys were all such scintillating companions, do you think I would've spent the whole goddam summer getting plastered with you?"

"No," Andy said. He didn't know whether to take it as a compliment or a backhanded put-down.

In any case, they had arrived at McCauley's. The place was jammed. They got four large beers and headed for a table in the back where they could watch everybody. Before he sat down, Andy noticed that Kathy Craig was slow dancing with Jeff Blum to a Beach Boys ballad titled "God Only Knows."

"They're going to have such beautiful children," Tim observed.

Andy could only pretend to laugh. He remembered the way her kisses tasted that night on the dunes, the creaminess of her breasts—it seemed like years ago—and recalling it left him a little dizzy. Out on the dance floor Blum engulfed Kathy in his huge arms like King Kong.

"Beautiful children but very dim," Tim added. "Maybe twenty-five watts each."

Also among the dancers were Kelly Donovan and her "steady" boyfriend Robbie Kugel. They were swaying together like the truest of lovers. After two months in the sun Kelly never looked more beautiful. She lay her head on Robbie's shoulder and closed her eyes dreamily. As she did this, Andy pictured her pussyfooting out of Bass's quarters in the harsh morning light. How could she be so two-faced? But then he noticed Kathy Craig again—she had her arms looped around Blum's waist now—and he recalled how infatuated with her he had been, and he remembered how Karen Koenigsburg had looked naked in the blue light of her television, and he thought of how warm and sweet Franny Flannery felt pressed up against him, and he began to understand how hungry the human heart could be, and how its hungers operated despite what the mind thought, or what people preached, or what the rules supposedly said.

"The human race is hopeless," he said and chugged his beer.

"I've been telling you that all summer," Tim said.

"Your turn to buy a round."

By midnight they had accomplished their objective, though Tim was drunker than Andy because of his head start. Tim had also gotten into one of his hostile-aggressive moods and was loudly making remarks about people out on the dance floor. Andy was still alert enough to sense that it might cause them problems if Tim kept it up.

"Whaddya say we go over to the Sea Witch," he suggested. In the Sea Witch, with the band playing real loud, it would be harder for Tim to make provocative cracks.

"Sure," Tim readily agreed, to Andy's surprise. "I'm totally sick of this dive. Same old assholes, week after week. Complete bummer. Hey, gotta go take a wee-wee first, though."

Andy watched Tim lurch across the dance floor to the men's room. He bounced off several dancers along the way—all girls—and Andy noticed the angry glances that the girls' boyfriends shot at Tim as he lurched through. A while later Tim walked out of the toilet just as Jeff Blum headed in. Kathy Craig had been left standing unattended nearby. Tim went up to her. Andy couldn't hear what was said over Sam the Sham and the Pharaohs singing "Woolly Bully," but Kathy was apparently not enjoying Tim's company. She shook her head emphatically. Tim put his hands around her waist and tried to drag her out on the dance floor. Kathy slapped Tim's chest as though fending him off. About this time, Jeff Blum came out of the toilet. Andy got up and tried to weave through the dancers to get to Tim, but it was too late. Tim obviously made some kind of crack to Blum and Blum popped him one in the face. Blood streamed from Tim's nose, all over his wrinkled blue oxford shirt and then onto the hardwood floor, where it dropped in dark stars. Kathy Craig screamed.

Tim just stood there defiantly, as though he enjoyed the display of gore and the distress it was causing others. By now, Andy fought his way through the crowd that had gathered.

"You better get your sidekick out of here if you know what's good for him," Blum said to Andy.

"I could snap you in half like a goddam lobster, you know," Tim told Blum in a continued show of drunken bravado.

"C'mon, Tim," Andy said in his ear. "This is crazy."

"The two of us could tie the guy up like a pretzel," Tim went on. "Let's give it a try. Whaddya say?"

"I say we get out of here."

"You're disgusting, Flannery," the younger Blum, Seth, now said, stepping up beside his brother. "Look at yourself."

"Why doesn't everybody just be cool," Robbie Kugel suggested, ever the diplomat.

"Why don't you go fuck yourself," Tim told him. "Better yet, go fuck somebody's sister—"

Andy cringed, thinking again that Tim was making some oblique reference to him and Franny, even though it was also obvious that Tim was referring to Kelly Donovan.

"—or maybe someone's mother."

"We better get him out of here," Robbie Kugel said decisively and put a hand on Tim's shoulder. "Come on, Tim, you're polluted."

Though everyone in McCauley's back room had stopped dancing, the jukebox was still playing loudly, a song called "Happy Together" by the Turtles.

"You're right, I'm polluted," Tim admitted, and then pointed to Blum, saying, "But he's an asshole. Tomorrow I'll be sober and he'll still be an asshole."

Jeff Blum lunged for Tim and it seemed as though every lifeguard and surfer in Ocean Breeze had to step in to separate them. Robbie Kugel and Hughie Donovan grabbed Tim while Van Donovan and four other guys struggled to restrain the Blum brothers. Then there was a kind of general surge through the crowd while Tim was escorted—shoved—through the bar and out the front door. Andy followed the surging mob.

"Go home, man," Robbie advised Tim calmly once they were outside in the cool night air. "There's enough fighting going on in the world."

"Hey, I'm just trying to bring a little of that Vietnam spirit back home, where it belongs," Tim said, still bleeding, still cocky. "I dare that stupid moron to come out and fight. Go on, tell him to come outside."

"You're being ridiculous," Robbie Kugel said, starting to get bored with Tim's antics. "'Go home and wash up."

"He's right, Tim," Andy said.

"Hey, whose side are you on?"

"I'm on your side."

"If you're on my side, why don'tcha act like it."

"You want me to get a bloody nose too?"

"No! But you don't have to agree with the goddam enemy."

"He's not the goddam enemy. He's your goddam friend."

"Goddam right," Robbie Kugel said.

"Well goddam all of you, then," Tim said as though he had discovered a general conspiracy. He spun on his heels and lurched in the direction of the Sea Witch. Then he suddenly stopped and turned back. "Wanna come with me?"

"No," Andy said. "I'm going back to the Club."

"Fine. Suit yourself. Be an asshole too."

CHAPTER SIXTEEN

F ranny had already been there and gone. Andy found a note from her on his pillow when he got back to the Club. It said, *Waited until 12:30. Maybe I'll see you tomorrow night instead. Love! Franny.* The dots over her i's were little circles, Andy noticed. It reminded him that she was fourteen. And the exclamation point after *Love!* brought a little bubble of panic up in his throat. Their relationship was sick, he thought, a sick thing on a sick island in a sick decade. He felt sick to his stomach and his head was spinning, but when he lay down the room whirled around him, even in the darkness, and he had to sit up again. Eventually he went to the bathroom and made himself throw up.

When he returned to bed his belly no longer ached but he could not go to sleep. He felt as though someone had switched on a kleig light inside his brain, starkly illuminating what looked like a parched desert landscape at high noon. He grew terribly thirsty and then, after he had guzzled more than a quart of water from the bathroom faucet, he had to get up every fifteen minutes and take a pee. As his drunkenness ebbed, all the terrors of his life began to crowd the parched desert landscape inside his head like so many scary tarantulas, scorpions, and lizards.

Foremost among these creeping terrors was the prospect of having to run off to Canada in the fall to escape the draft. It occurred to him that the Army might not necessarily call him up the moment he registered, and that therefore it might not be imperative for him to run off to Canada so soon. But what would his life be like in the meantime, he wondered? What would he do? Where would he go? He couldn't bear the thought of returning to New York City, living at his mother's. Perhaps he could stay out here, on Thunder Island, live in Mike Lovett's abandoned shack out in the Sunken Forest, at least through the fall. But no, he thought, that would be completely crazy. Everybody would be gone. He'd die of loneliness. And what would he do to make money—which brought him to the next fear, a more immediate one, the question of his job at the Club. Just what was the story with this new kid, John? Was Tim right, were they taking steps to get rid of him? What would he do if they fired him? He could possibly hang out at his Uncle Jack's for a while, but what would be the point? Why bother spending the last two weeks of the summer surfing when eventually you only had to run away to Canada where there is no surfing? He might as well take Lovett up on his offer and catch a ride north, get an early start on his new life in exile, whatever it might mean. But what really hurt most was that Andy didn't want to run away to Canada in the first place. He wanted to go to college, a nice, normal, American college somewhere far away from the scummy maw of New York City, where there were football games and girls and sunny quadrangles full of autumn leaves. And being deprived of this was so painful that he could no longer lie sleeplessly in bed being blinded by the light inside his head.

It was four-thirty in the morning. He put on his clothes and left the Club thinking that a walk might make him feel better, that it might even make him sleepy enough to get a few winks before noon. The day that lay ahead was Saturday, the busiest day of the week, and he dreaded it, especially the prospect of working on just a few hours sleep, or possibly no sleep at all.

The Club walk was full of sand again. He had just shoveled the goddam thing on Thursday, and now the wind had blown it all back. Not only that but the day after tomorrow was Sunday, meaning that a lot of the Club daddies would be heading back to the city, and they wouldn't be able to drag their little luggage wagons down to the ferry if the walk was covered with sand, meaning that Andy would have to shovel it off again. The futility of it was crushing, like a great dry wave.

The town was eerie at this hour, utterly dead. He'd never been in downtown Ocean Breeze when it was totally deserted. It would be desolate like this in the fall, when all the summer folk were gone. He vividly associated the emptiness of the town with the emptiness of his future and he began to shiver in the clammy predawn air. He was standing in front of the now-quiet Sea Witch when something rumbled around the corner on Juniper. A big garbage truck shot out of the narrow street that was hardly a street anyway in the normal sense of the word. The garbage truck had the huge, menacing, implacable military look of a tank, and the hollow-eyed teenagers who clung to the truck's side—native islanders who couldn't get a glamor job like being a lifeguard or waiter and had to settle for this—looked like the soldiers in Vietnam whose haunted faces were beginning to glower from the front pages of the newspapers and magazines.

The truck turned another corner and disappeared around the Dune Realty Company office, leaving Andy breathless in its blue diesel exhaust. The alcohol had completely worn off now and all that remained was a throbbing knot in his head just above his right eye. He was thirsty again and there was nowhere to get a drink of fresh water at this hour. Toward the east, past the spire of the old sailor's church—now an art gallery—the sky was turning a lighter peacock blue. If he didn't get back to the Club soon, before it got too bright, he'd never get to sleep at all, Andy thought, and so, fleeing from the dawn like a godforsaken creature accursed by a dark and terrible destiny, he hurried back to his quarters.

Andy was dreaming about Maine when Tim burst into his room without knocking.

"Surf's up," Tim said, yanking Andy's sheet and blanket off.

"Get outta here," Andy mumbled into his pillow.

"We've got a fine offshore breeze, beautiful glassy five-foot rollers. Let's go."

"Don't have a board."

"You can use Shawn's. He's at work."

"Don't want to."

"I've got an added surprise. Something wicked groovy to show you."

"Show me later."

"Hey, what's the matter with you, anyway?"

Andy made himself sit up, his eyes slits and his face puffy with sleeplessness. "What's the matter with me?" he echoed Tim. "Well, first of all, how about last night?"

"What about it?"

"You relegated me to the ranks of the assholes."

"Oh, that," Tim said. "Hey, I was drunk."

"Some excuse."

"Well, what do you want me to say?"

"You could apologize, for starters."

"Okay, I apologize. You shouldn't take me seriously when I'm like that."

"What time is it?"

"I dunno. Around ten."

Andy puffed out his cheeks as he calculated the amount of sleep he'd managed to get: four hours.

"I feel so shitty," he said.

"Couple of hours in the briny Atlantic and you'll feel like a million bucks."

"Hey, what are you doing here anyway?"

"You must be getting senile. I just told you: surf's up."

"No. I mean at this hour, on a Saturday."

"Oh. Well, that's another little surprise. I quit my job."

"You quit being a lifeguard?" Andy said, his eyes no longer slits but bugging out.

"Yup."

"What'd you do that for?"

"I was bored to death with it. Hummer gave me a hard time about being ten minutes late today so I told him to jam it."

"Great. What are you gonna do now?"

"I'm gonna goof off for the rest of the summer," Tim said as though it should have been obvious, and it took a moment for Andy to realize that, unlike himself, Tim didn't have to worry about a place to stay, about meals, about where he was going at the end of the summer, about anything, really.

"Oh," Andy finally said a little sadly.

"And lookit, if these assholes fire you from the Club, you can crash at our place for the rest of August."

"Jeez! You mean it!"

"Absolutely."

"Well, God, I don't know what to say," Andy said, thinking of Franny and how impossibly awkward the situation might be. "You sure your parents won't mind?"

"They don't know what the hell's going on around the house. Believe me. And my brothers have had their friends coming and going all summer. It's my turn."

"Well, it's awful nice of you to offer."

"Don't mention it. Just shag your ass out of the rack and let's catch some heavies."

"All right," Andy said, "but only until noon. I've got to shovel the goddam walk and then do goddam prep all afternoon in the goddam kitchen for goddam Benito."

"Who's goddam Benito?"

"The new goddam chef. They fired poor goddam Anatole. Remember?"

"Dear old goddam Anatole," Tim said wistfully. "Well, goddammit, get up."

Bass had Dylan on the Club P.A. system downstairs, a plaintive ballad about the murder of a Negro waitress in Baltimore. Bass himself was in the bar, cleaning up the mess from late Friday night.

"How did John work out?" he inquired as Andy and Tim passed through. Tim poked Andy in the ribs, which Andy took as a warning to be careful.

"He's a little slow," Andy said deviously.

"Really? He looked all right to me."

"By the end of the summer he'll probably be okay. Then he'll be all trained so he can have my job next summer."

"You're not coming back, then?"

Andy was surprised that Bass had assumed as much.

"No," he said. "I might not even be in the country."

"Going abroad?"

"If Canada's abroad," Andy said. "That letter I got last week—it was another rejection from a college. I might have to go north to escape the draft."

"Gosh," Bass said. "That's too bad. Well, if there's anything I can do . . ."

"What can you do?"

"I don't know," Bass admitted.

"Come on, let's catch those heavies," Tim said.

Outside, Mrs. Dern was in the front yard of her nearby cottage, pruning her rugosa hedge. It seemed to Andy that she made a special point of glowering at them as they passed by.

"Good morning, Edna," Tim said, waving as they passed, then muttered under his breath, *"You vicious old twat."*

Instead of proceeding straight to the beach, Tim led Andy down a path through the largest tract of undeveloped land within the Club holdings, a three-acre patch of scrub pine and wild rose farthest from the Ocean Breeze town line. The path led to a small clearing. In it was a jury-rigged structure that was part shack and part tent. It was made up of a large cardboard shipping crate, some planks pilfered from a construction site, a sheet of plastic staked out like a crude awning, and various wooden flotsam from the beach. A clothesline was strung up between two small pine trees and on it was a sweatshirt with the word *Loomis* printed across the front. The sweatshirt was blotchy with food stains. Tim stuck his head inside to see if anyone was there.

"Nobody home," he said. "My brother Matt and his buddies found this yesterday."

Andy didn't say anything. He just nodded his head, taking it in.

Tim pulled out his Zippo lighter, flipped the cap, and struck the flint. "This would take care of your problem."

"No, don't do that!"

"Hey, there's no one inside."

"Still, you can't burn it down."

"Why not? He's a goddam squatter on private property."

"It's not right."

"Help me rip it apart then," Tim said.

"No."

"This kid's your enemy. He's after your job."

"He's not my enemy. And I doubt that he's after my job. He probably thinks he's only the helper, just like they told him."

"You're a sentimental slob. You feel sorry for him?"

"Yeah, I do. Look at this place. It's pathetic—"

"Ssshhh!" A rustling could be heard coming up the same path they'd just taken. "It's him."

John entered the clearing, looking chagrined to find Tim and Andy there beside his crude shelter. He was shirtless and carried a brown paper grocery bag.

"Howdy," Tim greeted him.

"What do you want?" John said, looking to Andy.

"Nothing," Andy said.

"My colleague speaks for himself," Tim said. "I, for one, would like a little information. Tell me about yourself."

"There's nothing interesting."

"Behind every squatter's shack there's an interesting story," Tim disagreed.

"What do you want to know?"

"The story of your life."

John smiled at that. He was so thin that when he

smiled, creases appeared at the corners of his mouth like a much older person.

"I was born. Now I'm here."

"Seems kind of sketchy to me. Didn't you leave out a few details? Ancestors, parents, place of birth, schooling, youthful adventures, awards, honors, and distinctions?"

John shifted his weight from one foot to another uncomfortably. "There's no story," he insisted.

"Let's go surf, Tim," Andy said.

"Just a second." Then to John: "No story. There are clues, aren't there?" He snatched the sweatshirt off the clothesline. "For instance, what does it mean: Loomis?"

"It's a school."

"A prep school?"

"Yes."

"Aha! Do you go to it?"

"I did."

"What? Not going back?"

"If I can help it."

"We're making headway here."

"I couldn't be more bored," Andy said. "Let's go."

"Bear with me," Tim said. "Okay, picture this: a strange teenage kid lands on Thunder Island with nothing but the clothes on his back. Obviously he's a runaway. But from what? What else but a terrible crime!" Like a state prosecutor bearing down on a defendant, Tim suddenly thrust his arm out at John, pointing. "You slaughtered your entire family in East Hampton and ran away to here."

John laughed again, purely a laugh of discomfort, and crossed his arms as though holding onto himself.

"It couldn't have happened," Andy declared.

"Why not?" Tim asked.

"Because if a whole family got slaughtered out in the Hamptons, you would have read about it in the paper."

Then, to John: "He reads the whole goddam *New York Times* every day. I mean every *single* day."

"It pays to keep informed," Tim said.

"What about my point?" Andy said.

"There's something to it."

"Good. Let's go, then."

"Wait a second."

"I only have until noon, for godsake. Come on."

"Do you know this is private property?" Tim circled John. He had abandoned the theatrical courtroom manner.

"No," John said.

"Well it is. And you're trespassing. Look at this dump. It doesn't even meet the building codes."

"I'm going, Tim," Andy said, and he started down the path.

"If I were you I'd think about relocating," Tim told John. "And by the way, you better wear a shirt when you go downtown to buy groceries or you might get arrested." He tossed the sweatshirt to John and then followed Andy down the path. Once back on the concrete walk that led to the ocean, neither spoke until they almost reached the Flannery house up near the dunes. Then Tim said, "I guess that put the fear of God into him, huh?"

"I wish you would just leave him alone."

"I'm telling you, it's your job."

"Why do you care so much about my job?"

"Well, I'm unemployed now," Tim said, "and one of us has got to pay for the beer from now on."

Early that evening, after the roast beef dinners had all been sent out and the dirty dishes had not yet come back, Andy and John paused to eat some supper together. Andy had the distinct feeling that John was afraid of him. It made Andy uncomfortable and he tried to put John at ease.

"The Flannerys are all ballbusters," he said. "You shouldn't take what Tim said personally. They'd probably hassle anybody who camped out where you are. I mean, it's not aimed especially at you . . ."

John just glanced up at him intermittently as he gorged himself on beef and potatoes. Andy supposed that the kid hadn't eaten much all day, and this made him feel even sorrier for him. He also felt that he hadn't succeeded in reassuring John, either. Finally he gave up trying, and instead said, "John, what are you doing out here on Thunder Island?"

"I split from my folks' boat," he answered without evasion, to Andy's surprise.

"What kind of boat?"

"Sailboat."

"Really? Like a big one you can sleep on?"

"Uh-huh."

"Jeez. Where was it when you split?"

"Off the tip of Long Island somewhere. I don't know."

"How'd you get here?"

"Hitchhiked. Then took the ferry."

"How'd you get from the boat to land?"

"Swam it."

"Really? God. How far was it?"

"Just across the harbor. It was nothing, really."

"Oh. How come you ran away?"

"They were yelling at each other," John said. "Like always."

"Hey, at least they're still married."

John didn't seem cheered by the idea.

"Mine just gave up years ago. They're divorced," Andy

explained, but John just kept eating. "What are you going to do after the summer?"

"I don't know."

"What year of school are you supposed to be in?"

"Junior, this fall. But I'm not going back."

"You can't live out here. You'll starve," Andy said, watching John finish the last morsel of beef on his plate. "You'll freeze." John got up from the steel table where they were sitting and carried his eating utensils to the sinks. "Well, at least you don't have to worry about the goddam draft for a couple of years," Andy said. By then John had started to fill the sinks with hot water.

Franny was waitressing as usual and while Andy loaded up her tray with desserts, she asked, "Did you get my note last night?"

"Yes," he said.

"Are you getting sick of me?"

"No."

"Should I come by tonight?"

Andy hesitated.

"What's the matter?" she asked.

"Nothing," he said. The problem was that it was the first time he'd ever had to make a definite date to meet her, with no *maybe* to fall back on as a psychological escape hatch.

"Should I come or not?" she pressed him.

"Yes," he said. "Only you better make it around one, when all the old fogies are done drinking here."

"Okay," she said, and kissed her index finger and pressed it to the tip of his nose. The gesture embarrassed him wildly—John saw it from over at the sinks—and Andy made a mental note to tell her later not to ever do anything like that in front of other people again, because

232

he could get into serious trouble if people suspected they were fooling around.

They finished the cleanup a little after ten o'clock. John vanished out the back door with his slab of cake wrapped in foil. Tim was at his customary spot in the Club bar when Andy emerged from the kitchen.

"There he is: my partner in crime," Tim said. Andy could tell that Tim was already quite loaded, drunker even than he had been at the same point the night before. "Ready to rip the night to shreds?"

"I feel terrible. I only got a few hours of sleep last night."

"How could that be? You went home way before I did."

"I couldn't sleep."

"Someone keeping you up?"

"No!" Andy reacted strongly, hearing an accusation that hadn't really been made.

"You *are* strung out. What you need is a beer. Lemme buy you—"

"Tim, I can't drink here. You know that."

"Okay. Let's go downtown," he said, draining his glass.

"I don't feel like it tonight."

"What? You can't *not* go downtown. It's mandatory."

"I won't be any fun. Go without me."

Tim leaned over and whispered in his ear: "I got some wacky weed. That ought to start your engine."

"That'll totally knock me out."

"Come on. Get dressed and we'll go downtown. A few beers and you'll feel like your ridiculous old self again."

"Really, Tim, I just don't want to go out tonight."

"Great. What am I supposed to do?"

"Well, why don't you go home and take a night off yourself for a change? You could probably use it."

"What's that supposed to mean?"

"I think we're both drinking too much."

"Bullshit."

"No bullshit. I couldn't sleep last night."

"Maybe you've got a guilty conscience."

Andy felt the blood drain from his head. Once again he had to wonder whether Tim knew about him and Franny. "I think it's from all this liquor," was all he said.

"Beer isn't liquor."

"Oh no? What is it, then?"

"It's a wholesome, tasty beverage that builds strong bodies twelve ways. Hey, I don't have any trouble sleeping."

"Maybe not. Maybe it's affecting you in other ways."

"You should hear yourself. You sound like my goddam guidance counselor."

"You just lost your job today—"

"I didn't lose it. I quit," Tim retorted.

"Maybe if you weren't hungover every morning, you coulda got to the beach on time."

"You've got a lot of nerve thinking you know what it was like for me."

"Well, Christ, Tim, it's only the most desirable job on the whole goddam island, sitting out on the goddam beach getting a tan."

"Shit, I'd rather wait tables at the Sea Witch any day. You get much more money for less hours and you can surf all day and still get a tan."

"Okay. Fine." Andy gave up this line of argument. "How about last night then? You started a goddam fight and made a fool of yourself."

"I didn't make a fool of myself."

"You don't know. You were polluted."

"You were too. So who are you to judge?"

"I wasn't as drunk as you."

234

"Ah, this is stupid. You're stupid."

"What's stupid is that you can't take no for an answer. I feel like shit and I don't want to go out drinking. Can't you accept that?"

"Okay. Fuck you. I'll go by myself."

"Fine. And fuck you too. Only watch out that you don't end up like Lee Koenigsburg."

Tim angrily slapped down a 50 cent tip for Bass on the bar.

"Don't worry about me, buddy boy," he said. "Drunk or sober, I can swim like a goddam porpoise. I'll see you around."

Perhaps it was the bittersweet nearness of summer's end that kept Martin Donovan at the piano with a gang of diehards until almost two in the morning. Andy lay upstairs in his room unable to sleep again because of the racket, gnashing his teeth in worry and frustration. He supposed that Franny had given up waiting for the grownups to leave. He wished he had gone out drinking with Tim instead of starting an argument. And then there was the rest of his life to consider—the abyss that lay a few short weeks beyond whatever happened on Thunder Island.

Eventually the piano stopped, the rough drunken voices of the sing-along crowd faded as the screen door slapped, and they left the old Coast Guard station for their scattered cottages. Five minutes after they were all gone Franny appeared.

"I thought they'd never leave. Ooo, it's freezing," she whispered as she stepped out of her jeans and then climbed into the narrow bed beside him.

"Ssshh," he said, pointing at the wall. "The new cook."

Once under the covers she was avid, but Andy continued to worry.

235

"I think your brother knows about us," he breathed into her ear.

"He doesn't know," she whispered back, kissing his neck.

"He keeps on making these remarks. Does he ever see you sneaking back into the house late at night?"

"No. He's always out cold. One time I came home and Brian was up watching TV. But it doesn't mean he knew where I was."

"I suppose not."

"You're shivering."

"We need another blanket."

"I'll keep you warm," she said, and soon he was sliding down a slippery hill that led him ultimately to a deep, dreamless sleep.

It was dark when he woke up suddenly. Franny was still by his side in bed. A series of thumps could be heard in the staircase, then some giggling and more thumps. Andy propped himself up.

"Oh no," he groaned.

Franny now woke groggily. "What time—"

"Ssshhh."

More giggling and footsteps outside his door. Without Andy having to tell her, Franny shrank under the covers and pulled them over her head. The knob turned and the hinge squeaked as Tim pushed the door open.

"Hope we din' wake you up, ole buddy," he said, flipping the light switch that turned on an overhead sixty-watt bare bulb. Andy winced in the glare. Soon he discerned Meg Marvin standing behind Tim, a whacked-out smile on her face.

"Hi," she said and waggled her fingers over Tim's shoulders.

"Guess what we gotta have," Tim said.

"Key to the guest room."

"Thattaboy."

Meg stood on her tip-toes and whispered into Tim's ear. Tim's face lit up in a mischievous smile.

"You got someone in the sack with you."

"No I don't," Andy said.

" 'Course he does," Meg said.

"Give me a few seconds to put my pants on and I'll go get the key," Andy told them.

"Go ahead and put 'em on," Tim said, then over his shoulder to Meg: "Who's he tryin' to kid? There's someone under there."

"I know," Meg said and giggled.

"Would you two just leave the room a moment so I can—"

"Shut up out there!" the voice of Benito the chef called sharply from down the hall.

Tim ignored it, as he ignored Andy's request to leave the room. "Hey, Kelly, 'zat you under the covers?" he asked.

"It's nothing," Andy insisted. "Come on, you're drunk—"

"He's my new guidance counselor," Tim explained to Meg. "Thinks I'm a lush."

Suddenly Meg came out from behind Tim and stepped toward the bed. She grabbed the covers from the foot of the bed and started to slowly draw them down.

"Hey, don't do that," Andy said, clutching them back at his end.

Meg giggled. "This is fun!"

"You sly ole bastard," Tim said. "Found yourself a li'l side piece, huh?"

"Quit pulling the blankets!"

"I want to see you naked," Meg said.

"Shut up!" Benito yelled distantly.

"This is stupid, Tim. Tell her to cut it out."

"Why? I wanna see you naked too," Tim said and laughed. As he did, Meg jerked the blankets hard and Andy lost his grip on them. He and Franny were exposed. Franny lay on her stomach with her face against the pillow. "Hey, that's not Kelly Donovan," Tim said, and Andy could see suspicion gathering on Tim's puffy face like a wave rising. "Whoizzit?" he said and reached for the naked girl's arm.

"Don't, Tim," Andy said.

Tim ignored him and grabbed Franny's arm, twisting it in such a way that she was forced to turn over.

"Ow! You're hurting me!" she cried.

"You shit-heel," he muttered, glowering at Andy. "You goddam pervert!"

"I don't feel so good," Meg said.

"Get your clothes on," Tim said to Franny.

"Get out first."

"I said, put 'em on!"

"Not unless you get out!" Franny said, reaching desperately for the sheet to cover herself.

"At least have the decency to let her get dressed," Andy said.

"Decency! You sick fuck!"

"I'm gonna be sick," Meg said.

"I said, shut up!" Benito yelled again.

"Get out!" Franny screamed.

Andy lunged out of the bed trying to push Tim out of the room. Thinking he was being assaulted, Tim swung a fist at Andy. From the bed, Franny screamed at both of them to stop. Meg Marvin, wobbling backward into the wall, threw up virtually at the feet of Benito, who had at last emerged from his room to put an end to all the noise.

By this time Tim had wrestled Andy to the floor and had

landed several glancing blows. Franny, still clutching the sheet, flailed at her brother. Ted Bass suddenly appeared from below and collided with Meg at the top of the stairs. Finally, in a uproar of accusations, tears, vomit, and flying fists, Bass and Benito were able to separate Tim and Andy. Franny grabbed her jeans and T-shirt and fled from the room. Bass, a rugby player in his undergraduate days at Amherst, got Tim in a hammerlock, shoved him down the hall to the bathroom, and forced him under the shower with the cold water running. All the while Tim shouted objurgations at Bass and at Andy, screaming, "You're both fired, you chiseling low-life shit-heel pervert Jew bastards!"

Back in Andy's room, Benito paced back and forth in his shorts and undershirt like an angry father in an Italian movie while Andy sat slumped in defeat and despair on the bed. Eventually, Bass led a dripping and subdued Tim Flannery from the bathroom past Andy's quarters and finally downstairs.

"Good thin' we no have to work tomorrow," Benito said with weary disgust as he prepared to leave Andy alone in his room. "Clean up this goddam mess inna hall."

Andy had just finished mopping up Meg Marvin's vomit when Bass trudged back upstairs.

"Well, that was lovely," Bass quipped, but Andy sensed that Bass wasn't really mad at him.

"I knew it was going to cause a problem," Andy admitted. "I never should have started in with her."

"Sometimes it's easier to say that than do it," Bass observed.

"I know," Andy said and pressed his forehead to the wall just as the tears started to flow. He couldn't help blubbering. He felt as though all the confusion and unhappiness of his life had culminated in this dreary hallway reeking of vomit.

"For chrissake, shut up out there," Benito barked from his room.

Bass put a hand on Andy's shoulder. "Come on downstairs, let's have a nightcap."

Andy nodded without turning his head from the wall. When he heard Bass's footsteps on the stairs, he followed with the mop and wringer. He had just opened the back door in the kitchen to leave the mop on the rear deck outside when he saw what appeared to be a bonfire several hundred yards away in the scrub across the Club property. He knew at once that it was John's shack burning down. He ran back inside to get Bass.

Hearing Andy's shouts, Kelly Donovan, clad only in bikini briefs and one of Bass's oxford shirts, emerged from Bass's room behind the bar. She followed the two of them out into the orange-hued night, passing a stunned Edna Dern who stood bleary-eyed on the doorstep of her cottage in a housecoat muttering, "What in hell—?" They ran all the way up to the scene of the fire, where Martin Donovan and his sons, plus several other men whose cottages were nearby, had assembled with shovels and carbon dioxide fire extinguishers to put the blaze out. Their efforts were proving futile. Andy feared that John might have been inside the shack when it was torched, but he soon saw him standing in the shadows at the edge of the crowd, which eventually included most of the Club membership. When he approached the scrawny, younger boy, John appeared cowed.

"Did you see who did this?" Andy asked.

"No," John said, his teeth chattering.

"You're lucky you didn't get roasted."

"Someone yelled at me to get out before they torched it."

"That was nice of them," Andy said. He searched the crowd but saw no sign of Tim Flannery. Shawn, Brian, and Matt were there, though. "You want to come back to the Club and crash there?" he asked John.

"No," John said. "It'll be day soon."

"It's freezing out."

"It was cold inside anyway."

"Come on. I'll give you a blanket."

Shaking his head, John shrank away from the careening flashlights and vanished down the path that led out of the little clearing. The shack was rapidly consumed by flames as the crowd stood around and watched. Shrouded in blankets, the Club members looked like ancient Celtic tribespeople engaged in some kind of somber druid ceremony. Eventually Martin Donovan and the firefighters succeeded in burying the remaining embers under shovelfuls of sand. In his authoritative manner, Dale Hummer told everybody that it was all over, to go back home.

Andy returned to the Club with Bass and, too exhausted to brood further on his predicament in the world, he collapsed on his bed and went to sleep.

Later that Sunday morning, around ten o'clock, Bass returned to Andy's room and woke him up. The daylight oppressed Andy painfully. He wanted to sleep for a year and wake up to find the Vietnam War over. Bass sat beside Andy's bed in the plain wooden chair that was the room's only other piece of furniture.

"I've got some bad news for you," Bass said.

"Let me guess. I'm fired, right?"

"I'm afraid so," Bass said. "It wasn't my decision. Honest."

"It was Mrs. Dern's idea, right?"

"Pretty much." Bass nodded and sighed. "Well, she

just came roaring over here a little while ago all bent out of shape—"

"That's funny. I must have slept right through it."

"I'm sorry, Andy. She left me no choice."

"Is John going to take my place?"

"I guess so. He knows the ropes."

"He's an okay kid," Andy said. "To tell you the truth, I was getting pretty tired of the job, shoveling the goddam walk and everything."

"It's not the world's most exalted position," Bass admitted.

"What's the official reason for me getting canned?"

"Well, that's something I wanted to talk about with you," Bass said carefully. "Evidently, Mrs. Dern thinks you've been fooling around with Kelly Donovan—"

Andy burst out laughing. He lay on his back in bed, laughing into the ceiling until his eyes watered.

Bass cleared his throat and went on. "The thing is, I know you weren't fooling around with Kelly, and you know that you weren't, but everybody else thinks that you were—all the old farts, that is. And, well, I'd be mighty grateful if you would just bow out gracefully without putting up a big protest. I realize it's a lot to ask, but—"

"I'm not going to put up a big protest," Andy said. "Don't worry."

"I mean, there's no point in both of us getting fired. Is there?"

"No, there's not," Andy agreed and broke up laughing into the ceiling again.

Bass drew a little brown envelope out of his pocket.

"I've got your last paycheck in here," he said, "plus a little cash bonus for being a good kid."

Andy took the envelope. Along with the regular $58 check were five crisp $10 bills. It seemed like a lot of money to him, until he remembered his blank future in Canada.

"You don't have to worry about me, Bass," Andy said. "I'm not gonna go blabbing on you. But thanks for the dough. I'll keep it anyway, if you don't mind."

"By all means," Bass said.

"Give me an hour or so to get my stuff together."

"No hurry. Take all day if you like. It's Sunday. Are you going to stay out on the island?"

"What do you care?" Andy said, regretting the snippish tone of his reply.

"In case you get mail or somebody wants to get ahold of you. Weren't you staying at your uncle's house when we first met back in June?"

"Yes," Andy said. "It's on Pine, last house before the dunes."

"Well," Bass said, getting up and holding out his hand to shake. 'I'm sure I'll see you around, Andrew. You were one hell of a steward's assistant, whatever the old bitch says. Anytime you need a recommendation, let me know. And you were a real pal when the chips were down. I won't forget it."

Andy couldn't help feeling a little choked up, even though he knew Bass was mostly full of shit.

CHAPTER SEVENTEEN

When Andy stopped by his Uncle Jack's around noon that Sunday, sunk in anxiety and despair and lugging a large suitcase, Jack's wife Deanna immediately made him a pastrami sandwich. He ate it out on the deck with a bottle of Dutch beer in view of the ocean, listening to a Judy Collins record on the hi-fi, and slowly he began to feel he was back in a recognizable world—that his two-month sojourn among the Christians at the Thunder Island Club had been a kind of extended hallucination.

Early that evening he went downtown to McCauley's to ask Tommy Oldfield about the possibility of a job waiting tables. Tommy said they were set 'til Labor Day with the present crew, but that he'd heard the Sea Witch was looking for a dishwasher. This being in Andy's line of expertise, he went over there at once, presented himself as a candidate for the position, and was hired on the spot. It was a straight 6 P.M. to midnight deal, with no food prep or sandy walks to shovel. But he noticed quite a few amused grins among the waiters (so dapper in their white pants and polo shirts) when the owner showed him around the kitchen, and it didn't take Andy long to realize who the joke was on.

The twin sinks, it turned out, had been clogged since July. The owner refused to pay the extortionary rates of the two Ocean Breeze plumbers, so the sinks remained clogged. The working procedure, therefore, was to fill them up (one soapy, one rinse water), wash X number of dirty dishes, and, when the water became disgusting, to empty the sinks by bailing the dirty water out an adjoining window into an alleyway behind the restaurant using a plastic scoop cut out from a giant Clorox jug. The job required him to be there seven nights a week and paid the minimum wage of $2.65 an hour. However, this pay was strictly "under the table"—that is, no taxes were withheld—and so Andy figured to earn roughly $100 per week for the last two weeks of the summer. When the time came to leave for Canada, he wanted to have some cash in his pocket.

That first night on the job he heard about another position, a part-time day job breaking bottles at the dump. It sounded rather like fun—breaking bottles for money—and so bright and early Monday morning he went down to the Ocean Breeze dump to inquire about it. The paunchy chief of the O.B. garbage crew affirmed that the job was still available and took Andy deep into the reeking bowels of the dump to show him the procedure.

Because the island was so narrow, space was at a premium, and the town dump had been carefully designed to make the most efficient use of its 2.3 acres. Everyone in town, homes and businesses alike, were required to separate glass bottles and jars out of his or her garbage. This glass was then crushed to save space.

Andy was shown a strange two-story structure that looked like a widow's walk with no house attached. Along the open deck on top were several dozen peach baskets filled with bottles. At the front edge of the balcony was a steel hopper. You were supposed to take a basket of bottles, the garbage chief explained, and dump them into the hopper. He flicked an electric switch on a post. A loud grinding noise could be heard. Down below the balcony, glass fragments were spewed out in a heap. Over to the side was a much larger heap, truly an immense heap, of glass shards. Once X number of peach baskets full of glass had been run through the grinder, the chief said, you would have to go down and shovel the small heap under the grinder onto the giant heap. At the end of every summer, the giant heap was put on a barge and dumped out at sea.

All the rest of the garbage was burned in a pair of dual incinerators. The person who broke the bottles also had to clean out the ash pits of these incinerators with a kind of rake and then cart the debris—charred cans and metal odds and ends, over to a separate pile. Altogether, the job would take about three hours each morning, five days a week, starting at seven when the truck had finished its daily run. It paid $3.50 an hour, which amounted to just over $50 a week. Andy signed on.

Even with these two jobs, he still had most of the day to himself and plenty of time to ruminate about his past and his future. His Uncle Jack went back to the city on Monday and Andy was left alone with Deanna, who he already liked a great deal, and who showed a definite sympathy for his predicament in the world. Except for doing his job at the Sea Witch, he had quit going into the bars downtown and did not venture over to the lifeguard area up the beach where everybody hung out. The Club, the Flannerys, Karen Koenigsburg, those many drunken nights that now seemed a single blur, all felt like ancient history. So he remained around the house with Deanna, and they passed many long hours together, often in the brooding silence that Andy now gathered around himself like a protective cloak.

Then, late one morning after his shift at the dump, he was on the deck sketching a woman sunbathing on the beach and Deanna came out to find him so absorbed that he didn't discover she was behind him until she said, "That's an awfully nice drawing."

"I haven't sketched all summer long," he said in a voice full of embarrassment and regret.

"You're very good at it. Did you ever consider going to art school?"

"I just spent four years at one, Dee, for godsake. The High School of goddam Music and Art."

"I mean college."

"Oh. No," he said.

"Why not?"

"Look, I went to Music and Art because it was the only way I could keep from being stuck in some hell-hole of a regular city high school. I was never serious about art. It was just something I could do, something that helped me out of a jam."

"But why not take it seriously? You're obviously talented."

Andy sighed, growing fidgety in his chair and unconsciously doodling little cartoon piranha fish around his sketch of the woman sunbathing.

"Well, for one thing I don't fit in the modern age," Andy said. "What I like in art is things you can recognize: human figures, people doing things, a bunch of houses, a scene in the country. Nobody's interested in that kind of stuff anymore. Even at Music and Art, if you painted a picture of the goddam lily pond in Central Park everybody would laugh at it, including the teachers."

"My favorite painters are the Impressionists," Deanna said. "Monet, Pissaro, Sisley. When Monet painted a field of poppies, you *knew* it was a field of poppies."

"I like them too, but you can't paint like that today."

"Why not?"

"People won't accept it," Andy said, a little shrilly. "Look at the stuff my mother pushes. She's right in the thick of the whole art scene and she never shows an artist who paints anything you could recognize. In fact, with her lately it's got to be downright pointless or ugly to sell. You know this artist she handles, Kaspar Kraus—the guy who paints pictures that are totally black?"

"No. I'm not familiar with him."

"It's a joke. He paints those black canvases, big ones, bigger ones, gigantic ones, humongus ones. He's done about a thousand of the stupid things and they all look the same. And they sell like hotcakes. My mom can't get 'em fast enough. Now you tell me, what's the point of that?"

Deanna thought it over, squinting her blue midwestern eyes at the sun and setting her mouth in a ruminative line. "Well, to a certain extent it's just fashion. You know— novelty."

"Okay, fine. So some guy comes along and does a thousand stupid black paintings just because nobody else had the nerve to try it for the last two million years. It's still stupid even if it's a new idea that nobody ever thought of before."

"It can't be that stupid if people are willing to buy it."

"Sure it can. That's the whole point. It's not art. It's just a big con job. I'd love to grow up and be a painter, but what's the point if you have to do something completely stupid to be a success?"

"Who says you have to do what everybody else is doing?"

"If I painted what I'm interested in, I'd starve to death. Look at poor miserable Van Gogh. He did his thing and never sold a goddam painting in his whole life. Not a single goddam one. So he goes and puts a bullet in his head, poor bastard. It's sickening. That's what happens when you try to buck the tide."

"Gauguin bucked the tide," Deanna argued. "He went all the way to the South Seas and lived happily ever after. And he was a friend of Van Gogh's. Did you know that?"

"Yeah, we had art history and all."

"Gauguin even tried to help Van Gogh."

"I guess he didn't try hard enough, huh? Maybe he should have taken poor old Van Gogh along to the South Seas with him."

"The point is you don't have to make your life into a tragedy," Deanna said. "Van Gogh might have committed suicide even if he became a big success. Look at Lee Koenigsburg. His career was zooming straight up when he took his life."

"So then it doesn't matter whether you succeed or fail, painters just naturally end up committing suicide."

"I'm not saying that at all, Andy," Deanna protested. "You're twisting it all around. I just don't know why you can't accept the fact of your own talent and take it seriously."

"How can you take art seriously when guys like Max Pap exist," Andy said, standing up and raising his voice.

"Who's Max Pap?"

"He's this goddam phony idiot who makes giant hamburgers and hot dogs out of fiberglass. Hey, you know what? I could introduce you. He comes out here all the time to visit his teenage girlfriend—" Andy was overwhelmed by a flood of emotion—anger, longing, remorse—

as he thought first of Karen Koenigsburg and then of Franny Flannery.

"He's got a teenage girlfriend?" Deanna asked.

"This island is sick," Andy muttered, shaking his head and staring hard into the weathered cedar decking. "This whole world is so sick I can't stand it anymore."

He flung down his pad in disgust and leaped over the deck rail onto the dune below, leaving Deanna alone on the deck feeling that she had unwittingly injured him.

Andy began walking east along the beach with his eyes to the sand, past the Ocean Breeze line, past the mammoth Holly Wood Club and all the freckly stockbrokers' wives and their blond children, and out toward the Sunken Forest. Only there did he finally lift his eyes from the ground, and then it was to try and remember exactly where Mike Lovett's shack lay. The dunes between the ocean and the woods all looked the same. Andy climbed up the face of the dunes—ignoring the U.S. government signs to keep off—and trudged along the top searching for the little clearing with the driftwood shack in the middle. Eventually, a quarter mile up, he came to it.

The place seemed deserted. The various surfboards were gone. In the stiff offshore breeze the door to the shack slapped hollowly on rubber hinges cut out of an old inner tube.

"Hello, Mike . . . ?" Andy called. For a moment he thought he heard a voice say, "Hey there, ho-dad," but it was only the wind and his memory of a day that was now part of his personal history.

He proceeded down the lee side of the dune carefully so as to avoid the poison ivy, approached the shack warily, and peered inside the unlocked door. It was definitely vacated. There were various pieces of junk furniture in the eight-by-twelve room—a cheap aluminum and vinyl beach chair, a battered cable spool used as a table, a rusty iron cot with a mouldy mattress that had already been raided by mice to get stuffing for their nests—but there were no personal belongings to go with these. There were no clothes hanging on any of the nails along the wall, no blankets, no books, nothing. It was clear to Andy that Mike Lovett had moved out.

He entered the shack. Crude as it was, it seemed like the most enchanted dwelling in the world to him and once again he toyed with the idea of hiding out here for a while, perhaps through the fall at least. The walls were plastered with a hodgepodge of surfing photos and pinups from *Playboy* magazine. Andy brushed some tiny black pellets off the mattress—he didn't know they were mouse turds—and lay down on it. Directly overhead, painted on the ceiling in neat letters with rather ornate Gothic capitals, was a message from Lovett.

> *To whoever inherits this shack*
> *May your days be long and full*
> *of sunshine*
> *May the nights bring you many wahine*
> *May the fair offshore wind always blow*
> *and the sets be groovy*
> *May you always be happy*
> *May you always be brave*

Andy wished that he might have been the one to inherit Lovett's shack but with every second that passed he was more convinced that this was to be somebody else's destiny. Much as he loved being here, away from the world and all its torments, he realized that it would be crazy to stay here after the summer. Besides, Lovett himself was in

Toronto by now, where Andy would soon have to go. Perhaps Lovett would really be his friend there—

But when he tried to imagine any kind of a life in Canada, his mind went absolutely blank. Finally, all he could really imagine was the now-familiar scene of a sunny college quadrangle filled with autumn light and laughing students. He turned over on his stomach and buried his face in the mattress, sobbing and wishing that the summer was a bad dream he might wake from at any moment.

He remained there trying to shut out reality until he drifted off to sleep and had a real dream. In the dream, Tim Flannery was dead. Andy was in a fancy room having cocktails with a lot of people whose faces he recognized. They were members of the Thunder Island Club, including all the Flannery children. Only Tim was absent and his absence was terrifying. When Andy asked where Tim was, Franny told him very matter-of-factly that Tim had died. "But he's all right, now," she added enigmatically. Andy felt a suffocating terror at the thought that someone he knew so well could slip out of the world so easily, and he woke up gasping, disoriented, and unsure even who he was.

The confusion itself was so terrifying that he leaped from the cot and rushed out of the shack, where, breathless, he finally remembered who and where he was. The particulars of the dream had faded and all that remained was a vague feeling of unease about Tim. His wristwatch said three-thirty and he climbed back over the dunes to begin the long trek back to Ocean Breeze so he could make it to work at the Sea Witch on time. There were beautiful, massive, glassy rollers out at the bar break and nobody was surfing them.

Since that final disastrous night at the Club, Andy hadn't seen or spoken to Tim or Franny. Andy figured that he had done something unforgivable in full knowledge of the possible consequences and that now he was suffering those consequences. He had lost a good friend forever, perhaps one of the best friends he might ever have. That they had known each other for only one summer seemed hard to believe, and didn't make any difference. As for Franny, Andy missed her very much, but he'd felt that what they were doing together was wrong and that being cut off from her now was somehow logical and inevitable. Besides, he was afraid to call her on the phone at her house, where there were so many others who might answer and know it was him.

Early on a Wednesday morning, more than a week after his dismissal from the Club, Andy went into work at the dump as usual. As usual, one of the first things he did was peek inside the town jail. The jail was a little concrete block structure that contained two small cells and a narrow hallway fronting both. It stood between the incinerators and the glass smasher. The door to the jail was always left propped open for ventilation. About one day out of three the jail was occupied and Andy enjoyed visiting the prisoners. They were usually glad to see anybody, just to break the anxious monotony of their being there. Often they were innocent young hippies who had been locked up for trying to sleep on the beach.

This morning, however, Andy stole inside to find one cell occupied by a large, blond, frizzy-haired youth with his face turned to the wall. Andy assumed that this person was still passed out from being drunk. He was about to leave and attend to smashing his bottles when the figure rolled over and looked over his shoulder. It took Andy a moment to realize that he was looking at Duff Perleman.

"You," Perleman said mysteriously after a portentious pause.

"Me?" Andy replied.

"You're his friend."

"Who?"

"I took care of your buddy. Don't worry, I took care of him."

Andy stood there waiting to hear Perleman explain, but the older, larger boy just turned his face back to the wall.

"What'd you do?" Andy asked carefully. Perleman didn't answer but his body shuddered and Andy understood that he was not in any mood to discuss it.

Andy backed out of the little building dazed and worried. It was already a warm day, one of August's last hurrahs, and the sharp stink from the smashed bottles was dizzying. It was a very complicated odor composed of whiskey vapors, stale beer, ketchup, and rancid mayonnaise. For the first time since he had started working there, Andy felt like he was going to throw up, and he fled the dump without notifying the chief.

He was soon downtown in the phone booth outside the drugstore. The Flannerys' number was busy. He dialed the Club, hoping to get ahold of Bass. There was no answer. He waited and called the Flannerys' house again, and then again. The line remained busy. He imagined the Flannery house filled with shocked siblings and weeping parents. Finally, unable to stand the uncertainty another minute, he went to the police station—just a large room in the ferry terminal—and inquired there.

"Was anyone murdered in town last night?"

The two officers on the premises made bewildered faces at each other.

"Why? Is someone in your family missing, sonny?" one asked.

"There's this guy in jail over at the dump: Duff Perleman," Andy said. "What'd he do?"

"What are you? His attorney?" the other cop asked with a playful glance at his partner.

"No. But I'm afraid he killed my friend."

"What's he in for, anyway?" the first cop asked the second in a much lower voice.

"I dunno. Graveyard shift musta booked him."

"Look it up on the blotter, Jojo."

The second cop went and checked a large ledger book on top of a file cabinet.

"Assault," he said as his face suddenly descended to the page with sharp interest. "Hey, it says here he bit some other kid's ear off."

CHAPTER EIGHTEEN

"D o you think Dylan has brain damage, or what?"

Andy wheeled around to find Tim Flannery looming behind where he was sitting on the beach. Tim had a huge, lopsided bandage on his head that looked like something halfway between a turban and a fighter pilot's helmet. His left ear was swaddled in gauze and tape. His right eye was black and yellow and partially closed. Andy could only gape at him without a word.

"I hear that ever since the motorcycle accident, Dylan can only speak French," Tim went on. "He tries to say something in English and it comes out in French, even when he sings. Of course, what I hear and don't hear myself is subject to question these days—if you get my drift. How are you doing?"

"Okay," Andy croaked dryly.

"You know, it took a certain amount of intestinal fortitude for me to venture out of the house with this ridiculous headgear on. The least you could do is act like you were glad to see me."

"I'm awful glad to see you, Tim."

"Hey, that's a damn good drawing you've got there," Tim said, stooping down so that he wasn't looming over

Andy anymore. "Oops. She moved," he said, referring to the drawing's subject, a woman lying on a blanket fifty feet away. "There goes your pose."

"I was almost done anyway."

Tim finally sat down in the sand while an awkward silence prevailed between them. At length he took a newspaper out from under his arm and began to read:

"Get a load of this: 'Indian Nazi Party Formed.' Dateline: New Delhi. 'A new party called the Hindi Nazi Party was founded today at a meeting of fifty young Hindus and Sikhs. A program circulated at the meeting called for the abolition of parliamentary government and the enforcement of a dictatorship for twenty years.' So much for the radical youth of the great subcontinent." He folded the paper back up. "I guess I owe you an apology."

"You don't have to apologize," Andy said. "I knew I was headed for trouble. I never should have started in with Franny."

"Well, she's a cute kid. I can understand. Almost."

Another awkward interval stretched between them.

"Did you know it was going on, before you . . . before that night?"

"Didn't have a clue."

"You seemed to constantly be making references to it. It really made me paranoid."

"Made you what?" Tim leaned in with his good ear.

"Paranoid," Andy repeated loudly.

"Oh. Well, sure. That's a guilty conscience for you. Want to know something funny, though?"

"What?"

"I thought you were giving it to Kelly Donovan."

"No, not me. Bass was."

"That Bass. What an old weasel. Which reminds me: He says he's holding some mail for you back at the Club."

Andy emerged from his thoughts as from a dream.

"Mail?" he said urgently. "Did he say what?"

"I dunno. Just mail—"

"Was it from a college?"

"Could have been."

Andy jumped to his feet.

"Could you possibly get it for me?" he asked.

"Come down and get it yourself."

"I'd feel weird going back to the Club."

"It's Thursday. Nothing's going on down there. Come on, I'll go with you."

"Well, okay."

"Only let's not walk along the beach," Tim said. "It's not that I'm a coward or anything, but let's be realistic: I look like a fucking idiot with this bandage on."

They made their way over to the Club via the Midway. At eleven o'clock this weekday morning late in August there were few other pedestrians around to gawk at Tim.

"I saw Duff Perleman in jail," Andy remarked, trying to find out just what happened without asking point-blank.

"Oh?" Tim said. "What were you doing down there?"

"I have this job in the dump, smashing bottles."

"No kidding? That's one of the worst jobs on the whole island."

"I've come to realize that."

"My brother Terry did it one summer. He had so many little pieces of glass embedded under his skin that they kept on coming out for a year afterward. It was gross."

"Tell me about it."

"Not much more to it, really."

"Tell me about your ear, then?"

"My ear. Well now, that's a whale of tale," Tim said and sighed. "He bit off most of the top of it, the helix it's called. It won't have any effect on my hearing, the quack says, once the bandages are off, that is. I can have plastic surgery in a few months. They take some flesh off your butt and some cartilage from your rib cage and mold a new one. It's a good goddam thing that long hair is all the rage these days. Even with plastic surgery, I don't think it's ever going to be a great-looking ear again. Now the one he bit off, *that* was a great-looking ear."

"It's too bad Vincent van Gogh didn't have your outlook on life."

"What do you mean by that?"

"Never mind," Andy said, and they walked awhile in silence. In a cottage off Ivy someone was still playing the *Sgt. Pepper's* album. "Did he catch you in bed with his mother?" Andy finally asked.

"As a matter of fact, he did."

Andy stopped in his tracks. "You're sick," he said.

Tim also stopped. "Hey, you're sick too," he countered.

"I know. We're both hopeless," Andy said. They resumed walking. "What was she like?"

"She was unbelievable."

"Tell me."

"Hey, wait a minute. I had to sacrifice my goddam ear for this. You want all the juicy details for free?"

"I'll buy you a beer."

"I'm off the sauce."

"Get out of here."

"No shit. You were right. I was turning into a regular alkie."

"I suppose you're never going to have another drink again as long as you live."

"Of course I will. But for now I'm dry. It makes me feel righteous, pure, godly. Hey, I must need a drink. Ha ha, just kidding. Let me tell you something, my friend. There is *nothing* like an older woman with the right attitude. And Lilah Perleman has definitely got the right attitude."

"What's the right attitude?"

"She was grateful."

"It sounds pathetic."

"To you everything's pathetic. Take it from me, she was superb. I shall treasure our time together—fleeting though it may have been. And I regret having to press charges on her offspring, the old Duffer, but you can't very well go around maiming people, can you?"

"It was his *mother*, Tim."

"Hey, it wasn't my mother."

"That was sort of how I felt about Franny. She wasn't my sister."

"Yeah, but she's fourteen, for godsake. And she's *my* sister. I ought to bite off your goddam ear, you pervert—oh look, there's Edna Dern puttering in her garden. Dear old thing. Maybe we should both offer to give her a poke. Talk about gratitude! You'd never get rid of the old bitch—Hello, Edna dear."

Edna Dern stood up from attending her rugosas and scowled as she recognized Tim with his bandaged head and his odious companion, the former steward's assistant.

"Just picking up my mail," Andy explained.

Frowning, Mrs. Dern returned to her knees beside the rose hedge.

"Let's grab her," Tim whispered. "And violate her among the plantings.

"Shut up," Andy said. "These walks need shoveling."

"Nobody ever shoveled like you did. You shoveled your heart out for this great institution. Ah, here we are."

They mounted the steps to the old Coast Guard station.

"Hey, Bass," Tim shouted. "It's old home week. Get your paws off somebody's sister and come out here."

"Well, well, Andrew!" Bass greeted him ebulliently as he emerged from the room behind the bar. "I'm glad Tim got ahold of you."

"Me too."

"Things just aren't the same around here with you gone."

"I can see."

"John's a good kid, of course," Bass went on, "but he doesn't have his heart in it like you did."

"I didn't have my heart in it, either, Bass."

"No? Well, you certainly put your mind to it, then."

"I guess."

"John's less philosophical."

"I told Andy you had some mail for him," Tim said.

"Oh, yes. I do."

Bass vanished back into his office for a moment.

"Hey, put on a little Dylan while you're in there," Tim shouted. "Something old."

"*Another Side Of?*" Bass asked.

"Groovy," Tim said. "Good old Dylan."

Bass reemerged shortly with two letters. One was from a high school classmate of Andy's, a girl who had gone to Israel for the summer. The other was from a Seward State College. He ripped that one open first.

"I don't believe it," he mumbled.

"They turn you down too?" Tim asked. "I mean, a name like Seward. It sounds so much like sewer."

"I think they're accepting me."

"Lemme see." Tim plucked the letter out of his hands and scanned it quickly. "Kind of looks that way. What do you think, Bass?"

Bass read it over. "Oh, definitely," he said. "Lookit, they're telling you here at the bottom to send in for your dorm assignment."

"Is that what that was?"

"No question. You're in."

"I'm in?" Andy said, still astonished.

"You're in," Tim said. "Only maybe you want to think it over. Where is this sewer anyway?"

262

"Seward," Andy said, snatching the letter and rereading it. "It's in New York. They named it after William Henry Seward, the secretary of state under Lincoln. You've heard of him, haven't you?"

"He bought Alaska," Tim said. "Seward's Folly."

"Correct," Bass said.

"Well, where is it exactly? New York's a big state."

"I have no idea," Andy admitted. "But I think it's a long ways from the city."

"You'll have to call and ask for directions," Tim said. "I'd love to listen in on that call: uh, sir, I was just admitted to the freshman class. I wonder if you might tell me how to get there from down in the city. What's that? You say a left at Poughkeepsie . . . ?"

"This calls for a celebration," Bass said, stooping down to open a small refrigerator under the bar.

"This means I don't have to run away to Canada!"

"Lucky you," Tim said. "Maybe I'll take your place."

"Here we are, gentlemen," Bass said, dusting off a moldy bottle of Dom Perignon champagne.

"Whoa, that's the good stuff," Andy said.

"Thirty dollars a bottle," Bass said.

"Are you sure it's all right?"

Bass thought about it for a second.

"Yes, it's all right," he said, adding, "It's been sitting down there forever."

"Martin Donovan bought that bottle the year Kelly was born," Tim said. "But he was too cheap to open it. Or so the legend goes."

"Three glasses, please, Andrew."

"Tim's off the sauce."

"Get serious," Tim said. "This is a momentous occasion."

Bass wiped the bottle with a bar rag, eased out the cork without any wasteful explosion of foam, and filled the three glasses.

"To our fighting forces far across the sea in Vietnam," Tim said, lifting a glass. "Sorry, guys, but you'll have to carry on the war without us."

"Hear, hear," Bass said. "And to Andrew Newmark, possibly the best dishwasher in the history of the Thunder Island Club—"

"What do you mean 'possibly'?"

"Okay, indubitably."

"Better believe it."

"'And to his future at—what was the name of that college?"

"Sewer State," Tim said. "Mmmmm. God that tastes good. I've been dry for days."

"Wait, I've got a toast," Andy said.

"Well?"

"To Dylan. May he not have brain damage."

"I'll drink to that," Bass said.

"You're both assholes," Tim said.

Bass was refilling their glasses when John, the new steward's assistant, came in the dining room entrance and passed through the bar on his way to the kitchen. When he saw the three of them sitting in the bar, the expression on his face was grim and frightened. He hesitated a half step, trying to take in the odd-looking bandage on Tim's head, and then, without saying anything, continued on through.

"He doesn't like me since I torched his shack," Tim said.

"I'd say he has rather good reason," Bass observed.

"Hey, I gave him plenty of time to get out," Tim said. "But I suppose when you get right down to it, it was one of those things you regret later in life. Hell, I was drunk."

"You always say that."

"And extremely pissed off."

264

"I'll be back in a minute," Andy said, leaving his barstool and heading into the kitchen

"You better be," Tim said. "Surf's up."

John had made himself a sandwich and was sitting alone at the big steel table eating as Andy had also done so many afternoons when he worked at the Club. John seemed to regard Andy with deep suspicion. His stare was intense, and the long stringy blond hair gave him altogether the look of a wild boy who had barely been housebroken and trained to perform a few menial domestic chores.

"I'm sorry about your shack," Andy said.

John continued to eat, paying rapt attention to Andy but saying nothing.

"Tim's sorry too, when you really get down to it. He was drunk and pissed off at me and I guess he took it out on you."

"It doesn't matter anymore," John said. "I live here now."

"I don't blame you for getting my job, either. I just wanted you to know that. My getting canned had nothing to do with you."

John just nodded his head slightly, still devouring his sandwich.

"Are you going back home after the summer?"

At this John smiled as though anyone ought to know better than to ask such a question.

"You're not, then?"

"Never," John said.

"What are you going to do? Where are you going to go?"

"Don't know. California maybe."

"Well, you can't stay here at the Club after Labor Day."

John shrugged his eyebrows.

"There's this really groovy shack about two miles down the beach from here. It's just over the dunes in the Sunken Forest. It used to belong to the best surfer on the whole island, Mike Lovett. He was the most amazing person you ever met. He could tell what you were thinking before you even said it. He's gone up to Toronto now to get out of the draft. If you ever have to get out of the Army, you ought to go up there and look him up. He'll help you out. Especially if he finds out you've been out at Thunder Island. Anyway, his shack is vacant right now. It's a cool shack."

"I'm going to California," was all John said in reply. No matter how much he ate, he always looked hungry.

"Well, just thought I'd let you know about that shack," Andy said.

"Surf's up," Tim said, sticking his head in the swinging door.

"Good luck out there in California," Andy said to John.

John nodded his head, looking wise and old beyond his years.

"I wanna go on a surfin' safari," Tim said.

Andy left the kitchen with him.

"Thanks for the champagne, Bass," Andy said.

"Don't mention it."

"He means don't mention it to Martin Donovan," Tim said as they headed out the door into the strong August sunshine.

"Can you surf with that stupid thing on your head?" Andy asked as they passed Edna Dern's cottage.

"I'm not supposed to," Tim said. "But, hey, you're only young once."